Fire Plague

A Rory Mack Steele Novel, Volume 5

Eugene Lloyd MacRae

Published by CreateSpace, 2017.

This is a work of fiction. Similarities to real people, places, or events are entirely coincidental.

FIRE PLAGUE

First edition. May 3, 2017.

ISBN: 139780991739257

Written by Eugene Lloyd MacRae.

Chapter 1

"**WE NEED TO CULL** the world's population of undesirable elements if we are to survive," Helmer Postigan said. He sat back in his plush office chair and observed the young lady across from him.

"Cull?" Nan Bacon repeated. Her body went rigid. She couldn't have heard that right. "You mean kill off people you don't like?"

"No, of course not," Helmer Postigan answered with a wave of his hand.

Nan Bacon relaxed in her chair on the other side of the broad oak desk.

"It has nothing to do with people we don't like, Ms. Bacon," Postigan said. "It's about those who are not useful to society. It's about protecting the interests of those who are the best of our world."

Nan Bacon now looked at him like he had two heads. "Protecting the best of our world?"

"Everyone knows the world is in danger from overpopulation," Postigan told her, "and it's only going to get worse." The rotund man got up from behind his desk and stepped over to a

1

cherry liquor cabinet. He opened one of the doors and took out a bottle of Schnapps and a glass.

"But that doesn't mean you simply kill people off!" Nan objected. She watched him pour a drink and drop some ice into it.

"The world's population has grown since the black death of 1350 when there were only 370 million people worldwide," Helmer Postigan said. "Now, it's just over 7 billion. 7 billion! Can you imagine that?" He closed the liquor cabinet and shook his head. "And expert estimates say we will reach over 10 billion by the year 2050. That can't be allowed to happen."

"So you feel the need to simply kill them off," Nan said as she crossed her arms.

"We need to *cull* those populations for the rest of us to survive, Ms. Bacon," Postigan countered. He sat back down in his chair behind the desk.

"Us? You mean old white dudes," she said.

Postigan smiled as he raised his glass towards her, "And young white ladies as well."

She shook her head, "Is this one of those New World Order ideas people turn to when they feel their corner of humanity is threatened? Well, you can count me out. I don't want any part of it."

Postigan set his glass down hard enough to send liquor splashing onto the desk. "You may not have a choice! Experts say the population surpassed the world's ability to renew its resources back in 2007. Yet, we've continued to grow. China and India have nearly 40 percent of the world's population and they are soaking up the world's resources by leaps and bounds every single day. Society as we know it is on the verge of collapse and you may not like what you wind up with, Ms. Bacon."

Nan jutted her chin out, "I'll take my chances."

"I see," Postigan said. He took a sip of his drink and his brow furrowed as he considered the young lady across from him.

Nan stood up abruptly and headed for the door out of Helmer Postigan's study. "Now, if you don't mind Mr. Postigan, you can have me taken back to the NYU Genetics Laboratory. I'd like to get back to my work, actually *helping* people."

Postigan swirled the ice in his drink, "I do wish you would reconsider, Ms. Bacon. I really do."

"*Not* going to happen," Nan answered emphatically. But when she opened the door to leave the room, a large man blocked her way out.

Nan turned to Postigan with a firm look on her face. "Tell him to move. This conversation is over."

Postigan looked at her and shook his head slowly. "I'm afraid we can't let you leave, Ms. Bacon."

Taking a step back in anger, Nan yelled, "You can't stop me from leaving! Do you understand me? You can't–"

Postigan slammed his glass down on the desk again, the caramel colored liquid splashing across the oak desk, "Yes we can. We can and we will. There is too much at stake and we need you."

"Need me? Need me for what? What are you talking about?" Nan shook her head, "Never mind. I just want out of here. And I want out of here *now*."

Postigan took a deep breath to calm himself. His voice returned to a polite tone, "My daughter tells me you are quite brilliant when it comes to genetic splicing."

Nan crossed her arms, "I thought she was my friend. I can't believe it. All those years we spent together at school, I thought

I knew her. But all of a sudden she starts spouting this same crap nonsense that you are. Both of you are total nut jobs!"

"Well, she still thinks a lot of you, Ms. Bacon," Postigan said. "I wish you would reconsider. We need your expertise."

"To do what?" Nan asked him.

Postigan sat back in his chair as he looked thoughtfully at the young woman. "I understand that you are quite familiar with the Black Death that struck Europe in the 1300s," he said. "In fact, I've been told it's a great passion of yours."

Nan cocked her head. "The Black Plague? Is that what you're talking about?"

"Yes, exactly." Postigan answered with great enthusiasm. "I'm sure you'll be quite interested to know that we have a strain of the plague that the CDC collected from that case that occurred in Colorado last year."

Nan's eyes shot open in alarm, "You do? How in the world did you get that?"

"That doesn't concern you," Postigan told her curtly. "All you need to know is that we have it."

Alarmed, Nan took another step back towards Postigan, an intense look of concern on her face. "Is it safely contained?"

"Oh, yes," Postigan said. He puffed his chest out. "I can assure you we have a top-notch genetic facility here. We built it specifically to contain the various strains of pandemic diseases, such as the plague."

Nan's eyes narrowed, "What do *you* need a strain of the plague for?"

"For our research project. And that's where you come in. We need you to modify it," Postigan explained.

Her body stiffened in surprise, "Modify it? To do what?"

"To genetically engineer it to attack specific populations," Postigan said.

Nan Bacon's mouth opened but she couldn't speak.

"We can start with the Chinese, who are becoming too powerful today," Postigan said. "Then we can move on to India, then perhaps the African continent." Postigan waved his hand dismissively, "Actually, the sequence of events doesn't really matter in the long run. Just as long as we remodel the world in the proper way."

Nan shook her head slowly and took a step back in shock but the large man was right behind her. He placed his hands on her shoulders and held her rooted to the spot. Nan continued to stare at Postigan as she weakly tried to move the man's hands away from her.

"Of course, we can start your tests on sample populations here in the United States first," Postigan told her. He pressed a button on his desk. "It doesn't matter which ones, as long as we get things started."

"You're crazy," she said weakly as the full extent of his plans struck her with force.

Postigan ignored the comment, "As I said, we have a fully equipped lab on the premises, Ms. Bacon. You will be pleased to see we have every cutting edge piece of equipment available today. But we can buy whatever else you need to help you with your work. I can assure you, we will spare no expense to advance this project."

A door opened on Nan's right and a man in a tweed jacket entered the room. He looked over at Postigan, who nodded his head once. The man in the tweed jacket walked directly over to Nan Bacon and pulled a syringe out of his side pocket.

Nan struggled to escape the large man's grasp on her shoulders but he was simply too strong for her.

The man in the tweed jacket removed the safety cap from the syringe.

Her eyes wide, Nan's voice quivered, "What are you doing?"

The man with the syringe pressed the plunger, squirting some liquid in the air to push out any air bubbles.

Nan struggled to twist away.

The needle was plunged into Nan's right arm.

"No!" Nan cried.

Helmer Postigan sat back in his chair, a satisfied look on his face, "Welcome to your new home, Miss Bacon,"

A world of darkness closed in and within seconds Nan Bacon lost consciousness.

Chapter 2

UPPER WEST SIDE, MANHATTAN, New York

RORY MACK STEELE walked up the six steps of the old brownstone building to the front door. The black letter stenciling on the upper window of the door read 'Cordell Reece Bacon - Defense Attorney'. Rory opened the door and stepped inside. This was obviously the waiting area for the lawyer's clients but Rory felt like he was stepping back in time. The entire room looked like something out of the 1930s. It reminded him of the old detective movies he used to love watching on TV when he was a kid. There were a number of red leather chairs with brass buttons lining the walls just inside the door. The intricate architectural details on the cherry lintels, door casings, and crown molding were amazing. A scent of vanilla hung in the air.

An elderly lady, with beautiful ebony skin and snow white hair, was sitting behind a large, ornate, cherry wood desk. The only thing out of place was the large computer screen in front of her. She looked up at him and smiled; a Brooklyn accent very evident as she said, "Yes sir, how may I help you?"

"My name is Rory Mack Steele. Mr. Bacon called my office and asked me to drop by."

"Ah yes, Mr. Steele," the lady said amiably. "I was told you would be coming. Would you please take a seat for a moment and I'll tell Mr. Bacon you're here." The lady gestured to one of the plushy red leather chairs.

Rory took a seat as the woman got up and walked across the room to her right. She pulled open a door to another room, then disappeared through the doorway. Rory settled in for a long wait. A Private Investigator with Highland Investigative Services, the family business started by his Uncle Murdock MacLeod in New York City, Rory was used to long waits at times. It came with the territory. But he was pleasantly surprised when the elderly lady came back into the waiting room only a moment later.

"Mr. Bacon will see you now. Please go in." She indicated the open door beside her.

Rory got up and walked across the room. "Thank you," he said as he walked through the open door. The woman shut it behind him. Bacon's office was also redone to a 1930s feel. And no expense had been spared inside here either. The dark paneled walls were satiny and rich looking. A large oak desk sat like a looming presence on the far side of the room. Behind the desk was a large bookshelf that contained a number of books behind glass doors. Rory assumed they would be law books.

Just then another door opened on the right-hand side and a tall, round gentlemen with curly white hair stepped into the office. He closed the door behind him. "Sorry to keep you waiting, Mr. Steele," the man said as he strode up to Rory and stuck out his hand, "I'm Cordell Bacon."

Rory noted the man had a Brooklyn accent as well as he shook his hand, "Very nice to meet you, sir."

"I just live upstairs," Bacon said as he hustled over behind the large desk, "makes the commute much easier. Sit down please, Mr. Steele." He indicated one of the two comfortable red leather chairs sitting in front of the oak desk.

Rory sat down as Bacon did the same thing on the other side of the desk. "I understand you want us to find your daughter," Rory said, getting right to the heart of the matter.

"Yes, that's right." The man sat forward in his chair and clasped his hands on the desk. "She's been missing about three weeks. No one has any idea where she is or what happened to her."

"Have you talked to the police?" Rory asked him.

"Oh yes," Bacon said. "But they haven't been able to find anything. Like I said, they have no idea what happened to her or where she is. She has simply vanished without a trace and they haven't found a single lead."

"Okay. Let's start at the beginning then. When was the last time you saw your daughter, Mr. Bacon?"

Cordell Bacon looked down at his hands, still clasped on the desk in front of him. He didn't say anything for a few moments. He seemed to be struggling for an answer. Then his body sagged a little, "Personally, it's been quite a few years, I'm afraid."

Rory cocked his head, "Then, how did you find out she was missing? Who told you?"

The lawyer didn't say anything more for a few more minutes. He just continued looking down at the desk.

"Mr. Bacon," Rory said firmly, "I hope you won't withhold *anything* from me. I'll need to talk to whoever it was that let you know your daughter's missing."

"It's just a little embarrassing, Mr. Steele. It's probably best if I start from the beginning." Bacon seemed to gather his thoughts for a moment and then started, "My wife died giving birth to my daughter. I named her after my wife, Nanette Marlayne Bacon. When I hired my receptionist, Denelle Atkinson, she was raising her own granddaughter Bella and she took Nanette under her wing. Both children started school at the same time...but Nan turned out to be a brilliant child and she bounded ahead of her peers through school. She graduated with a medical degree from Harvard University in Boston at age 18. Three years later, she graduated with a PhD in genetic engineering from the University of California-Los Angeles."

"Brilliant is an understatement," Rory said.

"You're right. But for all her brilliance, she's also a very naïve young lady," Bacon added. "She stopped talking to me a long time ago because I was a defense lawyer. According to her, if you're arrested, or you're charged by the police, you must be guilty. Law enforcement doesn't arrest innocent people, according to her. And people like me...defense lawyers...all *we* do is get people off."

"She's not the first person I've heard say that," Rory said. "But I think people like you and me know a lot better than that."

Bacon nodded his head in agreement, "I've had a lot of clients who were guilty and a lot who were innocent. But that doesn't matter. Innocent or guilty, my job is simply to work within the legal system. To give them the best defense possible. But my daughter has never seen it that way. She has despised me for my job. Anyway, for the past two years she has worked at the New York University Genetics Laboratory. It's part of the NYU School of Medicine. They set up the teaching-research laboratory for genetics three years ago to teach cutting-edge techniques. I have a couple of friends there who are on the board. I've given a lot of money in donations to NYU over the years and they've been kind enough to keep an eye on my daughter for me. Nanette would be furious with me if she knew. That's why I was hesitant to say anything."

"So, one of *them* let you know she was missing," Rory concluded.

Bacon nodded, "I was called when she hadn't shown up for work in the laboratory one morning. That was not like her. She loved her work and never missed a day. She never missed one single day, Mr. Steele."

"What exactly did she do there?" Rory asked.

"My friends there have told me she is one of the top genetic scientists in the world," Bacon replied with a smile. "Apparently, she is capable of doing genetic engineering and gene splicing that others can only dream about. I'm very, very proud of my daughter and her accomplishments, Mr. Steele."

"Did she have any trouble at work? Any problems with coworkers?" Rory asked.

"Not as far as I know," Bacon said with a shake of his head. "I'm told she was well-liked by everyone. She was very quiet and really didn't socialize much after work. As you and I both know, workplaces can sometimes create a great deal of friction that can result in terrible things happening to people. But everyone I talk to at NYU said that was not true in Nan's case. The police asked that same question as well. They told me they couldn't find one single incident along those lines."

"Do you know what she was working on specifically?" Rory asked.

Bacon nodded, "Yes. A large food company heard about her and approached the University. They offered a great deal of money if she could assist them in a few of their projects. The University thought it would be great training in genetic engineering for the students working with her. Her most recent project was working on genetic modifications for crops. She was working to increase yields for areas that had short growing seasons, as well as increasing the micronutrients in the crops for additional health benefits."

"There are a lot of people who don't like crop modifications. They call them Frankenfoods," Rory said suspiciously. "Maybe she was targeted by some extremist group against genetically modified food?"

"I thought of the same thing. But the laboratory has had absolutely no problem like that according to my contacts there," Bacon countered. "They've had no demonstrations or sit-ins. And they haven't had one single phone call, letter or e-mail making any threats. The police followed up on that angle very thoroughly and they couldn't find anything. To put it bluntly, there doesn't seem to find *any* reason why she's gone missing."

Rory nodded his head slightly, thinking deeply, "Did she have any close friends? Anyone I could talk to?"

Bacon shook his head softly, "No. I'm afraid I don't know of any. As I said, she didn't really socialize much outside of school or outside of work over the years. Even while she was growing up here, she rarely associated with children in the neighborhood. Bella was probably her best and only friend until she moved ahead in school. She was purely driven by intellectual challenges and had little time for people."

"How about at work?"

"If there is someone in the last few years...." His voice faded away.

Rory nodded in understanding, "All right. Perhaps the best thing for me to do is to go to the laboratory where she worked. Maybe I'll dig up something the police missed."

"You can talk to Dr. Leo Bonifay when you go there. Leo is a professor there and he is one of the friends who keeps an eye on Nan for me. I'll let him know you're coming." Mr. Bacon reached for a large brown envelope that sat on the corner of his desk and gave it to Rory, "There are pictures of my daughter in this package. I've also included her vital statistics, background information as well as the background security check the University did on her. There's also a check in there that your office said would be your starting fee. If you need anything else, please don't hesitate to call me, Mr. Steele."

"Thank you," Rory said. He took the package and stood up. "Do you know where your daughter was living?"

Cordell Bacon nodded and he pulled open a wide desk drawer in front of him. "The police went to her apartment and didn't find anything. But I'm sure you'll want to do your own investigation there as well." He pulled out a small brown envelope and passed it over to Rory, "She didn't know it, but I am part owner of the Madison Green Residential Plaza she lives in. The address is on the front of the envelope. The number below it is the code that will let you into the building. The key inside the envelope will let you into her apartment. The superintendent of the building is one of those guilty people the system nearly railroaded into prison. I helped him get back on his feet and he takes care of several buildings for me. He also watches out for my daughter as well."

Rory took the envelope and slipped it into his pocket, "I'll keep you updated on anything that I find Mr. Bacon. I'll do everything I can to return your daughter to you. Let's just hope she didn't get herself into something that makes it difficult to get her back out."

Chapter 3

NEW YORK UNIVERSITY School of Medicine

WHEN HIS CAR wouldn't start, Rory took a Yellow Cab to the NYU Genetics Laboratory. He wondered if this was a bad omen. Starting a case this way couldn't be good. Sitting in the back seat, Rory opened up the package Cordell Bacon had given him. The picture showed Nan Bacon to be a pretty young blonde with a very earnest look on her face. The brilliant young woman looked to be someone who was determined to succeed against all costs. But Rory also detected the vulnerability her father had alluded to. If she had been kidnapped for some reason, Rory wondered how long she could last. He hoped someone so young and brilliant was still alive. He took a deep breath and let it out slowly. The fact was, Nan's youth reminded him of someone else. His teenage bride, Kitty Black, who had died from cancer less than six months after their wedding. Rory had found it difficult to forgive himself for not being able to save her and his life drifted aimlessly for months afterward. He made the decision to join the Canadian Army, serving most of the time over ten years with Joint Task Force 2, the special forces unit, volunteering for every mission available. One army shrink said he was haunted by Kitty's death. Another said it drove him. Both agreed it had created a need to help others, despite personal danger. Rory wasn't sure about the haunted part, or if it was self-inflicted punishment or penance, but it gave his life purpose. And right now, Rory was determined to find Nan Bacon and bring her back safely to her father.

The cab exited FDR Drive, drove up East 30th Street and then turned right on 1st Avenue, where Rory got out in front of the NYU Medical Center cluster of buildings. The whole block was a hub of activity. Men and women in business attire were mixed in with the larger population of eager students, many crowded around the street vendors, attracted by the delicious aroma of hot dogs, fried onions, and fresh hot pretzels.

Rory ignored his own taste buds and climbed the stairs to the front doors of the NYU Genetics Laboratory. Inside, one of the security guards on duty directed Rory down the hallway to his right. A small plaque on the third door on the right read 'Professor Leonard Bonifay, PhD'. Rory opened the door and stepped inside. The room wasn't very big and contained a gray metal desk and a few filing cabinets against the back wall. A small man with thinning black hair, dark spectacles and dressed in a white lab coat, was hunched over the desk, reading something closely.

"Yes?" inquired the man as he looked up over the spectacles.

"Professor Bonifay?"

"Yes," the man answered. He sat up a little straighter and removed his spectacles.

"I'm Rory Mack Steele. Mr. Bacon sent me," Rory said as he closed the door behind him.

The small man's face lit up, "Yes of course." He stood up and moved quickly around the desk to shake Rory's hand. "Cordell said you would be coming down. I was delighted to hear he was going to have someone working on Nanette's disappearance. The police have simply given up, I'm afraid. We're *very* worried here about her and I'm hoping we can find her safe and sound."

"I'm going to do everything I can to make that happen," Rory said.

"Cordell said you wanted to see where Nanette worked. I'll take you up to her office in the laboratory right now if you want?" Bonifay's eyebrows went up, eagerly awaiting Rory's answer.

"Yes, that would be great," Rory said.

Professor Bonifay reached for a keycard on the desk. He placed it around his neck and then reached for a card labeled 'Visitor' and passed it over to Rory, "Where we are going, you'll need to wear this."

Rory placed the card around his neck and followed Professor Bonifay into the hallway.

Bonifay was very emphatic in his words and gestures as he hustled them back down the hallway, "While you're here, *whatever* you need, all you have to do is ask. No matter what it is. The University will cooperate in *any* way."

Nodding, Rory asked, "I take it you've known Cordell Bacon for some time?"

"Yes," Bonifay said as they headed for a bank of elevators. "Cordell helped a member of my family with a personal, legal matter some years ago. I liked him very much and when his daughter came to work here, I was very happy to keep an eye on her for him."

"I'm sure the donations he's made to NYU helped as well," Rory prodded.

"The donations came after," Bonifay said, without the least look of guilt or concern on his face. He pushed the 'up' elevator button and one of the elevator doors opened immediately. "We all liked Nan very much," he said as he led Rory inside the elevator. He stabbed his finger on the elevator button for the eighth floor and the doors closed.

The elevator car rose under Rory's feet, "Mr. Bacon said you called because his daughter didn't show up for work one day?"

Bonifay nodded solemnly and let out a short breath, "Yes. We were very concerned when she didn't show up for work. That was very, very unusual for her. In fact, it had *never* happened before. Never. She was always here. I telephoned Cordell right away and he suggested we bring the police in immediately. They were a little hesitant, but Cordell called in a few favors. Unfortunately, it appears nothing has come of their investigation. She's simply disappeared off the face of the earth. I always heard that phrase in movies but I never thought I would experience it. It's a most unsettling feeling, to not know where a loved one is."

Rory nodded. He had seen a lot of people fall apart with the worry. "I understand she was working on genetic modifications for crops," he asked.

"That's right," Bonifay confirmed as the elevator gently rose towards the eighth floor. "She was working under a very large grant from General Dynamics Food Incorporated. She had already done marvelous work on modifying plums for growing in short season climates. She had also increased certain micronutrients in the crop as well. Our graduate students were very excited about what they were learning while working under her direction. Nan had begun working on other fruits just before she disappeared."

"And that brings me to an important question. Have there been any threats against the University for working on genetically modified foods?" Rory asked.

"Absolutely nothing," Bonifay said as the elevator doors opened. "The only problems we've *ever* had here occurred some years ago when we had animals in the lab. But we don't do that anymore. We haven't received a single threat on any of the projects the university is working on, including this food crop one. And there haven't been any demonstrations either," he added as they exited the elevator. He turned right and walked a few feet down the hallway to a door on the left. Bonifay inserted his key card in a reader and began punching a code into the keypad.

Rory watched the Professor with interest, "You keep everything locked up? Everyone has to have keycards and codes?"

"Oh yes. Definitely," Bonifay said. "The work being done here is potentially worth billions of dollars. But we're not worried so much about somebody breaking in and stealing things. We're far more worried about things being contaminated. Besides, this is a teaching facility and we run things exactly the way the students will encounter them in a private laboratory setting once they graduate. Out there in the real world, this is exactly what you'll find, everything under lock and key."

The door unlocked and Rory stepped through the doorway ahead of Bonifay. He found himself in a wide hallway that ran at least one hundred feet. He was surprised by the fact the walls on both sides of the hallway were glass. It was like being in a huge fishbowl. Behind the glass wall on the right, he could see a long string of offices. The glass wall on the left gave him an open view of a large laboratory filled with students and staff in white lab coats. The entrance to the laboratory was an eight-foot archway in the glass wall down the hallway. The lab itself was divided in half by a frosted glass wall with four archways equally spaced across the room. Through the archways, he could see more students and staff. The air smelled 'dead' so Rory assumed air scrubbers were at work.

"Impressive isn't it?" Bonifay said as the door softly closed behind him.

"That's an understatement."

"Beyond that frosted wall are millions of dollars worth of scientific equipment," Bonifay told him proudly. "We've been very fortunate to have an alumnus that has been very generous in donations. We have a laboratory for teaching that is the envy of universities around the world. Now, if you'll follow me, Mr. Steele, Nan's office is just down here."

As Rory followed Bonifay, he noted a number of biosafety suites on the far side of the laboratory. He knew that agricultural containment rooms, to prevent contamination on agents undergoing study, were necessary for the type of work Nan did. But these looked more like biosafety level four rooms for studying dangerous pathogens. He made a mental note to ask Bonifay about it.

The professor led Rory twenty feet down the glass hallway and into one of the offices on the right. "This was the Nan's office, Mr. Steele," Bonifay told him. "While you get started on your search in here, I'm going to get one of the staff who was closest with Nan. I'll be back in one moment."

As the professor left, Rory took a look around the office. There were some bookshelves with a number of books on genetic engineering and gene splicing. Rory sat down in the chair behind the desk and looked through the drawers. All he found were office items, some paper and a bit of change. A large computer monitor sat on the desk. The tower was under the desk and Rory pressed a button to turn it on. He watched the monitor as it booted. It required a password. Rory looked around on the desk. He didn't see anything that might give him a clue as to the password. Then he thought back to what her father had said about his daughter being naïve. Rory typed 'nan' into the password box, pressed enter and he was in. He began looking through the computer files. He opened up each one but they were filled with a lot of scientific gobbledygook that made little sense to him. He sifted through Nan's e-mail but all of it was based around scientific research. And all the e-mails appeared to come from somebody within the University. He noted there was nothing of a personal nature. He checked out the websites she visited. There were only a couple in the computer history and they dealt with scientific papers. There were no social media sites or any online forums that she visited. Nanette Bacon was definitely different. Rory felt it was unusual for someone who had grown up in the digital age to never use the Internet for a little surfing now and then.

Professor Bonifay came back into the room, followed by a young, dark-haired woman. He came around the desk and looked at what Rory was doing. "How in the world were you able to get into that computer so fast? All of these computers are supposed to be airtight secure."

"Hidden talent," was all that Rory said.

He shook his head in bewilderment, "I'm glad you're on our side, Mr. Steele." He was half-serious when he added, "Maybe we should have you work downstairs in our computer labs."

"I'll keep that in mind, in case I need a job," Rory said.

Bonifay shook his head again and then turned his attention to the young woman he had brought into the office, "Mr. Steele, this is Cora-Anne Junkins."

Rory stood up and shook her hand, "Ms. Junkins."

Junkins seemed to blush slightly as she looked into his silver-blue eyes and gave him a shy nod, "Mr. Steele."

"Cora-Anne worked in the lab with Ms. Bacon and was probably the closest to her," Bonifay said. "She'll work with you in here and give you access to anything else that you need in the laboratory. Although, from the looks of it I don't think you need our help to access anything. Well, I'll be downstairs if you need me anymore." He shook hands with Rory and left.

Cora-Anne Junkins crossed her arms over her chest, "Professor Bonifay said you were hired to find Nan?"

"That's right," Rory confirmed. "So you knew her well?"

"Despite what Professor Bonifay said, none of us here really knew her well or were close to her. I worked with Nan for the past two years but learned very little about her personally," Junkins said. "Don't get me wrong, Nan got along with everyone, but she really wasn't a social person. It was all about the work with her."

"Is there anything that you can think of that would cause her to disappear? Did she have any problems in her personal life? Were there any bad boyfriends?" Rory asked her.

"No, nothing that I can think of," Junkins said. "A number of us got together at a pub once a month, but when she joined us she never talked about anything beyond her work. If she had a boyfriend, she never talked about him. But to be honest with you, I don't know where or when she could have gotten into trouble. She was always working. And she was working even longer hours lately so she could finish her present project and get back to her other work."

Rory cocked his head, "What do you mean her other work? You mean outside of the lab?"

Cora-Anne Junkins shook her head, "Oh no, no. Nothing like that. Nan was talked into doing a genetics food project by Professor Bonifay. It was going to bring millions of dollars into the University and he promised Nan to put more money into her pet research."

"What did she normally do?"

"She was into genetic research on diseases," Cora answered. "That was her passion. She wanted to cure every disease known to mankind. She was almost obsessive about it. She's already made some amazing breakthroughs on Cholera and Malaria."

"I see." Rory chewed on his lower lip for a moment, wondering if there was a reason there for her disappearance. "Then he asked, "Was she worried about anything? Was there anyone bothering her?"

"The police asked the same questions," Cora-Anne replied, "and there was nothing like that at all. Everything seemed perfectly normal the last day we saw her. She left the lab to go home and never showed up the next morning."

"And she never said anything about not coming back? Maybe there was something she said to someone else in the lab?"

Junkins shook her head no, "The police talked to everyone and we talked about it after they were gone. I was the only one she really talked to that day. And just like every other day, she never said anything to me beyond the work we were doing. That was all she knew."

"Can you think of anyone else I can talk to? How about at the pub you talked about, anyone outside of your workgroup that she talked to?"

"Not that I can think of. There was someone that used to work here that Nan knew from her University days. Her name was Lillian Safford and the two got along famously. She's the only real friend I ever saw Nan Bacon have. I haven't seen her since she left and Nan never mentioned her after that. Maybe if you talk to her she might know something more."

Rory nodded to himself. This was at least a trail he could follow, no matter how tenuous, "Where is this Lillian Safford now?"

"She left the University about six months ago and went to work for a large laboratory," Cora-Anne told him. "I don't remember the name, but the lab itself is supposed to be in Brooklyn somewhere. She had an office up on Madison Avenue and East 23rd Street though."

"That's close to where Nan Bacon lived at Broadway and East 22nd Street in the Flatiron District," Rory mused. "But that's a long way from a lab that's supposed to be in Brooklyn."

"Like I said," Cora replied, "they were close. Lillian tried to talk her into joining her but Nan wanted to stay with the NYU Genetics Laboratory. She loved the research we were doing here. And she loved helping others to learn."

"All right. Would you mind looking at the files on her computer for me while I do a little more looking in here?"

Cora-Anne's eyebrows rose at the request, "Of course." She sat down in front of the computer, still looking puzzled, "Am I looking for anything specifically?"

"I'm just wondering if you see anything that stands out. Something that would not be part of her normal work here at the

University," Rory told her. As Cora-Anne began looking through the computer files, Rory moved to the books on the bookshelves again. This time he took each one and leafed through them quickly. He was looking for a clue, maybe a note in a margin or some kind of loose paper that might be inside. He looked for anything that might give him an idea about what had happened to Nanette Bacon.

"I'm afraid I don't see anything here that could help," Cora-Anne said after 15 minutes of looking through the files. "Everything here is dealing with her work in the laboratory, either her present research on crop modifications or what she was doing in the past on various diseases. I'm sorry I can't help you more."

Rory was finished with the last scientific book as well and hadn't found a thing. "Thank you for all your help," Rory said. "I'll go and see if I can find Lillian Safford. Hopefully, she'll have some information that can lead me to find Nan Bacon."

Chapter 4

RORY TOOK ANOTHER Yellow Cab up to Madison Avenue and East 23rd Street. Not having much to go on, he simply began looking through the various office lobbies on the block. There were dozens and dozens of companies that made for a long, boring search. Rory had to stop twice at a Starbucks for coffee and the energy boost. He finally found a lobby directory that had an office on the 15th floor for a MetaTech Laboratories Inc. What caught his eye was the name below the company name. Dr. L. Safford, PhD. Rory took the swift elevator up to the 15th floor. When he exited the elevator, a MetaTech sign on the wall in front of him pointed down the hallway to the left. He wandered down the hallway until he found a door that read MetaTech Laboratories Inc. He went inside and found a large, impressive plush office space with a small, pretty blond receptionist behind a large curved counter. Behind her, in big bold letters on the wall, was the name again: MetaTech Laboratories Inc.

"May I help you sir?" asked the perky blond behind the counter.

"I'm looking for Dr. Lillian Safford," Rory said as he approached the counter.

The receptionist went into a protective mode as if she were protecting the keys to the kingdom, "Do you have an appointment with Dr. Safford?" she asked him curtly.

"No," Rory said, "my name is Rory Mack Steele. I've been hired to look into the disappearance of a good friend of hers, Nanette Marlayne Bacon."

"Oh!" the young blond said in surprise. "I met Dr. Bacon a couple of times when she came here to see Dr. Safford. A couple of detectives came here to talk to Dr. Safford as well after Dr. Bacon disappeared. Just a moment and I'll let Dr. Safford know you're here. I'm sure she'll want to see you." The young blond hurried out from behind the counter and disappeared down a long hallway to the left. Rory could hear her heels clicking away. It was only a few moments before he heard two sets of heels clicking and coming back this way. The young blond appeared again and right behind her strode a tall, attractive brunette dressed in a black sheath dress and black high heel shoes. The strong floral scent of roses arrived before her. She flashed a bright smile and looked directly into Rory's silver-blue eyes as she held her hand out, "I'm Dr. Lillian Safford. Mr. Steele is it?"

"Yes," Rory replied as he noted she had a very firm handshake for a woman. It was the kind of handshake that usually came from a man who was trying to convey his strength and manliness. But this beauty sure wasn't a man.

"Please follow me," she said as she spun on her heels and began walking towards the long hallway. "We can talk in my office," she said back over her shoulder. She was obviously used to people following her directions.

Rory's gaze fell to her long, shapely, tanned legs. And her swinging hips. When he saw the doctor designation downstairs in the lobby, he hadn't expected a doctor in a hot body. Beauty, brains and probably a lot of money all in one package, a woman to dream about. Rory looked up and realized she was looking back at him as she opened the door into an office. The smile on her face said she knew exactly what he was looking at it and what he was thinking. Caught like a dumb schoolboy, Rory cleared his throat as he stepped through the doorway behind her.

Dr. Safford stepped around behind a large metal desk and simply stood there. She waited until Rory was on the other side of the desk before she sat down. She crossed her legs very slowly, lifting her knee fairly high and giving Rory an obvious glimpse of her shapely thighs before her black dress settled back down. She indicated Rory could take a seat in the chair on the other side. "Now, what exactly can I do for you Mr. Steele?" she said with a knowing smile.

Rory realized she had watched him looking under her skirt when she had crossed her legs. Rory cleared his throat and sat down. "As I said to your receptionist, I've been hired to try and figure out what happened to Nanette Bacon. I understand you were her best friend."

"That's right," Dr. Safford confirmed, "we met at Harvard. She was just a kid and I was 10 years older than her but we hit it off right from the start. We both did our PhD in genetic engineering in Los Angeles but she graduated long before I did. She just blew through everything. Everything came so easy to her. She was amazing. Nan Bacon has a once-in-a-lifetime brilliant mind."

"And you both ended up working at the New York University genetics laboratory," Rory stated.

Dr. Safford nodded, "Yes. I was fortunate enough to get a position there after I graduated. It worked out great because we were such good friends and we were able to work very closely together. To tell you the truth, I actually learned a lot from Nan while I was there."

"And then you left," Rory said.

"Yes," Dr. Safford said with a nod. "I was actually sent to school by my father. He is the sole owner of MetaTech Laboratories and the plan was for me to come to work here all along, once I gained some experience in other laboratory settings. He wants me to eventually run the company. When I left, I tried to get Nan to come with me, but she wanted to finish up on some of her research at the laboratory. She's very loyal that way and I figured eventually she would come to work with me at MetaTech. We talked about it several times."

"I understand you've already talked to the police, Dr. Safford?" Rory asked her.

"Call me Lillian, please," she said. She flashed him a brilliant smile.

Rory nodded, "Okay Lillian. You can call me Rory."

Lillian Safford stood up. "Okay Rory," she said as she reached for a handbag on a small credenza behind her. "I'll only answer more of your questions if you take me to lunch."

Rory stood up, a little confused at the sudden turn in the conversation.

Lillian Safford came striding around the desk. She hooked her arm into his, gave him another bright smile and guided him out into the hallway and down to the reception area. "Hold all my calls, Carolyn," she said to the young blond behind the counter, "I'm going to lunch with Mr. Steele." She led Rory out the door and back down the hallway towards the elevator. The elevator door opened with the first punch of the button and they stepped inside. As the elevator dropped swiftly to the lobby floor Lillian held onto his arm and placed her other hand over his bicep. "I love a man with muscles," she said with a twinkle in her eye.

Rory wasn't quite sure where this was going. The elevator quickly reached the ground floor and he was guided out of the elevator by Lillian Safford and across the lobby to a wood and brass door marked Las Tosca. Rory was guided into a small, intimate restaurant, filled with the aroma of roast beef and fine wine.

The maître d' met her and greeted her by name. He immediately took them to a secluded table near the back.

When Rory sat down, he was surprised when Lillian sat down on his right instead of across from him.

The Maître d' called a waiter over who took their orders for drinks and a small lunch special for each.

"Now, where were we," said Lillian Safford as she turned her attention to Rory.

"I was asking you about talking to the police," Rory stated.

"Oh yes," Lillian said as she slowly crossed her legs again, lifting her knee high enough to give Rory another inviting glimpse of her shapely thigh under the black dress. Rory was also surprised when the toe of her foot actually touched against his left leg and stayed there.

"I was actually the one who called them," Lillian said as she leaned a little in his direction. "Nan was supposed to meet me on Wednesday for lunch here in this restaurant. But she never showed up. I never thought much about it because Nan was sometimes obsessed with her work and would forget things. But when I couldn't get her at home that night, I called the NYU Genetics Laboratory in the morning. They said they hadn't seen her for a couple of days and the police were looking into it. I called them immediately to see what was happening. They came down to my office and they interviewed me but I never heard from them again. And I guess they haven't found Nan either."

"No," Rory said, "that's why I was asked to look into it."

"Who hired you?" Lillian asked. She sat back a little as the waiter put her drink in front of her.

"Her father," Rory said as he picked up his own scotch on the rocks.

That remark immediately caught Lillian's attention, "Her father? I remember Nan saying her mother was dead but I never heard anything about her father. I just presumed he was dead as well." Lillian seemed to drift off, lost in thought as she sipped on her martini.

"No, he's alive," Rory said, watching her reaction. She was definitely surprised by the mention of Nan's father. "Was there anything that was bothering Nan?" he asked after a few moments. "Was there anything that you could point to as a reason why she would simply vanish?"

Lillian took a few moments to answer. Then she seemed to come out of her deep thoughts and turned her attention back to Rory. She shook her head, "No. Nothing that I can think of." She casually placed a hand on her black dress and pulled the hem back of a couple of inches, exposing more of her tanned legs.

"You two were friends," Rory asked as he admired her legs. "What she romantically involved with anyone?"

Lillian laughed, "God no. Nan and I used to make comments about some of the good-looking guys in school and at work. But she never had any time for a personal relationship. She was too wrapped up in her work. And she was brilliant at it as well. She was the best at gene splicing that I ever saw. She was the best either university ever saw. I tried to emulate her when we were in university, we all did, but she was light years ahead of us. She was just someone special when it came to genetics and gene splicing."

"So there was nothing bothering her," Rory asked, "no one she was having problems with?"

Lillian thought for a moment as the waiter placed their lunches in front of them. "There was something, but I don't know if it's relevant," she said finally.

"Even the smallest thing might help," Rory said as he picked up a fork.

"Well, she was working on something in her apartment," Lillian told him as she picked up a fork and lightly touched her lunch. "She was working on some puzzle that had to do with old diseases. She talked to me about it a bit, then never mentioned it again. I do remember her saying someone wanted her information but she was determined not to share it with them."

That comment really piqued Rory's interest. "Was she defensive about her work?"

"Oh no, nothing like that," Lillian answered as she set her fork down. "There are some people in the scientific profession that are very possessive or very guarded about their work. They don't want to share any information or credit with anyone else. But that wasn't Nan. Not by a long shot. She was always willing to share her work as well as the credit."

"Then why wouldn't she want to share her work in this particular case?" Rory asked her.

Lillian thought for a moment and then shook her head, "I'm not sure why. All I know is there was someone she didn't want to share this particular aspect of her research with."

"Do you know who it was?"

Lillian Safford shook her head no again, "I never really thought too much about it after she stopped talking about it. In fact, you're the only one I've ever mentioned it to." She placed her left hand on Rory's right, "But it's such a small thing. I can't imagine a puzzle about some old diseases would have anything to do with her disappearance. Do you?"

Rory looked into Safford's hazel eyes, "I've seen people get into fights over the stupidest things. You never know."

"Well in that case, why don't you and I go up to her apartment after lunch and see what we can find," Lillian said as she rubbed his hand gently. "Nan and I exchanged keys. I know I seem all bubbly and bright, but that's how I deal with things. Nan was always serious and studious and I was the opposite. I think that's why we hit it off so well. But I really am worried about her and I would like to help you if I can." Her hazel eyes looked directly into Rory's silver-blue ones. Will you let me?" she pleaded.

Rory nodded. "Of course. You two were good friends –"

Lillian Safford leaned over and took something gently off the side of Rory's mouth, "Nan and I were the best of friends. I'm sure you and I will be just as close."

Chapter 5

AFTER LUNCH, Lillian Safford led Rory outside the restaurant to her Ferrari 458 Spider parked at the curb.

Rory thought it was a flashy car for someone who was friends with a quiet academic person like Nanette Bacon. He was barely sitting in his seat before Lillian put it in gear and shot away from the curb, squeezing into tight spaces between the traffic as she headed over to Nan Bacon's apartment at Broadway and East 22nd Street.

Rory struggled to buckle in and looked over at Lillian. Her black dress crept up her thighs as she handled the stick shift, giving Rory a nice view of her shapely legs. He enjoyed the view as the dress slid higher. He glanced up.

Lillian gave Rory a wink.

Rory felt a little like a peeping tom. Then a thought struck him...was she letting her dress ride up on purpose?

A few moments later, Lillian pulled over to the curb and parked the car. She turned and looked at Rory through her thick eyelashes, "Would you be a dear and go around and giving me a helping hand to get out? Sometimes these cars are just a little too low for a lady."

Rory got out and jogged around the front of the vehicle. He opened her passenger door and held his hand out. Lillian turned in her seat and slowly lifted her left leg up. She kept her right foot on the car floor and opened her legs wide, giving Rory a full view of the lacy black panties between her legs! He averted his eyes to look up the street.

Lillian slowly set her black, high heel shoe on the pavement and then got out of the Ferrari. She tapped Rory on the cheek and gave him a small smile. Walking around the front of the car, she strutted towards the lobby entrance.

Rory felt like a dumb schoolboy getting caught again. But he couldn't help himself. He watched her shapely legs and bottom as she walked in front of him down the short walkway to the front door of the building. He played back the mental image of her getting out of the car and the full display of her black silk panties between those long, shapely legs. In fact, he played it back several times.

Safford punched in the code to gain access to the building. The door clicked and Rory pulled it open, allowing her to walk in ahead of him. She strutted across the large lobby towards an elevator, allowing Rory to watch her legs again. But instead of taking the elevator, she turned left and walked down a long hallway.

"Nan hated heights, so she insisted on an apartment on the ground floor," Lillian said. She looked back at Rory and caught him looking at her legs again. When Rory looked up, she wiggled her eyebrows a couple of times. A moment later, she stopped midway down the hallway and put a key into the lock of the door on the left. Unlocking it, they went inside.

Rory walked in behind Lillian, getting his first view of Nanette Bacon's home. The apartment was quite large but sparsely furnished. There was a small white sofa on the left with a couple of unmatched easy chairs in front of it and not much else. Rory didn't see a television anywhere. And no radio, sound system or iPod dock for music either. Nanette Bacon was definitely someone who didn't care about decorating, furniture shopping or entertaining. There was a very light scent of woody potpourri, which meant she was too busy to even keep that fresh. To his right was a fairly large kitchen area, filled with stainless steel appliances. Everything looked brand new and untouched. "It doesn't even look lived in," Rory said.

"No, but that was Nan," Lillian said. She strode across the living room and turned left, going down a hallway, "She had a computer room down here. That would be where she did most of her research when she was home." Lillian opened a door on the left and went inside the room.

Rory followed behind her. This room looked to be a large study. Unlike the living room, every bit of space in here was packed with something in it. On the left was a window that looked out onto the street. The window was covered with curly, black iron security bars. The rest of the wall space around the room consisted of built-in bookcases that were filled with books of every size and color. There were a couple of easy chairs around the room and books were piled high on them as well. In the center of the room and facing the window was a large desk with a computer and a 30-inch monitor on it. On the left-hand side of the computer desk were three open books, sitting one on top of the other. A brown folder, containing a pile of papers, was on the right side of the desk. There was a closet door on the right wall, in the middle of the bookcases.

"This is where Nan spent most of her time," Lillian said, sweeping a hand around the room. "She was either working on her computer or reading one of her books."

Rory wandered along the bookcases, running his hand along the spines of the books and browsing the titles.

"You won't find a romance novel or any other kind of book beyond science," Lillian said as she stood by one of the other bookcases. She ran her hand across the spines of the books as well but she was watching Rory as she said, "She was dedicated to her work and driven to increase her knowledge of genetics."

Rory walked back to the computer, sat down and turned it on, "Let's see if she has anything on here that helps us." As the computer booted up, Lillian Safford walked over behind Rory and put her hands on the back of the chair. The password on this computer was the same as the one at her workplace; nan. Rory looked through her e-mail messages. There were only a few messages from someone at work or from Lillian. That was it. All the bookmarks in her browser were to medical or science sites, nothing for any of the social media sites, hobbies or outside interests. Rory opened her document folder and leaned forward as he began looking through the various files.

Lillian Safford bent over and looked over Rory's shoulder, "Anything of interest?"

Rory was conscious of her breasts pressing gently against his back. It took his mind off the files for a moment and he had to refocus. "Most of the files seem to be about various diseases," Rory said finally.

"Uh huh," Lillian said. "That was Nan's specialty. Diseases. She was going to cure every disease known to man. She always said that. It was almost her mantra."

"That's similar to what Cora-Anne Junkins said as well at the University when I talked to her," Rory replied as he looked over a large number of folders.

"Her?" Lillian replied icily. "That one is a piece of work. She was always trying to horn in on everything. Trying to share in the credit for what Nan accomplished."

"She seemed nice," Rory said. He clicked open a folder to look through the files. Science was the theme for every file he looked at.

"Yeah, well don't let her fool you," Lillian said.

Rory heard the disdain in her voice. He also felt her breasts press a little more against his back. Not finding anything in the folders that piqued his curiosity, Rory looked over the items sitting on top of the computer desk itself. He reached over for the brown folder that was on the right side of the desk. He laid it across the keyboard, flipped it open and looked at the pile of pages it contained.

"What's in there?" Lillian asked as she pressed her breasts firmly against him again.

"There are dozens of pages that look like copies of an old manuscript," Rory replied. He looked back at the front page. "The title is De re Militari by Publius Flavius Vegetius Renatus. That's a mouthful."

"Oh, right!" Lillian exclaimed as she quickly moved around Rory's right to look through the pages in the folder herself, "Nan told me she had found something in an old Roman military book from the 4th or 5th century when she was researching the puzzle she was working on. She said it was a military manual and every European country used it for training, strategy, and tactics right up to the 19th century. Actually, now that I think about it, it was a late 17th-century Italian version of the original that she'd found. It was in the New York Library special collections department if I recall correctly."

"Why was she looking in the special collections? What was she looking for?" Rory asked her.

Lillian and shook her head slowly as she looked closely at the pages, "I have no idea. But she said it piqued her interest because what she found had an additional section on biological warfare that wasn't in the original version. I was surprised because I didn't even think they used biological warfare that far back. I think she said it referred to the Italian bubonic plague outbreak of 1629. But don't quote me on that."

"This whole thing seems to be written in Italian," Rory said as he watched Lillian flip through the pages.

"You're right, it does," Lillian agreed.

Rory sat back in the chair. "Why was she interested in the bubonic plague from hundreds of years ago?"

Lillian gave him a shrug, "That was Nan for you." Picking up the entire brown folder, Lillian continued to leaf through the loose pages, "The Black Plague was probably the worst disease in the history of mankind and she was fascinated by it. The Great Plague of Milan in the 1600s took about 280,000 people. The Black Death in the 1300s is estimated to have killed up to 60% of Europe's population. And from what Nan said, the plague had struck in areas of the Asian continent before that."

Rory shook his head at how she had taken over the folder. He turned his attention to the three books piled one on top of the other on the left-hand side of the desk. While Lillian continued looking through the papers in the folder, Rory reached over and pulled the books closer to him. The top book was on the Italian plague Lillian had referred to. The next book was on the European plague. But the third book wasn't about Europe at all. It concentrated on China and the reports of the Plague that broke out there almost 2,600 years before it hit Europe. This book had a number of small pieces of paper inserted as bookmarks. Rory checked each one out. Each page discussed some aspect of the plague reports. A couple of the reports referenced biological warfare using the black plague over the centuries. He pushed the books back to their original spot and sat back in the chair.

Lillian rustled through the pages for a few more moments and then looked down at him."What are you thinking?"

Rory didn't say anything for a moment and then, without looking up, he said, "You say she found something someone wanted. Do you think someone could have wanted this type of information on the plague?"

"You mean like terrorists?" Lillian asked him.

Rory looked up and nodded.

Lillian put down the folder, one eyebrow rising, "You think someone kidnapped Nan for this information?"

Rory gave her a shrug, "I'm just throwing out ideas here."

Putting a hand to her chest, Lillian said, "Do you think I might be in danger? I was Nan's friend and maybe they think I know something." She moved her body against Rory, one hand on his far shoulder and the hand moving softly over his black hair, before settling on the far side of his head, "I'm so glad you're here."

Rory felt her breast press against his right ear as she pulled his head into the softness, "I'm not sure that's actually happened but you don't have to worry." He was enjoying the closeness and his thoughts went to the erotic memory of the black panties between her open legs. After a moment of letting her breast press against his ear, he cleared his throat, aware of something stirring between his own legs, "Maybe we should check out the rest of the apartment."

Lillian stepped back and let Rory get up. But as he headed out the study door, Lillian stayed glued to him.

Rory opened the door right across the hall. It was a bathroom. Seeing nothing of interest in there, he turned left. Lillian was right there, pressed up against him. He walked down to the next door on the left. He opened the door and went inside. He saw a bed, a table, and a lamp. There was nothing else in the room. *Probably a guest room.* He stepped across the hall and opened the door. It led to a larger bedroom. This one had a large Queen sized bed with a bedside table on either side topped by a lamp. And beside each bedside table was a bookcase filled with books. Rory stepped inside and walked over towards the bed. On the right-hand side was a long set of mirrored doors, probably leading to a bedroom closet.

Lillian moved in close behind him, her voice soft and purring, "What exactly do you have in mind by leading me into a room with a bed, in the middle of all this danger, Mr. Steele?" She put her hand over his shoulder and rubbed his cheek. She moved closer, pressing her breasts against him, whispering something in his ear.

But Rory wasn't listening. He was staring at the bedroom wall to his left.

Lillian emitted a chuffing sound, miffed that he wasn't paying any attention to her. She slowly turned her head to see what he was staring at. "Oh!"

The entire wall was written on in black magic marker. Someone had printed out a message in very painstaking detail:

¿ÕßµþôÄ♀§↕§○§òôÅÖÉÿÜøÉ×æìÆÓƒ×ôëåôÆßÒrÇüⵉÇçØ×Ù

"What in the world is that?" whispered Lillian in amazement.

"You're the one with the PhD. You tell me," Rory muttered.

Lillian's voice sounded awe-struck as she walked forward, staring intently at the wall, "I have absolutely no idea. This must be what Nan was working on."

Chapter 6

LILLIAN SAFFORD was a foot from the bedroom wall, staring intently at the strange writing. "How do we figure out what it says?" she asked him.

"Don't look at me," Rory said. "I'm no expert in decoding. Besides, why would we spend time trying to figure it out?" Rory was actually looking down at her long legs.

Lillian Safford turned and looked at him intently, "As I said before, Nan told me she had found something in her research, a puzzle that somebody else wanted. If Nan found something important in that message on the wall, maybe that's why she was kidnapped. It must be important, Rory. Why else would she write it on her wall? How many people do that?"

Rory mulled over that thought as he glanced at her bust. The strange writing was the last thing on his mind.

Lillian Safford walked back to him, put her arms around his neck and looked deeply into his silver-blue eyes, "Please. I'm afraid for Nan. Maybe if we figure out what's in that message, we'll be able to figure out why she's missing. Or who took her." Lillian moved in close, pressed the full length of her shapely body against him and whispered in his ear, "Please, Rory."

Rory felt her breasts pressing against his chest and he gave in, "Okay, what you're saying makes a lot of sense. And it's the only lead we've got." He looked over her soft shoulder at the strange writing, "But I'm not even sure where to start."

Lillian gave him a kiss on the cheek, "Thank you."

"But I do have an idea," Rory said as he reached into his pocket.

"Mmm, hmm, I can tell."

Rory didn't look at her as a wry smile crossed his lips. He shook his head as he pulled out his cell phone and held it up, wiggling it in the air.

Lillian gave him a wink as stepped back.

Rory stepped closer to the wall and took a picture of the strange writing. After he checked to make sure the image was readable, he said, "Okay, let's go back into her study." Rory stepped out into the hallway, followed closely by Lillian, and went back into Nan's study room. He went right to the brown folder on the right-hand side of the computer desk. Picking up the folder, he began looking through the pages inside.

"What are you looking for?" Lillian asked as she stood close beside him.

Rory tapped on the top sheet of the thick pile of papers in the folder, "It's a long shot, but I think this set of copies from the New York Library Special Collections is the last thing Nanette Bacon was working on. They might provide a clue to unravel the meaning of the writing on the wall."

Lillian crossed her arms across her ample chest, "But I didn't see anything like that strange writing on any of those pieces of papers. And I looked at every one of them."

Rory nodded as he continued looking, "You're right. I didn't see anything either. But you said Nan told you she found something that had to do with biological warfare. To me, that means diseases, right?"

"Well, it could also deal with a deadly fungus, but I get your point," Lillian answered.

Closing the folder, Rory took a breath and let it out slowly, tapping the folder against the palm of his hand. Then he gestured to the books on the desk, "Okay. All those have to do with the plague, which is a disease. You told me she said she was working on some puzzle that had to do with old diseases. If she found some centuries-old puzzle, connected to the document in this folder, maybe she hid that part somewhere, when she realized someone else wanted it, probably for the wrong reasons."

Lillian looked skeptical as she glanced around the room, "Maybe. But...."

Rory nodded, "I know, it's a needle in the haystack."

"And we don't know what the needle looks like," Lillian said.

"No," Rory said. He held the folder up, "But we do know one of the original haystacks she was looking through. And since this is the only lead we have to go on...."

Lillian looked at Rory for a moment and then nodded, "Then I guess we're headed to the New York Library Special Collections. What are we waiting for?" She took the thick brown folder from his hands and headed out of the study.

Rory had to smile to himself as he shook his head. Lillian Safford was an assertive woman who definitely didn't wait for someone else to take the lead. He followed Lillian out, enjoying the sway of her hips as she led the way to the Ferrari parked at the curb.

Once they were in the car, Lillian set the brown folder on his lap. He barely got his seatbelt on before she left the curb with a screech of tires, heading swiftly for the New York Special Collections building.

As she drove, Rory called ahead on his cell phone to speed things up. After explaining who he was and what he was doing, he was put through to the head of Manuscript and Rare Books, Dr. Enrico Gonzalez. As Rory talked to Gonzalez he watched Lillian's black dress climb higher up her long legs as she worked the clutch and brake. He fully expected...and hoped...to see a glimpse of her black panties again.

Lillian looked over and gave him a knowing smile.

Rory winked back at her as he ended the call. When she finally pulled to the curb in front of the New York City Library, Rory was disappointed when Lillian didn't ask for help getting out of the car. Instead, she got out on her side quite easily and moved around to the sidewalk in a hurry. Rory simply chalked it up to her being eager to further the search for her best friend. Rory called the library again to let Gonzalez know he and Lillian had arrived. A lady told him to wait inside the front entrance and someone would be right down. They climbed the stairs, flanked by two amazing marble lions, and stepped inside the busy and beautiful, marble library building. Astor hall was a soaring space that took your breath away. Two beautiful staircases led up to the second floor but they stayed put as requested. The rich scent of old books filled the air and the hushed voices and light footsteps of the other visitors echoed off the walls.

"Mr. Steele?"

Rory looked to his right and saw a tall gentleman with curly black hair, a pencil-thin mustache, and movie idol good looks approaching them.

"I am Dr. Enrico Gonzalez," the tall gentleman said. He flashed a smile of white teeth and stuck out his right hand towards Rory, "We spoke on the telephone."

Rory shook his hand, "Yes sir, thank you for seeing us so quickly."

"No problem," Dr. Gonzalez said, "I'm happy to do anything to help where Ms. Bacon is involved."

When Rory introduced Lillian, he noted the good doctor was also a charming Casanova who held her hand a little longer than necessary for a simple hello. Rory broke into the flirting doctor's act and extended the brown folder. "This is the document I was talking about when I talked to you on our way over here."

Dr. Gonzalez took a few more seconds before he removed his attention from Lillian and took the folder. He looked at the contents. "Ah yes, I remember this. This is part of an extensive collection left to us a number of years ago by a generous patron of the library. This particular part of the collection related to the genealogy of his family that went back for centuries. The family had been part of the Italian military and they had collected medals, citations and other records for each member of their ancestors who had been involved."

"Can we look at the original?" Lillian asked him with some eagerness.

"Yes, of course," Gonzalez said as he flashed another smile at her. He pulled out a cell phone and hit speed dial. "Hello, Amanda. Would you please check on your computer for the Guimonti collection for me? Thank you."

Rory saw him flash another smile at Lillian as he waited for an answer. *This guy is Casanova x 2.*

Gonzalez's attention went back to the call, "Good, good. Please take it to room 14. We'll be right up. Thank you, Amanda." He closed the call and nodded, "You can go upstairs right now to look at it. Usually, a collection like this is kept in the vaults because it doesn't relate to a lot of the things our patrons are looking for here in New York. But Ms. Bacon had it out not long ago and it hasn't been returned to the vault yet." He took Lillian's elbow and began walking with her towards the elevators.

"Is it also possible to get a list of any other parts of your collections Nan Bacon may have been looking at over the last few months?" Rory asked him from behind. He felt like a third wheel at the moment.

Dr. Gonzalez looked over his shoulder at Rory and shook his head, "No. I'm afraid we wouldn't be able to do that." Reaching the elevator, Gonzales pushed the call button. The doors opened immediately and he ushered Lillian inside the elevator car.

"If you're concerned about privacy issues, I can put you in touch with her father," Rory said as he stepped into the elevator. "He can verify she is missing and that I've been hired to find her."

Dr. Gonzalez pushed a floor button and the elevator rose. "That's not necessary Mr. Steele. That's not the problem, I am very happy to cooperate in any way I can," Dr. Gonzalez replied. "I'm afraid we simply don't have a list like that for Ms. Bacon."

"You don't keep track of who looks at items in your Special Collections? Even items kept in the vaults?" Rory asked. "I would've thought the library would've automatically done that for any of your collections."

"Oh yes, we do, Mr. Steele," Dr. Gonzalez replied as the elevator stopped and the doors opened. "We are very conscious of security, as well as knowing what subjects interests our patrons. We always want to know what type of collections to pursue."

Rory's brow furrowed and he rubbed his chin, "Then why not in this case?"

"Because Ms. Bacon was staff," Gonzalez replied as they all exited the elevator.

Lillian looked at Gonzalez in surprise, "She was a staff member of the library?"

"Oh yes," Dr. Gonzalez replied, "Ms. Bacon was a very brilliant young lady. I don't think she was 13 when she first came here during summer vacation. She used some of our collections to write her Master's thesis, as well as a number of other scholarly papers. The surprising thing was she also helped us to sort out parts of the collection we never had the time to get to. This collection you're asking about was one of them. She was a remarkable young lady. My area of expertise is linguistics and she could have been the best in my field if she had chosen to apply herself to it. When we realized how much she could help us, we made her a staff member with full access to the library. Once she went through our exhaustive collection and satisfied her curiosities there, she began working on anything un-cataloged. She would make reports on anything she had analyzed and sent it to the head of the specific department. She was amazingly helpful. We would've hired her full-time if possible."

"I had no idea she was doing this," Lillian said in astonishment.

Shaking his head, Dr. Gonzalez said, "She did all of that while spending only a short amount of time here. It would have taken the rest of us working more than eighty hours weeks to accomplish even a fraction of what she did." He led them into a room with several tables and chairs, "You can work in here in private."

The smell of old paper, with an underlying trace of must, arrived a moment later, when a young woman appeared, wheeling a small cart carrying three boxes. "This is the part of the Guimonti collection that was still out, Dr. Gonzalez," she said.

"Thank you, Amanda." As she left, Dr. Gonzalez handed white gloves to Rory and Lillian, "Please use these as you look through the collection. The items are very old, so please use caution as you handle the papers. If you need anything else, please ask at the desk outside. I won't be very far away." He flashed another brilliant smile at Lillian and turned on his heels, disappearing out the door.

Lillian looked at the cart, "Okay. So where do we start?"

"How about I take this box and you look through that one?" Rory said. "Let's see what we can find."

Lillian nodded as she lifted a box and set it on one end of the table. Rory set his box down on the other end and they began going through the collection. It took them several hours of painstaking work before Rory came across what they were looking for in an old, leather-bound volume. He turned a page and there was the strange writing. Rory took out his cell phone and brought up the picture he had taken in Nan's bedroom.

Lillian was up out of her chair immediately and moved around to his side of the table, "Did you find something?"

Rory held the image on his cell phone next to the page of the leather-bound volume on the table, "Looks like this is where she got the writing from," he said. "It looks like other parts of the page had that strange writing as well but it's all faded."

Lillian lightly brushed her fingertips across the page as she bent over to look closer. "It was hand-lettered," she whispered. She gently turned a few pages of the leather-bound volume, "The rest of the pages are all hand-lettered as well. Gonzalez said it was part of someone's Italian family history...so I guess the writing is in Italian." She looked at Rory, "Do you have any idea what this is all about?"

Rory shook his head, "No, my Italian is nonexistent. Maybe Dr. Gonzalez can help us. It's part of his collection and he's also a linguist."

Lillian Safford stood up and turned, her high heels clicking across the floor as she went to fetch Dr. Gonzalez.

Rory enjoyed the view of her long, tanned legs until she disappeared out the door and then looked back at the strange writing, wondering how they could decipher it.

Returning with Gonzalez in tow a few moments later, Lillian slid the leather-bound volume from in front of Rory, to the edge of the table, and pointed at the page, "This is what I'm talking about."

Dr. Gonzalez leaned over and leafed gently through the pages. He shook his head softly, "This is amazing. This was inside this collection?"

"Yes," Lillian confirmed, "can you read that? What's it all about?"

"Which box was it in?" Gonzalez asked.

Rory stood up and tapped the box on the table, "This is the one I was working on. And it was in the middle of those other documents and leather-bound volumes, sitting on the desk."

Gonzalez had the look of someone worshiping at the altar of ancient history. He was quiet as he moved around the table and looked over the contents in the box. Then he leafed through the other items on the desk.

Lillian crossed her arms and chewed on her lower lip as she watched Gonzalez.

After a few moments, Dr. Gonzalez went to the leather-bound volume with the strange writing again and looked through it. "Are you familiar with De Re Militari by Vegetius from the 4th century?" he finally asked in a quiet voice.

"Yes," Lillian said, "we figured out that part."

Dr. Gonzalez nodded, without looking up, "Well, *this* is a 17th-century version, with some additional sections added to it by an Italian military specialist of his time. Most of it is written in the Italian vernacular of the time period, with some other sections written in old Latin. This particular leather-bound volume is much older than the rest and is a collection from various periods. Some of it is written in early Italian, possibly the 6th century. Other sections are in old Latin, possibly from the 2nd century BC. This page with the strange writing looks to be even older. *Much* older, in fact."

"Is there an overall theme for this volume?" Rory asked.

Dr. Gonzalez pursed his lips for a moment, "Theme?" He took the leather-bound volume in his hands, stood up and turned a few pages, considering the question, "At a glance, I would say it deals with biological warfare. The different sections talk about various poisons and other biological agents. The pages before the strange writing discuss the military use of disease and warfare. Parts refer specifically to the Great Plague of Milan."

"The Great Plague of Milan?" Lillian exclaimed. "You mean like the Black Plague? Are you sure?"

Chapter 7

"**OH YES**," Dr. Gonzalez confirmed, "the plague hit Italy, just like other parts of Europe centuries ago. From 1629 to 1631 it killed nearly 300,000 people in the Lombardi and Veneto regions alone. Famous cities like Milan, Venice, and Bologna were affected."

"So what does the page with the faded writing say about it?" Lillian pressed.

"I'm sorry Dr. Safford," Dr. Gonzalez said, "But I have no idea what the strange writing is. It must be some kind of code or cipher that would have to be unlocked."

Lillian's voice was filled with excitement, "Can you unlock it for me?"

Dr. Gonzalez closed the leather-bound volume, holding it against his stomach as he considered the question, "I'm not really sure. There have been some codes that have defied centuries of work to uncover their secret. The Copiale Cipher was the latest one to be cracked. And that took 300 years."

"I don't think we have 300 years," Lillian said. She moved close to Dr. Gonzalez, put her palms on the lapels of his jacket and looked up into his eyes, "Please help us. It may help us to find Nan."

Rory raised his eyebrows as he watched Lillian work the good doctor.

Dr. Gonzalez looked back into her eyes, "Give me a moment."

Rory watched as Gonzalez brought the slim volume up from his waist and the back of the good doctor's fingers and hands slowly pressed into the softness of her breasts.

"Hold this," Gonzalez whispered. His hands were now exactly where her nipples would be.

Lillian took the volume in her hands, not a word about the doctor feeling her up with the back of his hands. As he left the room, Lillian simply leafed through the bound volume again.

Rory actually felt a little jealousy course through his veins. He shook his head and, to distract himself, he went back and looked at the other papers contained in the collection.

A few minutes later about a dozen men and women entered the room. Dr. Gonzalez and a tall, white-haired man approached Rory and Lillian. "This is Dr. Bianchi," Dr. Gonzalez said. "Doctor Lillian Safford and Mr. Rory Mack Steele."

Rory and Lillian shook hands with Bianchi.

"Dr. Bianchi has quite a bit of experience with codes and ciphers," Gonzalez explained. He reached for the leather bound-volume again, taking it from Lillian's hands with a smile and opened it to show Bianchi the strange writing. Everyone else gathered around Bianchi and Gonzalez, talking excitedly as they looked at the strange symbols written across the page. After a few minutes, a few of the men and women walked over to look through the rest of the collection.

Lillian and Rory stepped back as they watched and listened to the group talk.

FIFTEEN MINUTES LATER, Dr. Gonzalez walked back to them, "As you can see everyone is very excited about this discovery. As I said, everything else is written in Italian and some in old Latin. But no one has ever seen writing like that and we are not really sure what it is, beyond some type of code. It doesn't appear to be a Caesar cipher like we would expect to see in Italian papers. But we're sure it would eventually translate into a variation of Italian or Latin."

"I heard someone talk about using a computer," Lillian said, "would that help?"

Dr. Gonzalez tugged at an earlobe, "Well, we do have a super-computer here that has been used to work on old languages. But time has to be scheduled behind other projects. We will do that eventually–"

"But can't we do it now?" Lillian asked as she moved towards him. "Nan is missing and...."

Rory watched her literally bat her eyelashes at the man. *The woman is shameless in her manipulation.*

Dr. Gonzalez looked into the pleading hazel eyes of this beautiful woman. After a moment he said, "All right–"

Lillian didn't waste a heartbeat as she got moved up against Gonzalez, "Great. Lead us to it."

Rory felt small pangs of jealousy again as he watched Lillian's body press against the doctor's.

Dr. Gonzalez asked them to follow him. He led them out of the room and down a hallway to another room that had a larger computer sitting on a desk. A woman sat behind the computer. Dr. Gonzalez walked over to her and spoke to her in a low voice.

The woman got up and left. "I had to promise her extra time," Gonzalez said with a sheepish grin on his face.

"How do we get the special writing into the computer?" Lillian asked him as she moved quickly towards the desk.

"Well, we normally don't do this with old documents, but I will just for you," Dr. Gonzalez said to Lillian.

Lillian flashed a smile at him.

Rory felt like the third wheel in the room again.

Dr. Gonzalez took the old document and placed it in a scanner beside the computer. The light on the scanner flashed and the result was entered into the computer. Dr. Gonzalez then brought up an optical character recognition program and converted the scanned image into text that the computer could try to translate. He then brought up a translation program, "Okay. This is the program we normally use to translate foreign languages into English," Gonzalez explained. "That being said, it has been used to try and decipher a few codes. But it hasn't always been very successful, I'm afraid. But I have used cut-and-paste to enter the strange language into the computer and I've set the output to Italian. If it doesn't output anything that looks like Italian, you can use the mouse to change this option to Latin, here on the screen. If either Italian or Latin appears, you can cut-and-paste what it says into the input again and ask for an English output. Do you understand?"

"Perfectly," Lillian said as she gave him a kiss on the cheek, "thank you very much for your help."

Dr. Gonzalez nodded and flashed a smile, "You can stop it and start it here on the screen as well. You can change the method it's using to try and translate the symbols. I warn you, it may take some hours at the very least. In the meantime, I'll be around if you need me, Ms. Safford."

Rory watched Dr. Gonzalez walk out of the room.

Lillian sat down in one of the chairs in front of the computer and crossed her legs.

Rory looked at Lillian, simply sitting there and then said, "Maybe I'll get us a couple of coffees. If it's gonna take a few hours–"

"That would be great," Lillian said as she watched the flashing computer screen.

Rory felt totally ignored. He wandered off and returned later with some coffees.

Lillian was sitting back in the chair with her arms and legs crossed and her foot jiggling.

"Anything happening?" he asked her.

With an annoyed tone, Lillian said, "No. It just keeps says it's working. That's it."

Rory nodded and sat down, passing her a coffee. The computer continued to show 'working' on the screen for the next hour.

Lillian was obviously anxious for a breakthrough. Her foot continued to bounce and she bit her nails.

Rory tried to engage her in conversation but she remained distracted by the flashing computer. Rory left an hour later and got a couple more coffees. When he returned, he suggested they change the output to Latin.

Lillian nodded eagerly, happy to do more than just sit there. She worked with Rory to figure out how to change the parameters and then restarted the deciphering program. Unfortunately, another two hours passed slowly while the computer continued to work.

"This is getting frustrating," Lillian said finally as she tossed her coffee cup forcefully into the garbage can. She stopped the program and looked at the various parameters they could set, "Caesar cipher, Vigenere cipher, I don't understand any of this stuff. This is ridiculous!" She got up out of her chair quickly, looking pissed.

"Where are you going?" Rory asked her as she headed for the door.

"To get Gonzalez," was her curt answer. A few minutes later she came back into the room. Her arm was threaded through the arm of Dr. Gonzalez like she was going to dinner with him. She walked him back over to her chair where she sat down and crossed her legs slowly. She looked up at Dr. Gonzalez, "Please help us. We don't seem to be getting anywhere."

Dr. Gonzalez looked at Rory. Then he looked back at Lillian, holding his hands out and shrugging, "I'm not really sure how else I can help–"

"Just give us a few hints on how we try to crack this," Lillian said. She gave him a gleaming smile.

Rory raised an eyebrow as Lillian pulled her black dress back a few inches above her knee.

Dr. Gonzalez cleared his throat as he looked down at her shapely, tanned legs.

Lillian's dress moved back another inch.

Dr. Gonzalez kept his eyes on her shapely thighs as he cleared his throat and finally spoke, "Well...you may have a problem because you don't have a key or–"

"What do you mean a key?" Lillian asked him. She pulled the dress back another inch.

Dr. Gonzalez raised an eyebrow as more of her bare thigh came into view.

Rory watched the whole thing like he was in the front row of a theater play.

Gonzalez glanced into Lillian's hazel eyes, then back down at her shapely thighs, "Well...a key is used when someone uses a cipher to hide a message. It can be as simple as taking every fourth letter in an encrypted message and those letters will form the words for the hidden message. The person who receives the encoded message would know the key to unlock it. This supercomputer is powerful enough to use brute force methods. It will just try every possible combination and method until it decodes the message. In this case, I would've expected a Caesar cipher because that was in use throughout Europe for centuries. Maybe you simply haven't given it enough time to go through all the permutations possible. I told you it could take a long time—"

"What's the difference between a cipher and a code?" Lillian asked him. "And why would someone use one or the other?"

"Well, think about the different kinds of writing we've seen over the millenniums," Dr. Gonzalez explained. "We use an alphabet in our modern day society to form words. But over thousands of years, you also find picture writing or pictography like Sumerian cuneiform, Egyptian hieroglyphics or the Chinese ideograms."

Rory took a step forward and interrupted their conversation, "Ideograms? I've ever heard that word before but I'm not sure...?"

"That means they use pictures for a word or a concept, *not* an alphabet," replied Dr. Gonzalez. "So in those languages, they couldn't use a cipher because that type of encoding requires individual letters in a word. In languages that used picture writing, they would have resorted to using a code to hide a message. When you use a code, entire words or concepts are replaced by a symbol, a number or even another word. And when you use a code, you would also have the need for a codebook to encrypt and decrypt each puzzle. If that codebook falls into the wrong hands, everybody can figure out your secret messages. A cipher can be much more secure. For example, you may have a Caesar shift cipher. And the key that unlocks the cipher text is to shift every letter in the message three places. You don't need a codebook that can fall into enemy hands, you can easily keep that key in your mind and it's much safer."

Lillian looked in frustration at the computer still running, "And these symbols don't mean *anything* to you, Dr. Gonzalez?"

"No, I'm afraid not," Dr. Gonzalez replied. "The Masons have used different writing systems like this to encode things over the centuries. The Malachim and the Celestial codes are symbols that look like this. But the computer would've applied that automatically to try and decipher it. It obviously didn't work. The Copiale Cipher is another method I already mentioned. That one used special symbols like this and the computer would've applied that one as well. But like I said earlier, it took 300 years to crack the Copiale Cipher. If you have a similar code...even if this supercomputer does it 100 times faster, it will still take three years to crack it."

Lillian sat back, looking dejected. Then she seemed to pout as she pushed her black dress forward to cover her legs again.

Rory noted the disappointment in the good doctor's face.

"I'm sorry," Dr. Gonzalez said. When there was nothing further from Lillian, he turned and walked out of the room.

"Three years or 300 years, it doesn't make much difference, does it? We need to solve it *now*," said Lillian in a quiet voice as she watched the computer working. When Rory didn't say anything, she looked over at him, "To find Nan quickly, I mean."

Something didn't sit right with Rory...but he wasn't quite sure what it was.

Chapter 8

RORY TAPPED A FINGER lightly on the arm of the chair, trying to pin down what he was feeling, but it was like a fleeting shadow at the corner of his mind. It was shapeless but definitely there. A moment later, he shook his head softly and stood up, "I guess I can get us a couple more coffees."

Lillian simply nodded. Her shoulders were slumped as she watched the computer work. She wasn't much company in her present state.

Rory left the computer room behind, intending to find those two coffees. Instead, he found himself simply walking aimlessly. That shadow - that *something* - nagged at him from the corner of his mind. But he couldn't figure out what it was. Rory found himself staring out a window, watching the traffic and pedestrians in the street far below him. This case was a frustrating one. He hadn't been able to find one single clue that could lead him to Nan Bacon. And this episode with the strange writing was turning out to be a wild goose chase–

Suddenly another thought rose from the depths of his subconscious and hit him hard. Rory turned around and began looking for a computer with Internet access. One of the librarians pointed him in the right direction and within moments he was doing an Internet search. When he felt he was on the right path, he hustled quickly back to the room with the supercomputer. When he walked back into the room, Lillian hardly noticed him at all. Rory picked up the ancient document they had been working from and sat in his chair, looking at the leather-bound volume in his hands, thinking.

Lillian finally noticed him after several minutes. She swung her chair in his direction. "What are you thinking?"

Rory didn't answer her right away. He leafed through the pages.

"Rory?"

He looked at her, "Maybe we're making the wrong assumption. Because this volume was written in Italian and Latin, those are the languages we're trying to use to translate the puzzle."

"But that's what all those experts said it should be. What else would we use?" Lillian asked him. She gave him a look like he was an idiot.

Rory ignored the look, "Have you ever read Sherlock Holmes?"

"Of course, I think everyone has," Lillian said. She was annoyed with him now. "But what does that have to do with this?"

"Throughout the books, there was *one* thing Sherlock Holmes always used to stress in his investigations. In the Sign of Four...he said you needed to eliminate all other factors...and the one which remains, must be the truth."

Lillian looked at Rory with a puzzled look on her face, "I still don't understand."

Rory leaned forward, "All the experts keep saying the language behind this puzzle is either Latin or the Italian vernacular they used at the time "Why?"

Lillian blinked several times, thinking, "Because the collection is from an Italian family...a family history thing...."

"Exactly. *But*...we've eliminated those language factors. They're not working. So what are we left with?"

Lillian shook her head slowly, still not comprehending.

Rory sat up a little straighter, "Gonzalez said this page with the strange writing looked older than all the rest. If I remember correctly, he said it was much, much older than 2 BC."

Lillian shook her head. She was getting more annoyed with him, "So how does that help us?"

"I was thinking about one of the books Nanette Bacon had beside her computer," Rory told her. "Two of them were on the European and Italian plagues like you would expect. But the third...it was different. It was on the plague outbreaks thousands of years ago in China. Maybe she was onto something. She was a pretty smart cookie." Rory chewed on his lower lip for a moment.

"So how does that help us?" said Lillian in a louder, harder voice.

Her anger caught Rory's attention. He looked at her for a moment and then chalked it up to concern and frustration over losing her best friend. He cleared his throat and continued, "Well, what if this particular page in the document doesn't have anything to do with a European language? Didn't Dr. Gonzalez say this is a 17th-century version of De Re Militari, with some additional sections added to it by an Italian military specialist of his time? What if someone took an ancient document *from China* and added it to the collection?"

Lillian Safford looked at Rory, blinking her eyes, "I never thought of that."

"And maybe everyone involved in looking at this single page in the leather-bound volume was thinking in a straight line," Rory said. "Their thinking was; everything else was Italian or Latin so *this* should be the same. They weren't thinking outside the box." Rory leaned forward and set the computer to code-breaking mode.

Lillian watched what he was doing and asked, "Why set it specifically to break a code?"

"Remember what Dr. Gonzalez said? It has to be a language with an alphabet to use a cipher to encode a message. But if it's Chinese...?"

"Ah, right, it's a picture language, so you need a code," Lillian said as she finally understood. "But didn't he also say you needed to have the code book to decrypt the code? How do we find that?" Lillian sat up straighter and perked up, "Do you think it might be back in one of those three boxes?"

"Maybe. But I used one of the library computers to do a little research on ancient code making," Rory told her. He began to type on the keyboard. "One of the things ancient societies used for a codebook was a poem. There is a collection called the Chinese Classic book of Poetry that goes back to the 10th century BC. I'm telling the supercomputer to use that as the code book. I'm hoping it can go out to the Internet and find the collection. It's a long shot, but we've got nothing so far anyway. If it doesn't work, we'll go take another look in those three boxes." Rory set the translation program to output the result in Traditional Chinese. He pressed enter and they both held their breath as the computer went to work again. Twenty agonizing minutes later the computer beeped and displayed this translation on the screen:

微楷体微楷体微楷体微楷体 微楷体微楷楷体微

"Unbelievable!" Lillian Safford said as she shot forward in her chair. She stared at the computer screen, "That looks like Chinese!"

Rory stared at the screen. "That it does," he said with a whisper.

"You did it!" Lillian said. She turned and gave Rory a big kiss on his lips.

Rory's eyes were wide open in total surprise throughout the long kiss.

Lillian Safford broke off the kiss and looked into Rory's silver-blue eyes, "Keep this up big boy and who knows what kind of reward you get next."

Rory wasn't sure if his elation was for solving the puzzle or getting the kiss.

"Now what do we do!" Lillian Safford asked him. She looked ready to burst with full-blown enthusiasm.

"I can think of a few things," Rory said with a grin.

Lillian Safford hit him on the shoulder with the back of her hand. "That's not what I meant. Although you can bring up those thoughts when we're alone later," she added with a wink. "But right now I'm talking about the decoded output. What do we do with these Chinese symbols on the screen?"

Rory was a little disappointed any extra reward would have to take place later. He gradually returned his attention to the keyboard, "Why don't we do like Dr. Gonzalez said and put the output into the translator?" Rory leaned over, did a cut and paste and put the Chinese lettering into the input box of the translation program. He set the output for English and pressed enter. They both watched in anticipation as the computer went to work. Once again, after long agonizing minutes, the output finally appeared on the screen:

'use the fire plague to kill your enemy ???? they will burn from the inside out burn everything after to occupy your enemies land find ???? lintong district held by the black warrior ???? buried with king of qin'

Both Rory and Lillian were too stunned to talk as they looked at the message on the LCD screen. After long agonizing hours, the solution turned out to be so simple. Hard to believe...but there was the message staring them in the face.

"What in the world is the 'fire plague'," Lillian Safford asked in a shaky voice

"I'm not sure," Rory said, equally subdued. "But considering what Dr. Gonzalez said about the theme of the volume, this looks to me like biological warfare instructions from ancient China."

"I'd say you're right," Lillian agreed. "But why the question marks?" Her fingers traced them lightly on the screen.

Rory shook his head, "I'm not sure. But...since this is a picture language, according to Dr. Gonzalez, maybe it's some words or concepts in the Chinese language that have been lost over the centuries. The supercomputer has no way of translating them."

"That makes sense," Lillian said after a moment. She took the computer mouse and brought up the web browser. She went to Google, typed in 'king of qin' and pressed enter. The first entry at the top of the page the search returned was a Wikipedia article on Qin Shi Huang. She clicked on the link to look at the information it contained. Lillian scanned quickly through the article.

"King of the State of Qin. He was the first Emperor of a unified China!" she said. Her voice was full of excitement.

Rory nodded as he looked over the information on the screen, "Look at what it says there; Date of reign: 247 BC to 221 BC. That's a long, long time ago."

"This is amazing," Lillian said as she looked at Rory. "You solved a puzzle none of those so-called experts would have solved."

"*We* solved it," Rory said.

"You are so sweet," Lillian said. She leaned over and gave him another kiss. She held this one a lot longer and it was a bit more passionate than the first one. When she broke the kiss off, her hazel eyes looked deep into his silver-blue ones. "How's that?" she whispered.

"Wow. I'll give you compliments all night long if that's what I get," Rory whispered in return.

"Would you give me a minute?" she said as she pulled out a cell phone, "I'm going to make one phone call and then you and I can go and have dinner to celebrate. And who knows what else might happen," she added with a wink.

Rory watched her long, shapely legs as she walked away. The sway of her hips was tantalizing. *This could prove to be a very interesting evening.*

Chapter 9

RORY AND LILLIAN SAFFORD left the opulence of the marble, New York Library building behind and walked down the steps towards her Ferrari 458 Spider. Halfway across the sidewalk, Lillian hooked her arm inside Rory's elbow and gave him a kiss on the cheek.

Rory gave her a wink. And then, just as they reached the Ferrari, he heard someone step up behind him. Rory caught a glimpse of something coming down towards his head. He ducked. It was just enough. The blow was glancing. But the blow was enough to make him see stars and he fell to the pavement. His training kicked and he instinctively rolled over onto his back and kicked the legs out from under his attacker.

A large man, wearing a black ski mask, fell hard onto his back, a blackjack falling to the sidewalk.

Lillian screamed.

A vehicle screeched to a stop in the street behind the Ferrari.

Rory received a kick in his side from another attacker and he nearly threw up with the pain. Fighting to ignore the nausea, Rory rolled towards the second assailant and threw a punch.

It caught another large man, wearing a black ski mask, on the inside of his thigh, just missing his genitals. The man screamed and fell to the pavement.

Rory rolled back, intending to get up.

The first attacker was on his feet now - a foot from Rory - and the blackjack was already coming down from over his head.

Rory instinctively raised an arm in defense. The blackjack glanced off his forearm and clipped him on the side of the head. Stars blurred his vision again and he fought to stay conscious.

Footsteps began running towards the street.

Rory shook his head to clear it, trying to see were Lillian was.

The two attackers were running for a large, black van, directly ahead, parked behind the Ferrari. The side door of the van was wide open.

Lillian Safford was being pulled into the opening by two other men, both wearing black ski masks.

Rory struggled to his feet.

Spreading her legs wide apart, Lillian pushed against each side of the open doorway, fighting against the men dragging her into the van.

Rory ran for the vehicle, his head still dizzy. The last thing he saw of Lillian Safford was the full crotch of her black panties between her wide open legs, her feet against the inside posts of the doorway.

The van door closed with a whump. The tires squealed and smoked as the van pulled away from the curb.

Rory stumbled into the street, trying to chase after the van. There was no license plate. There was not a single thing to identify the van other than it was black. There was no manufacturer's name, no make and no model that would identify it. There was not a single piece of chrome or a bumper sticker that would make it stand out.

The van disappeared into traffic.

Rory was left standing there behind the Ferrari 458 Spider, wondering what had just happened. This case now involved two missing people.

Chapter 10

RORY TOOK A CAB to the NYPD 10th precinct and reported the kidnapping to the desk sergeant. He was asked to sit for a moment in an old wooden chair. The police station was a zoo today. Rory was surrounded by tough-looking young men with tattoos from head to foot, by women chewing gum and dressed like hookers and by several people with cuts and bruises on their face. Two policemen were hauling another tough looking dude through the precinct doors in handcuffs. He imagined it was just a normal day in a New York City police station. Rory felt the bump on the back of his head. That was going to be really sore in the morning. His side was already sore. He cursed silently. How could he not find Nan Bacon and then lose Lillian? He felt like a loser.

After a few moments, a black man in a blue wrinkled suit approached him, "Mr. Steele?"

Rory pushed his self-sympathy away and stood up, "Yes."

"I'm Detective Ainsworth," he said as he shook hands with Rory. "Will you follow me please?"

Rory nodded and was led past the desk sergeant to a large room filled with desks in the back. Rory could hear the constant clicking of keyboards as nearly every chair beside a desk was filled with someone telling a story. At a glance, Rory saw every slice of society from bikers to a well-dressed women crying into a handkerchief.

Detective Ainsworth took a seat at an old, beat up desk and indicated for Rory to sit in the well-worn chair beside the desk. The Detective pulled a keyboard close to him and he began to type into a computer, "You told the desk sergeant someone was kidnapped?"

"Yes sir," Rory said, "her name is Dr. Lillian Safford."

"Doctor?" Detective Ainsworth repeated as he typed, "we don't get too many doctors kidnapped in this precinct."

"She's not a medical doctor," Rory said. "She has a doctorate with a PhD. She's a genetic scientist."

"Ah," Detective Ainsworth replied. He stopped typing and looked at Rory intently. "Can she write scripts for meds? Is that why she was kidnapped?"

"I imagine she can," Rory said, "but I'm not sure why she was kidnapped. I work for Highlander Investigative Services–"

"A *private* firm," Detective Ainsworth said, like it was a bad taste in his mouth.

Rory ignored that and moved on, "Yes. We were hired to find someone else who has disappeared, Nanette Marlayne Bacon. Rory spelled each name. She was reported missing a few weeks ago."

"Nanette Marlayne Bacon," Detective Ainsworth repeated as he typed the name into the computer. "Okay, here it is. Reported by her father Cordell Reese Bacon, attorney-at-law. How is Nanette Marlayne Bacon tied in with this Lillian Safford?"

"Nanette Bacon is also a doctor with a PhD. She works at the New York University Genetics Laboratory," Rory explained.

"Lillian Safford worked there for a while as well. I was told they were best friends going back to their school days. Dr. Safford now works at her father's company, MetaTech Laboratories Inc. She has an office at Madison Avenue and East 23rd Street. That's where I went to talk with Dr. Safford. I was hoping to get some kind of lead on what happened to Mr. Bacon's daughter."

"Uh huh," Detective Ainsworth said as he continued to type. "And did you find any kind of lead, Mr. Steele?"

"I'm not really sure," Rory said. "Mr. Bacon said the police couldn't find much and I couldn't find much either. I was trying to work an angle on the fact Ms. Bacon had been working on various diseases at the University."

Detective Ainsworth stop typing and sat back, "Diseases? Does she have access to diseases like they do down at the CDC in Atlanta?"

"I believe so," Rory replied, "although I don't think it would be as extensive as the CDC would have."

Mulling over that thought, Ainsworth asked, "Do you think these women might have been kidnapped by terrorists?" he asked. "Maybe they want access to these diseases?"

"I honestly don't know," Rory told him. He decided to keep the code Nan had been working on to himself for now.

Chewing his lip now, Ainsworth stared at Rory, "How was Dr. Safford kidnapped?"

"We were just leaving the New York Library Special Collections building when two men jumped me," Rory explained. "While I was fighting with them, she was pulled into a black van by another two men."

"Did you get a good look at this van?" Ainsworth asked. "Did you get a license plate number? Even a partial?"

"There wasn't any license plate," Rory said. "And I didn't see any manufacturer's name, make or model on the van either. It looked like every detail had been stripped from the van. And all the men wore black hoods."

"Sounds like a professional job to me," Ainsworth said as he rubbed his chin. "And if diseases are involved, this might be something that Homeland Security may want to be advised of."

Rory nodded his head, "I can understand your concern." Rory gave a description of Lillian Safford and the address where she worked. He also told Detective Ainsworth where they could find her Ferrari Spider. He gave his own contact information and cell phone number as well.

AN HOUR AFTER RORY had walked into the precinct to report a kidnapping, he was walking back out. Rory had no idea what was happening and where this case was going. Rory took a cab to his favorite restaurant. He asked the waiter for a double scotch on the rocks. He was feeling a little deflated. He was no closer to finding Nanette Bacon and now he had lost Lillian Safford. He'd been unable to protect her. Two huge failures in one day didn't feel right. Rory ordered the restaurant special for the night but only picked at his food. He was into his third double scotch on the rocks when his cell phone rang.

Pulling his cell phone out, Rory looked at the screen. He didn't recognize the number. Pressing the 'answer' button, he put the phone to his ear, wondering, "Hello."

"Mr. Steele, this is Detective Ainsworth. You were in the precinct to file a kidnapping report with me earlier today."

Rory sat up, "Yes Detective Ainsworth. Did you find something? Did you find Lillian?"

There was a pause at the other end. Detective Ainsworth spoke sternly, "You do realize you can be charged for filing a false police report?"

That comment caught Rory off guard. "Pardon? I don't understand. What do you mean?"

"We started following up on your report as soon as you left. We sent a couple of detectives over to Lillian Safford's office to get some more information," Ainsworth said.

"Okay," Rory said slowly, not sure where this was going.

Ainsworth's voice rose in intensity. "And not more than 20 minutes ago, Dr. Lillian Safford walked in here, wondering why we were at her office and claiming she had been kidnapped!"

Rory's back stiffened, "But she was. I saw it–"

"I'm not sure what you saw, pal," Ainsworth said angrily. "But the lady just left here driving her Ferrari - the very car you claimed was supposed to be at the New York Public Library - the scene of the supposed kidnapping!"

"I don't understand," Rory said. His head was starting to spin.

"And neither do I," Ainsworth yelled. "The lady said she went to lunch with you to discuss this other case and you hit on her. She said you wouldn't leave her alone. Did you file a false report trying to get even with her, buddy? Can't stand rejection? Is that it?

"No, she was–"

"Listen, pal, if I see you down here again using up valuable time, you'll regret it. Do you understand me?" Detective Ainsworth hung up.

Rory was left sitting there with his phone still against his ear. What in the world had just happened?

Chapter 11

AFTER BREAKFAST, Rory headed back to Nan Bacon's apartment. He had tossed and turned all night, going through the events of the day before over and over again. He had witnessed Lillian Safford being kidnapped. But she denied it. Nothing in the whole episode made any sense to him. He had thought about calling Lillian Safford or going to see her but decided against it. He was beginning to wonder if he had imagined the whole day. He walked up to the front entrance of the Madison Green condominium apartment tower and pulled out the brown envelope Nan's father had given him. He punched in the code and the door clicked opened. Once inside the lobby, he headed down the hallway toward Nan Bacon's apartment. He pulled the key from the brown envelope and unlocked her apartment door. Putting the key back into the envelope, Rory slipped it into his back pocket. Opening the door, he stepped inside, closed the door behind him and stood there. Everything looked the same as when he and Lillian had come in yesterday. Or had he imagined that as well?

Rory realized he had been holding his breath. He shook his head and let it out. *Let's see what we can find this time.* He took several steps across the floor and caught movement off to his right.

A screaming form came rushing out of the kitchen. A glint of steel flashed through the air.

Rory's study of Wing Chun, a martial arts form specializing in close-range combat, saved him. He was barely able to get his hand up in time, but he deflected the arm holding a large carving knife that was headed for his juggler vein. He used the attacker's momentum to push him passed. Turning, Rory took a step to attack.

But the attacker was quick. He did a front roll and came up on his feet, lunging at Rory's midsection with the knife.

Rory's shirt was nicked as he jumped back. He went into a defensive crouch.

The attacker turned and ran for the hallway instead of continuing the assault.

Rory quickly sized up the attacker at about 5 foot 6, slightly built with a blond ponytail. He wore a dirty jean jacket, faded blue jeans and red running shoes. Rory chased after him.

The attacker ran into the study on the left.

Rory's hand caught the door just before it closed and he pushed it open. Stepping inside, he took a relaxed, focused stance, preparing for battle.

The man was at the window, clutching at the fancy black bars. He was trapped. The man whirled around and held the knife out towards Rory.

Blinking, Rory felt like wiping at his eyes. The man was - Nanette Bacon? She looked dirty and disheveled. Tears streaked her face. Wherever she had been for the past few weeks, it hadn't been easy for her.

"Don't come near me," Nan Bacon yelled. "I won't work for your boss. Do you hear me? I won't!"

Rory held his hands out, palms down as he walked forward slowly, "It's all right. It's–"

"No. You want to take me back." Nan turned the large carving knife around and pressed the tip against her stomach, "I'll die first!"

Rory's heart leaped into his throat. He doubted she would commit harakiri - but her eyes were wild. An extreme emotional state could easily override self-preservation. His mind whirled - just reaching for his phone to call 9-1-1 could tip her over - he had to find a way to get through to her - there had to be a way to show he was non-threatening. Dropping to his knees, he placed his hands on top of his head. Speaking in a low, soft voice, he said, "I was hired to find you, Nan. My name is Rory Mack Steele. I'm on your side. I'm a friend."

Nan Bacon looked at him. Confusion was written all over her face. It looked like she wanted to believe him. But fear wouldn't let her. She pointed the knife back in this direction, stabbing it in the air as she spoke, "I don't believe you. You're...you're trying to trick me...."

"No, I'm not, Nan," Rory said. "I *was* hired me to find you. I've talked to Professor Leonard Bonifay and Cora-Anne Junkins at the University and they are very worried about you –"

"You're lying," Nan yelled. The knife glinted and flashed. "It doesn't take a genius to pick up a few names. And you don't look like a genius to me." Nan Bacon began to edge to her left, towards the far side of the computer desk. Her eyes flicked back and forth to the floor, so she wouldn't trip over something, and towards

Rory, keeping the knife up and ready. Her breathing was sharp and raspy, filled with fear.

Rory realized she was going to try to get around the desk and make a run for the open door. She would be close...but there was still the knife. He relaxed his muscles, getting ready.

Nan moved slow and steady around the desk. The only sound in the room was her shaky breathing. Nan licked her lips, keeping her eyes on Rory...she made a run for the door–

Rory spun around on his knees and to his feet, slapping at the hand that held the knife.

Nan lost her grip and the knife tumbled through the air and away from her. "No," she screamed, running for the door.

But Rory was faster. Two long steps and he reached out, catching her around the waist with his right arm. She began crying as he picked her up off the floor, pulling her towards him. She desperately beat against his arm with her fists, trying to free herself. He put his other arm around her as he held her close. "It's okay," he said in a soothing voice. "It's okay, Nan. I *am* a friend." Rory could feel the tension go out of her body. Nan Bacon broke down and cried as Rory held her.

Chapter 12

ONCE NAN BACON stopped crying, Rory gently sat her in one of the chairs by the computer. He reached for a box of Kleenex on the computer desk and handed one to Nan, "What happened to you? The police have been looking for you for several weeks."

Nan Bacon blew her nose, sniffed back another tear and said, "I was taken to see Mr. Postigan. He owns a large laboratory and he's wanted to hire me for some time. I've always said I wasn't interested but his daughter talked me into going to see him. But when I realized what he really wanted me to do, I said no. I tried to leave but he wouldn't let me go."

Rory knelt in front of her. "What did he want you to do?"

"He has these stupid ideas about changing the shape of the world," she said. "He wanted me to modify some diseases, so he could attack specific populations around the world."

"He was talking about genocide on a worldwide scale?" Rory asked her. He shook his head, finding it difficult to believe.

Nan nodded as she wiped away her tears, "He's a freak. He's part of some old secret society. Like some old Nazi super race thing. When I refused to cooperate, he had someone drug me and they put me in a room. When I woke up, I realized they intended to keep me locked up until I cooperated."

"How did you get away?" Rory asked.

"I told the guy who was guarding me I had to pee. The pig kept the door open but I insisted he had to turn his back. There was a partly open window and I jumped out when he wasn't looking." She grimaced, "I didn't realize I was on the second floor but I fell through the window onto a tree and it broke my fall. It was dark and I just ran."

"Do you know where you were being kept?" Rory asked her.

Nan shook her head as she blew her nose again, "No. I was taken there in a limousine with blacked out windows. We drove into an underground garage and they took me upstairs to see Mr. Postigan. When I escaped, it was too dark to really see any details. All I remember is that the grounds were large and there was a wire fence that I had to climb to get out. There was also a forest or a park outside the fence that I had to run through. I just kept running when I hit the streets."

Rory cocked his head, "If you escaped right away, where have you been for the last few weeks?"

"I stayed in homeless shelters," Nan answered. "The first ones were in Brooklyn and I worked my way slowly across to this side of town. I just kept moving."

Shaking his head softly, Rory asked, "But...why didn't you go to the police...or call your father?"

Nan gave him a slight shrug and sniffled, "I was afraid they would kidnap me again if I went back to my old life. And I didn't want them threatening anybody else to make me do their work. I figured it would be better if I just disappeared."

Rory nodded, "Well, your father was very worried about you."

Nan just sniffled again and stayed quiet.

"And your friends will be glad to see you," Rory said. "Lillian Safford was very worried. She was helping me to find you–"

"What?" Nan yelled. Anger filled her eyes and she stood up with her fists clenched, "What did she say, what did she do?"

Rory was surprised by the sudden change in her demeanor. This was now a young woman ready to kill again, "Well for one thing, she helped me solve that writing on your bedroom wall. We thought it might lead to whoever kidnapped you–"

Nan's attitude changed again in a heartbeat. Fear now filled her eyes, "What are you talking about? What writing?"

Rory shrugged, confused by the wide swing in her mood changes. "The writing on your bedroom wall," he told her. "The one that came from that special leather-bound volume of De Re Militari." He gestured to the desk, "You had the copy here in that folder."

Nan's eyebrows pulled together and she took a step back into the chair, stumbling slightly, "Are - are you serious? Are you telling me she deciphered it?"

Putting a hand on her hand to steady her, Rory then reached into his pocket, pulled out his printouts and passed them up to her, "Yeah. Well - *we* deciphered it - we used a computer program at the New York Library."

Nanette Bacon opened the two pieces of paper, held one in each hand and looked from code to solution several times. Her mouth moved silently as she read the words - her chin trembling.

Rory shook his head, not sure why she wasn't happy with their help and the results.

A moment later, Nan squeezed her eyes shut, her words a raspy whisper, "Are you telling me Lillian Safford has this information?"

"Like I already said, Lillian helped me solve the puzzle but...." Rory didn't finish the sentence. He suddenly had a bad feeling.

Nan angrily crushed the pieces of paper in each hand. She looked up to the ceiling and screamed in rage. She crumpled the two pieces of paper together and threw them forcefully to the floor. She turned and swept her computer and the books off the desk. The computer smashed to the floor, cracking the plastic case. She picked up a ceramic lamp from the desk and tossed it against the wall, smashing it into a million pieces. She screamed at the top of her lungs as she looked up at the ceiling again.

Rory stood up, "Nan, what's wrong? Nan, talk to me."

Nan looked at him with rage in her eyes as she yelled at him, "The man who kidnapped me was Helmer Auguste Postigan. His daughter is Lillian Safford-Postigan. She dropped the Postigan part. She said Safford sounded more American and professional. They both spouted nonsense about modifying diseases to kill people they didn't want in the world. You fool. You may have just given them the original strain of the deadliest disease to ever hit mankind, the Black Plague!"

Chapter 13

RORY SAT ON THE EDGE of the small sofa in the living room. His elbows were on his knees, and he cradled his head in his hands. He couldn't believe what he had done. Rory thought back to the last thing he saw of Lillian Safford, a full view of her black panties. He saw that because she had spread her legs and *pushed* against each side of the open doorway in the van. She wasn't fighting against the men dragging her into the van. She was helping to get herself inside so they could make a quick getaway. He had been thinking with the wrong head. What an idiot. He felt shaken to his very core.

Nanette Bacon came out of the bathroom. She had a pink towel over her right shoulder and was tying her hair back into a ponytail again after taking a shower. She walked into the living room and sat on one of the chairs across from Rory.

Rory looked up at her. Nan had on a black and white blouse, blue slacks and white running shoes. Fashion was obviously not her forte either. She wasn't wearing any makeup but she was actually quite pretty. "How are you feeling now?" Rory asked.

"Not much better than you, from the looks of you," Nan said.

Rory took a deep breath and let it out. "I can't believe what I did. I can't believe I let her play me like that."

"Don't beat yourself up over it," Nan replied as she pulled her feet up under her on the chair. "I saw Lillian charm her way through a lot of University and grad school professors and students. She had a lot of practice at it. I always thought it was cute. I always wished I could be like her, flirting and getting every male around her to fawn over her. She had this one trick, if she wanted to catch someone's attention - she wanted me to do it, but I was too chicken." Nan gestured with her hands, "When she was wearing a dress, she would just open her knees and flash her underwear—"

Rory groaned.

Nan's eyebrows flicked upward, "Like I said, a lot were taken in—"

"That still doesn't excuse how I acted like a stupid love-struck teenager instead of a professional investigator looking for someone who was missing," Rory said with anger in his voice. "Instead, I was too busy looking at her legs and her underwear!"

"No, it was my fault, not yours," Nan said. "If I hadn't been so arrogant, we wouldn't be in this spot in the first place. I was going to be the greatest scientist the world ever saw. I was going to be the genius who cured every disease known to mankind. I'm the one that dug relentlessly into the greatest plague that ever hit mankind, the Black Plague. No one knows what it really was, but I was going to be the one to solve the mystery. I was going to be a one to find the original strain and then find a cure for it." She shook her head and added forcefully, "I was such a jackass." Her eyes filled with tears and she threw the towel hard across the room.

Rory looked at her. Nan looked like a broken little girl. For all her brilliance academically, she looked like a broken rag doll. Rory rubbed his beard, thinking.

Nan continued in a broken voice, tears filling her eyes, "The black plague of the 1300s killed up to 60% of the population. And in China, where it started, some researchers claim it killed up to 90% of the population in some Chinese districts. Do we now lose 60% of China? Do we lose 90% of the people in Africa? And the entire world can thank me, the brilliant Nanette Marlayne Bacon for it all. The world will forget Typhoid Mary and forever memorialize Black Plague Bacon."

"Black Plague Bacon?" Rory repeated He couldn't help but smile

Nan Bacon looked at him through the tears. She finally gave him a little hiccup laugh, "Look at me, I'm even giving myself a famous historical name."

Rory nodded as he took a deep breath and let it out slowly, "Well...we can do that....or we can try to do something about it. I don't think Lillian took a copy of the output –"

"Wouldn't matter," Nan said, "she had an eidetic memory. Once she saw it, she wouldn't forget it. There was her greatest strength, a photographic memory that never failed her."

"Oh great," Rory mumbled. Things were only going from bad to worse.

"Great mind and great body," Nan said, "you didn't have a chance."

"Thanks for the vote of confidence," Rory grumbled. "Look. We can continue to stay here and be sorry for ourselves –"

"Or we can do something about it, like you said." Nan got to her feet and headed for the hallway, "Let's get those printouts."

Rory got up and followed her.

Nan walked with determination into her study. Picking up the crumpled papers, she sat down on a chair and placed the papers on the computer desk, where she began to smooth them out.

Rory went behind the chair and looked over her shoulder.

"So this is what that writing was translated into," Nan said as she looked down at the first piece of paper:

微楷体微楷体微楷体微楷体 微楷体微楷楷体微

Nan nodded, "I had a suspicion that it was a Chinese document added to the collection. But I didn't have time to study it any further. When I started talking to Lillian about what I was looking into, she started spouting her crazy nonsense."

"What did she say?" Rory asked her.

"Just like her father," Nan said, "she started to talk about the great opportunity we had in our hands. That if we could figure it out, we had an opportunity to change the world. As genetic scientists we could modify the disease to cull certain populations. That was the phrase they both used; to cull certain populations. Like father, like daughter. They belong to some stupid secret society that wants to reshape the world. And then we give her this," she said as she looked at the second piece of paper:

'use the fire plague to kill your enemy ???? they will burn from the inside out burn everything after to occupy your enemies land find ???? lintong district held by the black warrior ???? buried with king of qin'

"The question marks must be placeholders for words or concepts the computer couldn't interpret," Nan said.

"That's what I figured as well."

"It's hard to say whether the extra information would be valuable or not," Nan mused.

"Do you know why it's referred to as the fire plague?"

Nan shook her head no, "No one really knows what the Black Plague of the 1300s was. And we have even less understanding of what the original plague in China was. There is very little documentation. One genetic study concluded it was a form of the Yersinia Pestis bacterium. But others are still convinced it was a combination of some other pandemics such as Anthrax and Ebola. Whatever it was, it was deadly."

"Okay, we figured out the king of qin refers to the first Emperor of China," Rory told her. "Did you run across him in your research? Do you remember anything about him?"

Nan shook her head slowly, "Not really." She looked over at the floor, "Too bad I destroyed my computer. Wait. Hold on a minute." She turned and gave Rory the two wrinkled pieces of paper. Getting up, Nan walked over to the closet in the corner behind the desk and retrieved a large laptop from inside. She set it up on the desk and started it up. "I'm on Wi-Fi, so we should be able to do a search," she said. She typed 'king of qin' into Google and clicked on the first Wikipedia link the search returned. They read quickly through the page on Qin Shi Huang.

"The decoded message referred to something buried with the King of Qin," Rory said, "try that link."

Nan clicked on the link entitled 'Mausoleum of the First Qin Emperor'.

"Look there," Rory said. He pointed to the web page and read, "While Sima Qian never mentioned the Terracotta Army, the statues were discovered by a group of farmers digging wells in March 29, 1974. The soldiers were created with a series of mix-

and-match clay molds and then further individualized by the artist's hands. Han Purple was also used on some of the warriors. There are around 6000 Terracotta warriors and their purpose was to protect the Emperor in the afterlife from evil spirits."

Nan clicked on the link 'terracotta army' and up popped a page discussing it. There was an amazing picture of a line of statues in an excavated pit covered over by a hangar-like structure.

Rory glanced at the paper with the English translation, "The puzzle says something was held by the black warrior buried with king of qin. One of those 6000 Terracotta warriors must be the black warrior the message refers to. Do you think it's possible they could bury something holding the plague and it could last all this time?"

Nan mulled over the question, "I don't really know. I highly doubt it, But I'm sure Lillian and her father will go to China to try and find out. Mr. Postigan basically said they had unlimited funds for their mad scheme. I'm positive they'll spare no expense and overturn heaven and earth to find this fire plague in China. That's a guarantee."

Rory stood up instantly, "I never thought about that. They'll have a head start on us too."

Nan turned around in her chair to look at him. There was fear in her eyes again. "You're right. What are we going to do? If it is buried among those terracotta figures, we *can't* let her get her hands on it. That would give them a deadly biological agent to use in their stupid plan."

"Presuming it's there, do you think Lillian can modify it?" Rory asked.

"She's a pretty good geneticist in her own right," Nan told him, "but even if she couldn't modify it, they could still unleash it in areas where they want to kill off people. Since it could be an entirely different and more powerful strain then the modern-day plague, our drugs may not be able to cope with it. In fact, I can almost guarantee it."

Rory pulled out his cell phone and made a call. "Uncle Murdock, it's Rory," he said. "Is Skye with you? Good. I'm going to put you on speaker." Rory quickly filled them in on what had happened in the case.

"What do you need us to do?" Murdock MacLeod asked. His voice was deep and firm.

"I need Skye to head to China," Rory said.

Skye Steele spoke up, "I'll leave right away."

"Thank you, I appreciate it," Rory said. He looked over at Nan, "I don't want to leave Nan Bacon's side, in case they try to kidnap her again. I'll be staying at her apartment. We should be safe here. I'll text you the address. Maybe I can figure out where she was kept when they held her. If I can...I'll make a visit."

"Sounds like a good plan," Murdock said. "Anything else we can do?"

"Yeah," Rory said, "I want Skye to keep a low profile while she's over there."

Uncle Murdoch laughed heartily, "Skye Steele keeping a low profile in the land of the Chinese? Fat chance of that happening!"

Chapter 14

SKYE STEELE STEPPED OFF the Learjet 85 at Xi'an Xianyang International Airport and walked towards the black, stretch limousine, waiting on the tarmac. The Chinese driver came around and held open the back door for her. At 6'-2" inches tall, Skye Steele towered over him. Her fiery red hair flowed behind her as she moved panther-like towards the open door. Her black leather jacket and pants whispered as she got into the back of the limo. Her green eyes sparkled as the driver appraised her Amazon-like body. Skye Steele was not going to 'blend in' very well, no matter where she went.

Skye was driven to a security company that had agreed to rent her an armored SUV. She ignored the leering looks of the manager as she got into the black, Mercedes-Benz GL550 and set the GPS for the Terracotta Army Museum. The reading said it was about 63 km away from where she was. She set her watch to local time. It was just past 9 a.m. Skye pulled out of the parking lot and began to maneuver across Xi'an. She kept a lookout for anything suspicious in the traffic around her or for signs of anyone following her. She passed Gaogou Village and took the exit off the highway, passing through Lintong. It wasn't long before she was passing the site of the Tomb of Qin Shihuang. She had two more kilometers to go and she became hyper-vigilant now. Her body was ready for anything.

Skye finally reached the Terracotta Army Museum. Parking the vehicle in the closest parking spot she could find, Skye walked quickly towards the gray museum with the green roof. She watched for anyone following her as she climbed the steps to the entrance. Once inside, Skye walked among the hundreds of noisy tourists, moving down a long hallway to an iron railing. This was Pit number one. It was huge, amazing sight and there was a rich, deep smell of earth and clay. The sign said more than 6,000 Terracotta warriors and horses were in this pit, with 1,000 already unearthed. The pit contained infantry, archers, crossbowmen, cavalry and generals, all in precise ancient battle formation. There were also figures that included acrobats, officials, and a strongman. The whole thing was spread out over four acres. How in the world was she going to find the Black Warrior? And what if he wasn't even uncovered yet?

SKYE WALKED AROUND the railing, looking for anything among the figures in the pit that would fit the bill. Skye took her time, also keeping watch for anyone around her that looked suspicious. A lot of the male tourists spent more time checking out this tall, beautiful redhead's sculpted figure than the historical ones below. Skye was used to it. She checked out vaults 1 and 2. Vault 3 was the army headquarters. There were so many figures to look at. Picking out one was not going to be easy. The hours passed as Skye studied the figures down below. She spent some time checking out other parts of the museum as well but nothing caught her eye. It was getting near 5:30 pm now, closing time. Skye decided she needed to find a way to search through all those figures up close. As Skye was passing a line of doors, one of them opened.

A young woman, carrying a purse over her shoulder, stepped out from a room. Standing in the doorway, she reached back and turned off the light off inside. Then she walked away, the door slowly swinging to close behind her.

Skye hesitated just a moment and then whirled around and stuck her foot out, keeping the door from closing completely. She looked discreetly around - no one had noticed her. She slowly pushed the door open and peered into the room. The light from the hallway showed enough to see it was a small office. There was no one inside. Slipping inside, Skye let the door close slowly.

There was a low click as the door locked.

Sky touched a button on her watch and an app lit up the face, giving her a small searchlight. There wasn't much in the room, simply a number of filing cabinets and a large desk. Walking over behind the desk, she sat down in the comfortable office chair and put her feet up. Turning off the searchlight app, she closed her eyes, her mind alert for anything but her muscles relaxing, getting ready for what might come.

SKYE STEELE LET A COUPLE of hours pass before she moved silently over to the door. Slowly turning the knob, she opened the door a crack and peered out. The lights were low outside. She opened the door a little wider. She imagined there would be security personnel around, or maybe a security guard, but she didn't see anyone. Slipping outside the office, Skye let the door lock behind her. She moved panther-like over to the area overlooking the exhibition of the Terracotta Warrior figures. Reaching the railing, she looked down at the dig. The lights had been dimmed over the closest figures but she could still see them quite well.

She began following the railing, again trying to figure out how she could find this Black Warrior. Ten minutes later, a flash of light over towards Vault 3 caught her eye. That was the area containing 72 warriors and horses and termed by the experts as the 'army headquarters' due to the number of high-ranking officers unearthed here. She watched carefully - another flash of light. Someone was definitely down there. Which meant she had company - someone probably looking for the same thing - the Black Warrior - and it made sense that a special figure would be in that area.

Skye moved as quickly as possible along the railing, peering into the dim light. She stopped.

Shadows moved through the figures of 'army headquarters'.

Watching for a few moments, Skye moved low again along the railing again. After twenty feet, she stopped dead in her tracks. A rope ladder was tied to the railing, dropping down into the darkness below.

If Skye remembered correctly, this was a new area being excavated in the pit below. Climbing over the railing, she slid down the rope ladder. The smell of the earth and clay was deeper and richer as she set her feet on the dirt floor. Crouching low once she reached the bottom of the pit, Skye slowly moved towards the area where the shadows had been.

Chapter 15

AS SHE CLOSED IN, Skye saw the beams of flashlights cut between terracotta figures. She crouched low behind a line of Terracotta warriors, watching for a moment. Shadows moved behind the flashlights until the beams were all converged on one spot.

Skye nimbly moved forward until she could almost touch the shadowy figures. It was three men crowded around a single figure.

Unlike the other figures, this one wasn't set up to hold any weapon. Instead, each arm held a terracotta urn to his chest. Even in the dim light, the level of detail was extraordinary. She could see the expression on the face, the hairstyle, the clothing - but unlike the faces she had seen on the other figures today, this one wasn't Oriental in appearance. The features were more of a black African. They had found the Black warrior.

Skye watched as two of the men set their flashlight down on the dirt floor. Then under the light from the third, each man slowly pulled an urn from its resting spot, leaving behind two round holes in the black figure's arms, where they had been slid into thousands of years ago.

A slight crunch of earth sounded behind Skye.

She whirled around to deflect a dagger headed for her kidney.

The bearded man behind the knife bent his arm and brought his elbow back, aiming for her jaw.

Bending back just enough, Skye allowed the elbow to miss and then brought her upper body back upright, shooting a palm against the man's chest.

Staggering backward from the blow, bearded-man grunted, putting a hand to his chest. A second later, snarling, he came back at her, thrusting the dagger at her stomach.

Skye simply waited a heartbeat, stepped sideways, grabbed his wrist and flipped him onto his back.

As his body thudded to the ground, pounding footsteps approached her from behind.

Turning, Skye went into a crouch as a husky man charged her. Like a matador Skye pivoted and let him go by, pushing on his back to use his own momentum against him. The man fought to stay upright, skidded to a stop in the dirt, turned and came back at her, teeth bared, hands seeking her throat. Skye turned slightly, caught an arm with hers and flipped him. As the husky man hit the dirt, she turned at the sound of the bearded man coming at her again. This time he swept the knife left to right, trying to eviscerate her. Pulling her abdomen, in, she let the knife swing past her. Then she thrust stiff fingers into his throat.

Bearded-man fell to the ground, holding his throat and gagging.

Skye turned back to the husky man but he was scrambling away from her. She heard a sound and glanced back. Bearded-man was stumbling off into the darkness, hands at his throat. She turned her attention back to the two men holding the urns.

They stood stock still, looking at her in surprise.

Skye took a step towards them.

One of the men tossed his urn high in the air, over to her left.

Skye reacted immediately. She ran swiftly in the direction of the urn as it arched through the air.

It began to fall towards the ground.

Skye left her feet and dove forward to the spot where the urn would land on the compacted earth. She stretched all 6'2" of her body and caught the terracotta urn with her right hand an inch before it landed. She lay outstretched for a brief moment, afraid to even breathe. Her eyes scanned the ancient vessel, wondering if the rough landing, even in her hand, had created cracks to allow whatever was inside to escape. But everything looked intact. Pulling her legs carefully underneath her, Skye slowly stood up, rotating the urn in her hands carefully to make sure. She sucked her breath in, suddenly remembering the men. Tucking the urn like a football under her arm, Skye peered into the darkness around her. It was pitch black.

Sounds came from the direction of the rope ladder.

Skye turned and looked up. In the dim light, she could a man scrambling up and over the railing.

A few moments later, the sounds of multiple footsteps were pounding across the floor above, heading towards the front entrance, sending echoes off the walls.

SKYE STEELE PEEKED out the front doors of the Terracotta Army Museum. The front stairs and the courtyard were bathed in lights. Not seeing anyone, she took off at a run carrying the ancient urn like a football. Her long strides moved her swiftly across the courtyard and into the semidarkness of the parking lot. She sprinted across the black asphalt to her SUV. Once inside, she laid the ancient urn on the passenger seat. Starting the vehicle, Skye kept the lights off as she scanned the parking lot. There was no evidence of the men but they had to be nearby.

Staying on alert, Skye slowly drove out of the parking lot and headed for the highway. She hadn't gone very far when she brought the vehicle to a stop.

Up ahead, a car was parked across the road, blocking her way.

Skye noticed the heads of several men behind the car, using it as a shield. When one of them lifted up a machine gun, she knew they were waiting for her. She turned on the headlights and hit the high beams. In the bright light, Skye recognized Kalashnikov AK-12 assault rifles and Croatian Agram 2000 submachine guns. These guys were serious and up-to-date. She jammed the gas pedal to the floor and the heavy SUV left black rubber marks on the pavement as the tires squealed. Skye aimed for the center of the car.

The men began to fire, using the car roof, hood, and trunk to steady their aim. But they weren't expecting an armored SUV. Their machine guns bounced hundreds of rounds off the ballistic armor plating and the bullet-proof glass as it bore down on them. At the last moment, they fled for their lives.

Skye steered for the front of the car. The larger SUV slammed into their car and sent it spinning to the side of the road. Skye hit the gravel shoulder on her side and heard several large bangs.

The men had anticipated her trying to drive around them. They had set down heavy spike strips and they had ripped through her run-flat tires.

Skye continued driving but the vehicle was hard to control and her speed was dropping. From her training, she knew she was only going to get a couple of miles before the tires would be totally deflated. She looked back in the rearview mirror and saw the men running for their damaged vehicle. They disappeared behind her in the darkness. But a few moments later she saw headlights behind her. She wondered if it was them. The headlights were moving back and forth like the car was drunk. Their vehicle was damaged as well and they didn't seem to be moving any faster than she was. But a low-speed chase was still a chase.

TIME PASSED AGONIZINGLY slow. The headlights behind her were slowly getting closer. They were mustering more speed out of their car than Skye could get out of the SUV. She was passing a commercial plaza on the right-hand side when she spotted a possible solution.

There was a small pizza delivery vehicle parked in front of a Pizza Hut. The vehicle was running and a young man was placing something in the passenger side. He went back inside the Pizza Hut.

Skye turned her headlights off and turned hard right without signaling. Parking the SUV to the left of the Pizza Hut, Skye picked up the ancient urn and ran for the delivery car. It was a Mini Cooper and a tight squeeze for the 6'-2" redhead. She placed the ancient urn on top of a hot pizza bag. Beside it was a large, red and white thermos. Putting the car in gear and cranking the steering wheel hard left, Skye was quickly headed for the roadway. Skidding into a fishtail on the pavement, Skye glanced into the rearview mirror as she worked to straighten out the Mini Cooper.

The herky-jerky headlights of the pursuing vehicle were close.

Skye pressed down hard on the accelerator and the herky-jerky headlights fell away behind her. The hot, double cheese and pepperoni pizza eased her hunger pangs as she headed for Xianyang.

IT WAS STILL DARK AS Skye Steele sat in the pizza delivery car just half a block away from the enclosed tarmac where the Learjet was parked. She had spotted six men waiting beside a black van near the gate in the wire fence. The bulges in their jackets told her they were armed with handguns. She had no doubt they had more powerful weapons in the car. How they knew she would be coming here puzzled her. But that would have to wait till later. Surprise would be her only weapon right now and she hoped the light bulk of the Mini Cooper could do the job. She pulled out her cell phone and called the Learjet.

Chapter 16

EXACTLY TEN MINUTES LATER, Skye put the Mini Cooper in gear. Time for the run to safety. She slowly increased her speed, so as not to attract attention. But by the time she hit the cross street, she was doing 75 mph.

The six men standing beside the black van near the gate heard the sound of the engine and swung their weapons up.

Skye anticipated the airbag deploying by leaning back against the seat and stretching her leg out to keep the gas pedal down. The Mini Cooper hit the wire gate at 80 mph and burst through with a metallic bang. The airbag deployed and Skye was now fighting to push it away while she drove blind. It was bulkier than she had anticipated and she had to fight the billowy fabric while she drove with one hand.

The sounds of automatic weapon fire exploded from the other side of the broken fence and the back glass of the Mini Cooper shattered into millions of pieces. Bullets ravaged the interior of the car on the left side.

The Mini Cooper jerked to the left and Skye felt like it was going to flip. She fought hard to keep it upright while still driving blind.

Automatic weapons fire sounded again and bullets ripped along the right side of the car.

Sky hammered away at the slowly deflating airbag and finally managed to push it down enough to see. Wind whipped through her red hair and she realized the front windshield was gone as well. Skye looked for the Learjet and saw it off to her right.

It was already slowly moving down the runway, heading for takeoff. The entry door was deployed and inviting.

Skye turned hard right to pursue the jet.

Tires squealed back at the gate.

Skye looked back in the cracked, rear-view mirror to see the black van pursuing the Mini Cooper.

A man leaned out the driver side window of the van and fired a burst.

Bullets tore up the tarmac in front of the Mini Cooper.

Skye braked for a heartbeat and then accelerated for the Learjet.

The gunman was thrown off by the maneuver and his bullets tore up the tarmac, behind the Mini Cooper this time.

Skye shot past the moving Learjet, keeping it ten feet off to the left. She counted to five and then applied the brakes, putting the Mini Cooper into a sliding stop. She threw the driver's side door open, while grabbing the red and white thermos from the passenger seat, and then sprang from her seat.

The Mini Cooper was just sliding to a stop when bullets tore through it.

Skye ran hard across the tarmac to meet the oncoming plane.

The engines on the Learjet began screaming, accelerating to takeoff speed.

Skye jumped on the entry door, grabbed the left-hand rail and fought to maintain her balance as she bounded up the steps.

Bullets ripped into the tarmac and the lower portion of the entry door.

Skye scrambled through the open doorway, hit the button to close the entry door and then dove for the floor.

Bullets pinged and ricocheted off the slowly closing entry door as the Learjet accelerated down the tarmac.

The Learjet went nearly vertical on takeoff.

Skye held the red and white thermos in one hand and the legs of a seat desperately with the other as the force of the takeoff threatened to send her sliding and crashing to the rear of the plane.

Bullets pinged and ricocheted off the body of the airplane.

The Learjet banked hard to the left.

Skye fought hard to hold on as her body was thrown sideways. The muscles of her left arm screamed in agony. Her legs swung across the floor from the force of the turn and she banged into another seat. She lost her grip on the thermos and it spun like a top on the floor, heading for a crash against the left side of the plane. Skye felt like her arm was going to come out of its socket as she turned her body hard and swung her feet out, desperate to grab the container before it smashed to pieces and contaminated them. At the last minute, she caught it between her boots and pulled it towards her butt as she reached down with her free hand. Her fingers curled around the top and she held it in place against her feet.

A few minutes later the Learjet leveled out.

Skye was able to pull the red and white thermos against her body and secure it. She felt immense relief as she was finally able to get on her knees and park the lethal container on a seat. But relief was short-lived.

The speaker system squawked to life and she heard the pilot's voice, "We have a problem."

Skye leaned her head against the seat for a two-second rest, used the seatbelt to secure the thermos and then made her way to the front cabin. "What's wrong?"

"A bullet must have nicked a fuel line," the pilot said. "The leak is slow but we'll have to divert from our original flight plan and set down before long, probably in Vietnam."

Skye rubbed her brow for a moment as she considered the situation. "Okay. I know someone who should be able to help us. Just do what you have to do and we'll play it by ear." She turned to head back to the container.

"That's not all. The airport is not too happy. I turned the yelling off, but I imagine we'll have company before too long," the pilot added.

"What you mean?" Skye asked him.

"You didn't exactly go through customs," the pilot said with a smile.

Skye realized he was right, "Crap. And no doubt they'll be contacting the authorities."

The pilot nodded, "I imagine the military will get involved." He turned off all the lights inside and outside the plane. "Better get seated," he added as he began a slow descent.

Skye worked her way back to the seat next to the red and white thermos and buckled herself in. She watched the lights of various buildings passing not far below the Learjet. The pilot was flying as low as possible, trying to stay under radar level.

Two hours later, the low sound of powerful jet engines outside the Learjet broke the silence. A pair of Chengdu J-10 fighter jets appeared beside them.

Skye now wondered if they were going to be shot down by the Chinese Air Force.

Another Chengdu J-10 fighter jet appeared just beyond the one on the left. The sound of their powerful jet engines was ominous but the fighter jets simply kept pace.

Skye could see the pilot on the left looking at the Learjet. He looked to the jet on his left for a moment and then back at the Learjet. He nodded his head. Skye was positive the fighter pilot had flipped the cover off the firing button on his joystick.

The Vietnam border was approaching rapidly but would they make it?

A few long, tense moments passed. Then the three fighter jets peeled off, allowing the Learjet to leave Chinese airspace.

Skye finally let out her breath. The only problem now was the fact the other urn would probably arrive in the U.S. two days before Skye could bring hers back. She pulled out her cell phone to give Rory a heads up.

Chapter 17

AFTER BREAKFAST, Rory and Nan Bacon headed down to the police precinct. Nan Bacon was positive once the police heard her story the authorities would begin an all-out search for Lillian Safford and her father. Rory was not so sure. They entered the precinct and spoke briefly to the desk sergeant. He asked them to sit for a moment. They took two chairs in the midst of tough-looking men and women. Rory detected the scent of alcohol on the breath of two men beside him and a number around the waiting area had the smell of marijuana on their clothes. He glanced at Nan and could tell she was uneasy around a group of people she probably only saw from a distance, if at all. He put his hand on hers to give her reassurance. About 20 minutes later, a large, white detective with thick black glasses approached them, "Mr. Steele, I'm Detective Nick Crenshaw. Will you folks please follow me?"

Rory and Nan Bacon followed him past the desk sergeant. The space beyond the front waiting area was packed again. Detective Crenshaw led them over to a desk.

Rory stopped in his tracks.

Detective Ainsworth was sitting behind the desk.

"Yeah, it's me again," Ainsworth said with a wry smile on his face. "I guess my partner and I have drawn you again, Mr. Steele. Please sit down, so we can see what *this one* is all about." He indicated two chairs by his desk.

Nan Bacon sat down, eager to get started.

Rory sat in the chair beside her, wondering just how badly this was about to go.

Crenshaw stood beside his partner looking down at Rory and Nan, his arms crossed over his barrel chest.

Ainsworth leaned forward and started working on his computer's keyboard, "And who did you tell the desk sergeant you were, young lady?"

"I'm Dr. Nanette Bacon," she said crisply.

Ainsworth nodded his head as he typed.

"I was kidnapped by Helmer Postigan," Nan added in a matter-of-fact way. "You need to arrest him."

Ainsworth stopped typing and he looked up at his partner.

Crenshaw looked down at Nan, "Your father reported you had disappeared but–"

Nan's eyebrows rose surprise, "My father? How did he know?" She looked over at Rory.

Rory's brow furrowed. He realized he had never actually said it was her father who had hired him.

"Why wouldn't he know? You don't talk to your father?" Ainsworth asked.

Nan looked at the detective and hesitated for a moment, "I...I haven't talked to him for a long time."

Ainsworth paused for a moment as he looked at her, "Okay. So you say you were kidnapped. Do you know where you were being held?"

"No."

"Were you blindfolded?" Crenshaw asked her.

"No."

"No?"

Nan's shoulders sagged a little, "I was taken to see Mr. Postigan in a big car but I didn't pay any attention to where we were going. And I don't drive so I don't know the city that well." She started to get fidgety in her chair.

"It's okay, Dr. Bacon, everything is fine," Ainsworth said as he held out a hand to calm her down. "Okay, you were held there for three weeks. Do you remember anything about the place where you were being kept? Any sounds? Any smells?"

"Actually...I was only there for one day," Nan said, "But–"

"You were only held for only one day?" Crenshaw asked her. "Where were you the rest of the time?"

"I was hiding out," Nan said, "I was afraid they'd make me work for them."

Crenshaw's eyes narrowed, "Work doing what?"

"Modifying diseases genetically," Nan replied. "If you arrest Mr. Postigan, he can tell you all about it–"

"Modifying diseases?" Crenshaw repeated. His brow knitted together as he looked at the young woman.

"Yes," Nan confirmed. "They have a plan to attack New York City and then the rest of the world–"

Detective Ainsworth sat back in his chair, "They what...?"

"They want to create an entirely new world order."

Crenshaw spoke slowly, "A new world order." He and Ainsworth exchanged glances.

Rory spoke up, "Look, detectives, I know how this looks but we're wasting time. These people are planning to unleash a deadly disease–"

"From the university where she works?" Detective Ainsworth asked him.

"No, one from China," Nan said.

Ainsworth's eyebrows shot up, "From China?" He looked at Rory "Didn't you tell me it had to do with diseases from the New York University Genetics Laboratory?"

"No," Rory said, "we were all speculating at the time–"

The detective's words came sharp and fast, "Look here. You were in here before telling us about another lady you *claimed* was kidnapped. Only the same lady comes in here *after* you leave and she tells us she *wasn't* kidnapped."

"I know how this might look–"

"And *now* you come back in here with *this* young lady who's been missing for three weeks. But she says it was for only one day. And now you two say someone is bringing a disease here from China. Is it SARS?"

"No," Nan said as she jumped in. "It's the Black Plague."

"The Black Plague?" Crenshaw said slowly. "Does that even exist anymore?"

"Yes, but in a modified strain," Nan explained. "And with the modern drugs we have today, it has been pretty well defeated, if we catch it in time."

"Then why the big worry if it's no longer a real problem?" Crenshaw asked her with a shrug. "Everybody just takes these drugs, right?"

"But the strain they're bringing back from China is several thousand years old," Nan told him, "and it could be much more powerful than anything we now know–"

"How in the world are they bringing back a disease from thousands of years ago?" Ainsworth asked her. He now looked like he was talking to someone from the loony bin.

"We're not really sure," Rory said. "We found an old puzzle–"

"Hold it, hold it, hold it," Detective Ainsworth said as he waved his hands in front of him. "Are you two making a movie? Is this some kind of publicity stunt! Is that what this is all about? Because I'm telling you right now–"

Nan lifted her hands in a pleading manner, "No, it isn't a publicity stunt, it's not a movie. This is *real*. I'm telling the truth. We're telling the truth."

Crenshaw pursed his lips and looked up at his partner.

Ainsworth had one eyebrow raised, his head shaking slowly as he looked at the young woman.

Nan moved to the edge of her chair and looked from one detective to the other, "Why won't you believe me? Why won't you believe us? You *need* to arrest Helmer Postigan and his daughter Lillian Safford–"

Detective Ainsworth shot forward in his chair, "Lillian Safford! The same lady he claims was kidnapped. The same lady who says she wasn't kidnapped. *That* Lillian Safford?"

Nan's voice was weak, "You don't understand–"

Detective Ainsworth stood up, "I think I understand well enough young lady. I want both of you to get out of this station right now. I should arrest both of you for being public nuisances."

"Please listen to me," Nan pleaded.

"Leave," Detective Crenshaw said sternly. *"Now.* Before we lock you both up."

Rory stood up and put his hand on the Nan's shoulder, "Let's go–"

"No," Nan said forcefully as she pushed his hand away and stood up. "They *have* to listen," she said to Rory. She turned to the two detectives, "You *have* to listen to me. I'm telling you the truth. Just give me some time and I can explain everything."

But both detectives just stood there with their arms crossed, unresponsive to her pleadings.

Rory gently took her by the elbow and guided Nan Bacon towards the exit.

Tears began to flow as Nan looked back over her shoulder, "Why won't they believe me?"

Rory led her outside the precinct door, his arm around her shoulders as she sobbed inconsolably. Rory hailed a cab and they got into the back seat. Nan leaned against the car door on her side, still sobbing. As they headed back to Nan's apartment, Rory contemplated their situation. The Postigan family had a plan and now they had the possible weapon to carry it out. And thanks to Lillian and her acting job to set up Rory, turning to the police for help was going to be useless. Helmer Postigan and Lillian were formidable foes and this was going to be a difficult fight. He wondered what the next few days would bring. And how close they all were to facing death at the hands of The Fire Plague.

Chapter 18

JOHN F. KENNEDY INTERNATIONAL Airport, New York

RORY AND NAN were waiting for Skye, who was just coming through customs at JFK airport. The terminal was jam-packed and noisy with people coming and going, the sounds of suitcase wheels rumbling everywhere. Announcements echoed and bounced off the terminals walls and high ceiling. Armed guards, working with trained detector dogs and their keen sense of smell, wandered among the crowds, looking for drugs, and prohibited meat and fruits.

Rory wondered if they would pick up on a strain of the Plague. He caught sight of Skye, coming through the crowd, "There she is."

Nan pushed herself up on her toes, trying to see.

Skye opened her arms and greeted her brother with a hug, "I'm sorry I wasn't able to retrieve both urns."

"No problem, little sister," Rory said, "I know you did your best. At least we cut their chances in half to hurt anyone. That's a partial victory at least."

"With the weapons those guys were using to stop me," Skye said, "they're playing for keeps. Don't let your guard down for a minute."

Rory nodded solemnly, "I'll keep that in mind." Rory then turned and introduced Skye to Nan.

Nan just blinked as she shook hands, looking somewhat intimidated by this tall, beautiful woman.

"I think I have something for you," Skye Steele told her. She was wearing a small backpack and she slid the straps off her shoulders, handing it over to Nan.

Nan unzipped the backpack and looked inside. She knelt down and placed the backpack on the floor, unzipping it.

"Maybe we should wait," Rory said.

But Nan wasn't listening. As the crowds flowed around them, she reached carefully inside the backpack, pulling out something that was shaped like a large thermos, wrapped in tissue paper.

Rory looked at Skye and then at the crowds around them, grimacing.

Skye just pursed her lips as she watched the young woman, concentrating solely on just unwrapping the tissue paper, in the midst of one of the world's busiest airports.

What Nan found was exactly what it had looked like, a large red and white plastic thermos. Nan looked up at Skye in confusion.

"It's actually just the outer case of the thermos," Skye told her. "I figured they weren't going to let me through customs with an ancient urn. So I took out the beverage bottle out of the thermos and inserted the urn."

Nan began unscrewing the two-piece thermos.

Rory bent over, whispering, "Nan. Wait–"

But Nan was already pulling the top part of the thermos off, revealing the top of a rich red colored urn with a beautiful glazed sheen. She handed the top piece of the thermos to Skye.

Skye took it in hand, glanced over at a guard with a dog passing nearby, "Hopefully...."

Rory straightened up and looked around as well, shaking his head.

Nan pulled the ancient urn from the bottom piece, handing that up to Skye as well. The ancient urn Nan now turned in her hands was decorated with intricate carvings.

Rory had to admit what Nan held in her hand was fascinating. He squatted down and peered closely at the urn."Can you tell what the carvings are?"

Skye squatted beside Nan as well and said, "I had a lot of time to look it over. The carvings are people."

"She's right," Nan said as she slowly turned the urn in her hand. "Some of the people look like they're dead. Others are in agony, tearing their clothes off."

Rory noted how Nan's eyes seemed to gleam as she looked at the urn and what it contained. He glanced around them at the sea of legs and rolling suitcases. *We shouldn't be doing this here.* He looked back at Nan and the urn, "Do you really think there's a live disease inside? Do you have any idea how they would've preserved it?"

"No. And that's part of the excitement. Figuring out what's inside and how they did it. This is amazing." Her eyes shone with excitement.

Rory exchanged glances with Skye and then said firmly to Nan, "Keep in mind that we are up against people who want to use the other urn to kill people. And we are looking at one in the middle of thousands of innocent people."

Nan frowned at herself, "Crap. You're right. I have to keep in mind this is not some abstract academic exercise. That's what got me into this trouble in the first place. This involves real people. Millions could die because of my arrogance and foolishness."

"Remember what you said to me? Don't beat yourself up too much."

A slight flush on her face, Nan said, "Words to live by. I'll try to keep that in mind. Just help me to stay grounded, please."

"I will. And the first thing I highly recommend you do is put that back inside the thermos. Then you wrap it back in the tissue paper and put it back in the backpack. I think this thing is too dangerous to have out in public."

Nan let out a small sigh. She had run through a whole gamut of emotions in such a short time. "You're right again. I'm sorry. We should take this right to the New York University Genetics Laboratory, where we can store it and handle it properly. If Helmer Postigan does use what's in the other urn to attack anyone, we need to make sure exactly what strain this urn contains and what drugs can stop it." Nan took the bottom piece of the thermos from Skye and slipped the urn gently back inside it. Then she took the top piece from Skye, slipped it over the top of the urn and began screwing the two pieces back together.

Skye stood up and glanced around.

Rory did the same.

The nearest guard said something into his shoulder mic, nodded and hurried off through the crowd. Several more passed by, headed with their dogs in the same direction as the first one.

Detecting urgency in their movements, Rory watched through the crowds for a moment, wondering what the problem was. He glanced down at Nan.

She was carefully re-wrapping the thermos in the tissue paper.

Rory felt some relief as she slipped it back inside the backpack. He looked at Skye, "Do you need a ride into town?"

Skye shook her head, "No. I have my car here." She gave him a kiss on the cheek, "If you need me for anything else, just call–"

"Oh, no."

Rory and Skye both looked down.

Nan was still kneeling on the floor and she looked intensely afraid as she clutched the backpack to her chest.

His heart went to his throat as Rory thought about the plague inside the backpack. He feared the worst and whispered, "What's wrong?"

Nan was shaking as she pointed past Rory's legs, at something behind him, "That man...."

Rory and Skye both turned their heads to look.

In the middle of the crowd, two large men wearing black bomber jackets were walking towards them. One was husky and one was bearded.

"Which one?" Rory asked Nan.

Nan's voice was raspy and tortured, "The one on the left. He's the big guy who blocked the door when I tried to leave Postigan's laboratory."

Skye looked down at her, "What are you talking about?"

"He was there when they kidnapped me," Nan said "He's one of the men who works for Helmer Postigan. I guess they're never going to stop until they get this urn...and me."

Rory and Skye looked at each other and their faces turned hard. Both turned slowly. Rory assumed these men were the ones who had created the diversion that attracted the security force.

The two men stopped a couple of feet away from them.

Skye looked to the bearded man and she raised an eyebrow, "I guess we meet again."

"You know these guys, too?" Rory asked her. The muscles in his jaw rippled as he clenched his teeth.

"I guess you could say that. We had a hot date in China at the Terracotta Army Museum," Skye said. She gave the bearded man a smile. "Unfortunately, he was shy and left before we could get really close."

As bearded-man stood there, trying to look menacing, he returned her smile. But there was a nervous twitch in his right eye. After a moment he turned his attention to Nan, "We want the urn. Now."

Rory took a step of warning.

Bearded-man opened his bomber jacket to show he had a gun in his hand. "This time it's different. I wouldn't move a muscle."

"How about if I move a whole bunch of them?" Skye asked him.

The bearded-man narrowed his eyes.

Skye pivoted on her left foot and shot a boot into bearded-man's arm, knocking the gun out of his hand. It clattered to the floor.

The husky man pulled his own gun from under the black jacket.

Rory moved in quickly with a block from his right hand and the gun discharged, the bullet ricocheting off the floor twenty feet behind Rory. Another strike by Rory and the gun clattered to the floor.

People in the terminal began to scream and run.

Bearded-man attacked Skye with a variety of Karate strikes and punches. She countered every one of them as she moved skillfully backward.

Now disarmed, Rory's opponent countered by bringing a knee up. Rory barely turned in time but still received a hard blow to his inner thigh. As his leg collapsed, Rory's opponent jumped on him.

Bearded-man now attacked Skye with a variety of Karate kicks. Skye blocked them all as she moved backward again and smiled at him. The man scowled back at her.

Nan Bacon screamed.

Skye looked over to see a third man holding Nan off the floor with one arm around her waist. He was trying to grab the backpack but Nan was holding it away from her body.

Bearded-man used the brief diversion to kick Skye's legs out from under her. She fell hard to the floor. He kicked her in the side - she grunted - then he lifted a foot and drove it down at her head. Skye shot her left arm straight up between his legs and her fist connected his genitals. She rolled away as bearded-man collapsed on the floor in agony.

Rory flipped his opponent sideways. The man landed on his back and rolled. He came up with the gun in his hand and aimed it at Rory. He fired but the shot went wide as a small suitcase, thrown by Skye, struck his hand.

Rory attacked quickly and drove his fist hard into the man's jaw. As the man collapsed, the handgun clattered to the terminal floor. Rory kicked it away. He spun around looking for Nan.

Not able to grab the backpack, the man holding Nan Bacon became frustrated and flipped Nan over his shoulder and slammed her onto the hard floor of the terminal.

The flip sent the backpack flying through the air. The thermos shot into the air as the flap on the backpack opened up. The backpack landed softly on the floor but the thermos casing hit hard. It cracked apart and the ancient urn clattered on the hard floor and began to roll across the terminal.

The man left Nan's prone body behind and ran after the ancient container.

Rory tackled him from behind, just before he reached the rolling urn.

Skye passed them on the run as they grappled on the floor.

"Don't let it break!" Nan yelled as she struggled to her feet. She was grimacing and holding her right shoulder as she began to run after Skye. Nan snared the empty backpack as she ran past it.

The husky man rolled away from him and got to his feet. Rory rose to his feet as well. When the man attacked again - Rory shot out a straight right hand. His palm hit the man in the chest. Husky-man grunted and fell heavily backward onto the floor. Rory turned and sprinted after Nan and Skye.

Skye was gradually gaining but the urn was headed for a flight of stairs. She strained to put in an extra burst of speed. At the last moment, Skye dove forward and grabbed the urn just as it reached the top step. She landed hard on the terminal floor, grunting from the pain, but she held the urn firmly in her right hand. Breathing heavy as she lay prone, Skye looked back.

Rory and Nan were ten feet away, running hard.

Skye spotted something else and she yelled, "Duck!"

Rory pushed Nan to the floor and dropped flat himself.

Skye slithered over the edge of the stairs.

Gunshots rang out.

Two bullets ricocheted off the stair railing were Skye had disappeared over the edge.

Rory and Nan scrambled on their hands and knees and slipped over the top step just as more shots sounded.

Five steps down, Skye ducked and pressed her body against the railing.

Rory pulled Nan down the stairs, pushed her head down and crouched over her against the other railing.

"Now what?" Skye asked him.

Shaking his head, Rory opened his mouth–

Pounding footsteps sounded from below them. A half-dozen security officers were running up the stairs towards them.

Rory pointed back up the stairs towards the terminal floor and yelled, "There are three guys in black jackets up there. They have guns."

"Just keep down," one of the security officers yelled as they took up a position three stairs from the top, peering over carefully.

Rory moved down a stair, pulling Nan to her feet. He gesturing to Skye, who was still carefully holding the ancient urn, "Let's get out of here." She nodded and followed them, keeping as low as possible as gunshots sounded behind them. They huddled together at the bottom of the stairs.

Nan she set her back pack down and gestured to the urn, "Is it cracked or broken?"

Skye held the urn out to Nan, "Don't even ask that question. And please take it off my hands. That's the second time I've had to dive for it and my body won't take a third."

Carefully taking the urn in her hands, Nan rotated it, narrowing her eyes as she looked for cracks, "It *looks* intact."

"That's a relief," Rory said.

"Yeah, but it needs to be examined under a microscope—"

More gunshots.

Nan startled.

Rory put a hand on Nan's arm to steady her. Then he looked up and saw the security guards disappear as they moved onto the terminal floor, "Secure it in the back pack. And we better get out of here quickly before the authorities come back start asking questions about what happened and why. I don't want that urn to end up in a police compound and out of our sight while we try to explain our way out of this."

Nan nodded agreement, "Someone hold the back pack open for me." As Skye did that, she carefully slipped the ancient urn inside.

Skye then looked at Rory, "Do you want me to drive you somewhere now?"

Rory shook his head as he got up, pulling Nan to her feet, "No. I think we should split up for now."

"Okay, call me if you need me." Skye took off at a run, heading down the hallway and towards the far parking lot.

Rory took Nan's arm and led her straight outside the airport terminal to the drop off and pickup area and hailed a cab.

As the cab was pulling up, Nan turned to Rory and spoke urgently "I just realized - we need to go back to my apartment."

Rory opened the back of the cab door, shaking his head, "No. We can't do that now. It's too dangerous. Postigan knows where you live—"

"And that's the problem," Nan said as she jumped into the back of the cab. She cradled the backpack with her arms and pleaded with Rory. "I have some genetic research papers on the plague that I *can't* let Lillian get. I was *stupid* thinking it would be safe there. If they get it..." Her voice trailed off with the implications of what could happen if they coupled her research with the ancient urn they already had.

Rory nodded reluctantly. "Okay, but we'll have to be fast, understand? These people will be looking for us to get that urn–"

"Or me," Nan whispered. Her eyes showed her fear and her body was shaking.

Chapter 19

THE CAB DRIVER dropped Rory and Nan Bacon off, near the corner of her apartment at the Madison Green Residential Plaza. The street was noisy and busy, as usual, and the air was hot and stuffy. As they walked back towards the tree-lined path to the front entrance, Rory noted a large, yellow Humvee parked right in front of the fire hydrant. When they turned between the two long planters and headed down the walkway to the front door of the Plaza, Rory glanced back. He couldn't see into the Humvee and he felt uneasy for some reason. Years of experience told him to trust his gut and he looked around.

Nan shifted the straps on the backpack and then reached up to enter her password to get into the building.

As she punched in the code, Rory looked through the glass door, into the lobby - and his heart jumped. He saw four large men, coming from the hallway leading to Nan Bacon's apartment.

The man in the lead looked up, and his eyes registered surprise when he saw Nan Bacon outside the front door.

Rory realized they must be more of Postigan's men. He quickly grabbed Nan's arm and pulled her away from the entrance and to the left, towards Broadway.

"What's wrong?" Nan asked in alarm.

"More of Postigan's men coming from the direction of your apartment inside," Rory answered quickly. They the sidewalk and Rory turned her to the right. "Run," he said.

"What? But...?"

"Run. I'm right behind you."

Nan took off running down Broadway.

Rory looked back at the entranceway. The men still weren't outside yet. *Good*. He took off running after Nan. Catching up to her halfway down the block, they reached East 23rd Street together and stopped at the back of the crowd waiting for the walk light. He looked back.

Postigan's men were already halfway down the block in hot pursuit.

Rory cursed under his breath. He grabbed Nan's hand, slipped through the waiting crowd and ran into the street against the walk light. Car horns blared as they stopped and started repeatedly, weaving their way dangerously across the fast traffic. Scrambling through the stunned crowd on the sidewalk, he glanced back to see the four men trying to pursue them through the traffic as well.

One of the cars slammed into one of the pursuers but it wasn't going fast enough to do any real damage. The large man rolled up the hood and then he was back on his feet, running between the cars again.

Rory looked for an avenue of escape. Spotting the entrance to Madison Square Park, he pulled Nan in that direction. There were three pathway and Rory took the central one. In a few minutes, they reached a circular walkway and skidded to a stop. There were several pathways leading off the circle.

"Which way?" Nan cried.

"I have no idea. Let's try that one." They took off at a run to the right and along the path lined with large trees, *hoping* to disappear from view.

The sounds of the traffic began to fade away.

But as they ran - despite the trees - Rory quickly realized there was no real place to hide. He changed directions, leaving the path and taking Nan across the grass and through more trees, hoping to find a building they could hide in. Cresting a low hill, he could see 5th Ave - it was only two hundred yards away. A cacophony of honking to the left caught his attention and Rory brought Nan to a stop. The large yellow Humvee that had been parked right in front of Nan's place was traveling aggressively *against* the traffic, coming up the curved section of Broadway in this direction. It wouldn't be long before it reached the junction where Broadway crossed 5th Ave - only half a block away - and Rory had no doubt it held more of Postigan's men and was coming up to cut them off. He looked around for the other men chasing them - they were heading their way quickly through the trees.

Rory cursed under his breath. Nan was still holding his hand but she was bent over, the other hand on her knee, breathing heavy, and he knew she was almost done. His mind whirled as he looked for a way out - he saw it.

Kids were clustered around a Mister Softee blue and white ice cream truck parked on a small side-road twenty feet from the main road. There was no one serving ice cream yet.

Nan squeaked as Rory took off, pulling her behind him as he headed directly for the ice cream truck. As they got closer, Rory still didn't see anyone inside the truck. He pulled Nan through the crowd of kids - they began asking where the ice cream was - pulled the driver side door open - saw the keys in the ignition - and pushed Nan into the truck.

Her chest was heaving as she scrambled across to the passenger side, struggled to take the backpack off and dropped it at her feet.

Rory shooed the kids to step away from the truck - they protested but moved away - he jumped in and started the vehicle–

"Hey!"

In the side mirror, Rory saw a man in a white jacket running towards the truck - a second man, dressed as the Mister Softee Mascot, was right behind him.

Rory checked the other mirrors for kids and then floored the gas. The tires screeched and smoked and the truck shot forward. He knew the Humvee would be faster so outrunning it right now wouldn't work. He cranked the steering wheel to the right, cut at an angle across the twenty feet of grass - blaring his horn to clear the sidewalk - and barreled into Broadway traffic, cutting off several cars. He veered to the right of the road and floored the gas, passing the yellow Humvee as it came this way.

Looking into the side mirror he saw the Humvee slide to a sideways stop. Two cars swerved to miss it, left the roadway, crossed the sidewalk and smashed into buildings. The rest of the traffic came to a sliding stop. Horns honked and drivers yelled as the Humvee made a U-turn. But it didn't take off in pursuit right away.

Rory could see the four men in the park passing the kids and running hard for the Humvee. It wouldn't be long before they began pursuit but at least it gave him some breathing room. Rory ran the light at East 23rd, barely passing between two vehicles.

The cars swerved and blared their horns at him.

Rory glanced into the side mirror.

The doors on the Humvee were closing as the big vehicle started coming after them.

Rory had to think fast. The more powerful Humvee wouldn't take long to run them down. Rory took a risk and turned right against the traffic on 22nd. He realized at the last moment there was no room on the road and the Mister Softee truck bounced up onto the sidewalk as he swerved away from a large van directly in front of them. Pedestrians scattered as he leaned on the horn. He saw a gap in the one way traffic and he turned left, squeezing between two large trucks. The Mister Softee truck shot across the street and across the sidewalk into a parking lot. Rory glimpsed the Humvee out of the corner of his eye.

The Humvee's tires screeched as it entered the intersection and plowed through a vehicle, knocking it aside easily as it made the turn towards the Mister Softee truck.

Rory stepped on the gas and the Mister Softee truck shot across the parking lot and out the other side. He narrowly missed a cube van as he turned right onto West 21st Street. He desperately tried to weave in and out of the traffic but there were few gaps. He kept having to take the sidewalk.

Irritated drivers leaned on their horns as they braked and swerved to avoid the Mister Softee truck barreling through the traffic.

Rory nearly lost control as he turned left onto Fifth Avenue. He pushed the pedal hard to the floor and wove in and out of traffic again. The Mister Softee truck shot across West 20th

Street. As he turned right on West 19th Street, Rory saw the yellow Humvee making the turn onto Fifth Avenue. Rory's desperate quick turns and weaving in of the traffic was not working. The Humvee was still on their tail. The only good thing about the traffic was that the larger Humvee couldn't make up a lot of ground. Rory floored the gas pedal again and passed as many cars as he could when he could. Rory shot through two more red lights, nearly missing vehicles both times. He could hear sirens in the background now.

The yellow Humvee tried to pass more cars behind the Mister Softee truck, taking more chances.

Rory realized they must be hearing the sirens as well and they wanted to finish this before the police arrived. The High Line elevated park appeared just up ahead Rory realized they were near the docks. Time for another plan. "Get ready to leave the truck with me," Rory yelled to Nan.

"Are they still following us?" she yelled back in fear. Nan reached down for the backpack.

"Yeah! Hold on!" he yelled.

Nan braced herself.

Rory made a hard left against the traffic on 10th. Then he made a hard right and the Mister Softee truck bounced into a parking lot. Rory quickly turned left and tried to hide the Mister Softee ice cream truck behind several parked cars. "Let's go," he yelled as he leaped out of the truck.

Nan was out the passenger side and around the front of the truck as fast as her legs could carry her.

Rory took her hand and they ran under the elevated park and down West 18th Street. They heard the screeching of tires behind them. Rory looked back and saw the yellow Humvee sliding to a stop in the intersection behind them. Rory kept checking behind as he led Nan across West 18th at an angle and then led her across another parking lot.

The yellow Humvee drove ahead twenty feet and started a quick right turn. Just before the yellow Humvee entered the parking lot, a car hit them. The Humvee was jolted and stopped.

Rory saw the collision and felt hope. He grabbed Nan's hand and took off at a run.

Chapter 20

RORY AND NAN ran hard across the parking lot. The sounds of squealing tires ripped through the air behind them. Both stopped and looked back.

The Humvee's tires screeched and smoked as it backed up. There was a bang as it came to a stop against another car. The wheels were cranked hard right. The tires squealing and smoked again and then they caught traction, driving the Humvee forward. It bounced up over the sidewalk and then the engine growled as the huge vehicle began to race through the parking lot.

Rory cursed. He grabbed Nan's hand and they ran hard. In a moment, they were running across 11th Avenue and Hudson River Greenway, dodging the traffic. A blue and gray building loomed ahead and they ran down the pier walkway to the left of it. Boats lined the pier just up ahead, offering another possible escape route. But Rory's heart dropped when he realized they were all cabin cruisers. There was no way they could fire one up one of these big boats in time to get away. They had to keep running. They reached the end of the pier walkway and turned right. Rory saw several smaller speedboats tied to the dock. Hope rose again and he led Nan towards the closest one, a Formula 353 FASTech powerboat. "Get in," he yelled to Nan as he began to undo a rope.

"I can't swim!" Nan said in fear.

"I think that's the least of your worries right now," Rory told her as he threw the first rope into the powerboat. He undid the second rope, "Just hurry up and get in."

But Nan didn't hurry - she was frustratingly slow - gingerly stepping across the gap into the powerboat - it rocked and her arms windmilled.

Rory jumped across the gap, dropped the rope and caught her before she went over.

Nan slumped to the floor of the powerboat, her chest heaving as she clutched the backpack.

The boat rocked harder as Rory moved up behind the steering wheel and started the twin MERC engine. He cranked hard to the left as the twin-engine growled. The powerboat slowly made the turn and then shot past the larger boats, heading for open water.

A gunshot sounded.

"Keep down," Rory yelled as he looked to his left.

Six men were standing on the walkway. Two of them were aiming guns.

Rory tried to stay as low as possible while he zigzagged the powerboat.

A bullet shattered the small windshield in front of him. His powerboat entered open water and he turned right at an angle away from the men. He heard the deep growl of an onboard engine starting up, then another. He looked back to see two speedboats maneuvering their way out of the dock. They were going to continue the chase on the water. Rory drove his powerboat hard down the Hudson River, wondering what he should do next.

Rory looked behind him and saw Nan curled on the floor the powerboat. "Are you all right?" he yelled above the noise of the speedboat. There was no answer. "Nan?" he yelled again.

Nan stirred just a little. There was blood on her left shoulder and she struggled to look up.

Rory could see the fear in her eyes. She said something but Rory couldn't hear the words above the noise of the growling powerboat. He desperately scanned the shoreline, looking for a place to hide or escape. There was nothing. He looked back

One of the speedboats was slowly gaining on them. The other seemed to be falling further back.

Rory saw a small marina coming up on the left. He glanced back, wondering how much time they would have to dock and run.

The speedboat was closing in.

Rory cursed. He had no idea how bad Nan's wound was or how well she could run. He looked for another escape route as he tried to coax more speed out of his powerboat. But it was already giving every ounce of horsepower it had. They were passing Battery Park now and Rory glanced back again.

The pursuing speedboat was slowly but surely closing in. In fact, it wouldn't be long before they were right on top of them.

Rory angled his powerboat to the right, trying to stay ahead. He glanced over his left shoulder and realized one of the men was standing up, getting ready to shoot at him. Rory zigzagged the boat, hoping to throw the man's aim off.

Crack!

Bits of fiberglass exploded just to Rory's left.

Crack!

A buzzing sound passed his right ear. He looked desperately for a way out. He saw it. It was a huge gamble but they had no choice. Rory cut hard to the left, cutting across the path of the pursuing speedboat.

The speedboat turned to give chase.

Rory did a looping right turn.

The pursuing speedboat matched his turn. One of the men stood up, holding onto the edge of the windshield to maintain his balance.

Letting off just a little on the power, Rory watched the pursuing speedboat.

The pursuing speedboat came closer. The standing gunman raised his weapon, getting ready to fire at Rory.

Rory returned to full power and turned hard left.

The pursuing speedboat did the same. The gunmen lowered his weapon, fighting to maintain his balance.

Holding his breath, Rory straightened out at the last minute and his speedboat passed under the shadow of the Staten Island Ferry boat.

The pursuing speedboat didn't. The gunmen yelled at the driver but it was too late. A fireball marked their contact with the front end of the Staten Island Ferry.

Rory looped back hard to the left, taking a heading back towards the Marina.

The second pursuing speedboat was closing the gap rapidly, now that Rory was headed back in their direction.

But Rory maintained his heading, gambling on the speedboat's next move.

The pursuing speedboat turned hard left, planning to cut him off at the Marina.

That's what he wanted. Rory made his move. He slowed briefly, turning at a right angle to the shore at Battery Park. Then he applied full power, aiming the bow of his speedboat for a cement boat ramp dead ahead. A few moments later, the speedboat hit the cement ramp, scraped harshly upwards and then ground to a halt with a jolt, throwing Rory against the shattered windshield. Rory ignored the pain, turned and jumped down beside Nan, "Where are you hit?"

"My shoulder," Nan said with a grimace.

"Can you run?" Rory asked her. He looked look back over the water, waiting for an answer.

"I...I...."

The other speedboat was bearing down on them.

"We have to go, Nan. *Now!*"

Nan grunted as she rolled, grabbing the backpack. She got to her feet with Rory's help and stepped off the beached boat, staggering.

People in the park were gathering beside the beached boat, asking if they were okay.

Rory ignored them and pushed his way past them, encouraging Nan to move as quickly as she could towards the ferry terminal. He looked back to see the other speedboat approaching another one of the cement ramps.

In a moment, they beached their boat hard as well.

Rory and Nan moved as quickly as possible to the South Ferry subway station. Rory paid for two fares and then helped Nan towards the stairs as he glanced back.

Three men were running hard after them.

The trip down the stairs was agonizingly slow for Rory but they finally made it to the platform. A train was entering the station. Rory glanced back.

No sign of the men yet.

As soon as a car door opened, Rory guided Nan inside. They sat side-by-side, breathing hard as they watched for the men chasing them. It was an agonizing wait but the doors finally started closing.

The men appeared at the bottom of the stairs. They ran to board the subway but it was too late. The three men ran along the moving cars, looking for Rory and Nan.

Rory's eyes met the man in the lead and saw him raise a handgun.

But they were into the subway tunnel before he could fire.

Rory finally let his breath out. He closed his eyes for a moment in relief and then turned his attention to Nan.

Nan held the backpack firmly with one hand as Rory checked inside her jacket.

"It looks like the bullet just grazed your shoulder," he said.

Nan grimaced in pain, "I'd hate to feel what it was like if one went inside. If we go to Penn Station, we can go to St. Jude Children's Research Hospital. I went to school with someone who works there. I'm sure she'll help us."

"Possibly," Rory said. "But I don't think we should take the chance. Hospitals have to report gunshot wounds. Even if your friend helped and stayed quiet, someone else might see you were shot and call it in."

Nan closed her eyes for a moment. "I have some bandages back at my apartment," Nan said as she gritted her teeth.

Rory slipped out his cell phone, "I don't think we should go back to your apartment either. I'm not sure how they knew we were at the airport, but we need to change things up–"

"But we have to!" Nan insisted as she grit her teeth against the pain. "If they get my research–"

"They probably already have it," Rory said firmly. "Those men were coming from the hallway to your apartment. I highly doubt they just knocked and walked away without going inside. What we can't do is let them get you as well. Your apartment is out. No more discussion."

Nan hammered her small right fist against the seat several times, swearing like a sailor.

"Just let me make a call and see what I can set up," Rory told her. Without telling Nan, he made a call to her father, Cordell Bacon. He would be used to helping clients hide in plain sight. He discussed the situation in a low voice. Bacon had several locations he used to hide clients and keep them safe. Rory chose one and closed the call. They rode to Penn Station where Rory bought some bandages and antiseptic. Then he helped Nan outside where he hailed a cab. Rory instructed the cab driver to take them to Union Square Inn on East 14th Street. The cab let them off the front curb and Rory led Nan through the front door.

"Do you think you can still walk for a while for me?" Rory asked her.

Nan nodded but he could tell she was in a lot of pain. She slipped the backpack over her good shoulder and they walked out the back of Union Square Inn and headed across to East 15th Street. Rory turned them left and they walked up to Irving Place. He kept glancing over his shoulder to make sure they weren't being followed. They turned right and walked five blocks into

Gramercy Park. Now feeling positive they were not being followed, Rory took Nan through the park and headed to the Gramercy Park Hotel where Cordell Bacon had set up the Penthouse Suite for them. The lawyer already alerted the security there and they said they were going to do everything in their power to keep his daughter safe.

Rory wondered if they could. Postigan and his men were determined to get Nan and the urn...or both. Rory also wondered about the other urn.

Chapter 21

IN THE MORNING, Rory was sipping coffee in front of the Stanford White fireplace in the penthouse suite. He had let Nan sleep soundly in the bedroom while he slept on the sofa in the living room. But there was actually little sleep since was constantly waking up with an eye on the front door. About 9:30 AM he had heard Nan go into the bathroom and take a shower. Right now, everything was quiet and peaceful. But he wondered how long that would last.

Nan came out of the bathroom wearing the clothes Rory had picked up for her. It was a blue pantsuit to replace the bloody and torn clothing from the long chase yesterday.

"How is the shoulder feeling this morning?" Rory asked her.

"Much better thank you," Nan said. Her voice was groggy, "I think all that Brandy might have helped numb the pain."

"You did drink a lot," Rory said.

"Do you realize you're the only man who has ever who gotten me drunk, seen me in my bra, and still nothing happened?" she said with an amused look on her face.

"Are you sure?" Rory asked her in a serious tone. "Was your underwear on straight this morning? Was the red rose on your panties at the front or the back?"

Nan's mouth dropped open and she turned red.

Rory laughed, "Don't worry. Nothing happened. I helped you to get into bed, that was all. I like my women sober in those situations. It prevents a lot of lawsuits from happening. That's how I've been able to hold onto my vast fortune."

Nan smiled sheepishly.

"There's some breakfast on that cart," Rory said, "room service brought it in about twenty minutes ago and it should still be hot."

Nan gave him a half-hearted shrug, "I'm not sure if I can eat anything–"

"Listen, Bacon, you need to keep your strength up or you won't be any good to anybody."

A flush crept across Nan's face, "Okay, Steele."

Rory gave her a thumbs-up and watched her closely as she got up and walked over to the cart.

"Aren't you having anything?" Nan asked as she lifted up the large lid. The smell of toast and scrambled eggs carried across the room, mingling with the rich scent of fresh coffee.

"I grabbed a little bit of the eggs and toast already," Rory told her. He indicated an empty plate in front of him on the coffee table.

Nan took a plateful herself, along with a cup of coffee, and wandered over to the love seat in front of the fireplace, opposite Rory.

Rory watched her eat as he gave the situation some thought. He wasn't really sure what his next move should be. Getting the other urn was a priority, but he how could he find it? And would she stay here in safety while he left to find it? The other problem was keeping her from falling into a deep depression at the thought of what the Postigan's might do with the other urn. There was no doubt she was still beating herself up mentally.

Halfway through her breakfast, Nan picked up the television clicker off the coffee table and clicked on the 60 inch LCD TV screen to their right, on the other side of the room. She scrolled through the various morning television programs and then left it on CNN. She picked up her plate to finish her breakfast.

CNN Breaking News flashed across the screen. A white-haired announcer talked solemnly into the television screen: "We're going to take you down to our remote location in Harlem where our correspondent Margaret Butterfield has been working to give us an update on about the events happening down there. Margaret, are you there?"

A young blonde woman, looking very earnest, appeared on the screen, "I'm here, Robert." The interview was taking place in front of a large crowd that included several policemen. Everything seemed to be in noisy chaos and there were a number of people crying. "I'm here with Dr. Simon Tamburri," Butterfield said. "I understand he just flew in from the Center for Disease Control in Atlanta just a few hours ago. Dr. Tamburri, we have reports of 227 people being sick so far. Can you confirm we have an outbreak of the Plague here in Harlem?"

Nan Bacon's breakfast plate crashed to the floor.

A thin bald man, wearing wire-rimmed glasses, appeared on the screen, "We're flying cultures down to the CDC for further analysis as we speak, Margaret. But all the symptoms point to an outbreak of the plague. Yes."

"Can you confirm we've had 43 deaths so far?" Margaret Butterfield asked him.

"We do have a number of dead, but I can't confirm any numbers right now," the CDC doctor told her.

"But there are a number of dead, isn't that right Dr. Tamburri," pushed Butterfield.

"Unfortunately, yes," Tamburri admitted. He looked very uncomfortable having to admit it.

"Do you know where it came from? How did these people get the plague in the middle of New York City?"

Tamburri grimaced, "There are a lot of possibilities but, at this time, we just don't know."

"All right. Can you confirm that Reverend Caufield is among the dead?" Butterfield asked him.

Tamburri gave her a shake of his head, "I'm afraid we can't say anything about any individuals until the next of kin are notified."

"But we understand that his entire family is also sick," Margaret Butterfield added. "Is that true?"

"Like I said, I'm afraid can't say anything at this time."

"But you are not denying it either," Butterfield challenged.

The CDC doctor let out a low frustrated breath, trying to maintain his composure.

Butterfield switched gears, "All right, Dr. Tamburri, I understand you have some important information you'd like to share with our viewers."

"That's right," Tamburri said. He looked directly into the camera, "The deaths and sickness reported so far have been between West 126th Street and West 124th Street. We're setting up a reporting center in the Apollo Theater right now. If anyone has *any* flu-like symptoms, we want you to let us know. That could include fevers and chills, abdominal pain, diarrhea, swollen lymph nodes or muscle aches. We don't care what it is. If you're not feeling well, let us know *immediately*. Don't hesitate. You can also call the New York City Police Department 28th Precinct at Frederick Douglass Boulevard. We're also setting up a hotline that people can call."

"I believe that hotline number is scrolling across the bottom of everyone's television screen right now," Margaret Butterfield said as she looked off to the side. She held a hand to her ear, "Yes. And I've just been told that we will keep that number on the screen so anyone can call 24-7. We're also showing the number for the NYPD 28th precinct. Please call if you have any of the symptoms that Dr. Tamburri described. Don't hesitate. Don't feel that you just have the flu. Just call and the doctors will help you out."

Nan Bacon jumped up out of her seat, "We have to get down there now!"

"What are we going to do?" Rory asked her as he jumped up from his seat.

"We have to go down there and tell that man, that Dr. Tamburri, what is happening," Nan Bacon said. She ran for the backpack. "Maybe that CDC doctor can have Lillian and her father arrested. They can find the other urn—"

Rory placed his hands on her shoulders and stopped her from rushing around. "That story didn't go over too well with the police already, remember?" Rory reminded her.

"But they *have* to believe us," Nan replied with conviction. "We're telling the truth. They'll be able to tell that—"

"And Lillian already shot down my version of a similar conspiracy. *And* made me look like a raving lunatic, who just wanted to get into her pants," Rory said.

"But...but...with what's happening..." Nan looked at the television screen and curled an arm over her head, desperate to do *something* to stop what was happening.

Rory couldn't blame her. His jaw clenched as he looked at the mass of humanity crying and pleading for help on the screen. "Look," he said after a moment. "You said they wanted to modify the disease to attack specific populations. I doubt they would've gotten back here that much faster than Skye did. Do you think Lillian would have accomplished that in just a few days?"

Nan had a hard time tearing her eyes away from the anguish on the screen and she simply shrugged, "It's...it's possible...."

"The fact that 43 people are possibly already dead tells me they either worked very quickly...or the disease is working very quickly. Which is it?"

Nan just continued staring at the crying and pain.

"Nan!" Rory yelled loudly.

That broke her out of her spell of despair and she jerked her head to look at Rory.

"Tell me *what* we are dealing with." He had to get her thinking like a scientist instead of a broken doll. "Did they modify it...or is the disease just fast acting?"

Nan swallowed and answered in a weak voice, "The Bubonic Plague takes 2-5 days to develop, the same with the Septicemic Plague. Pneumonic Plague can show signs and symptoms within a few hours and you have to start drugs within 24 hours to have a chance...but you're right...the fact that people are being infected and dying so quickly tells me we're dealing with a very virulent strain...." She glanced back over at the television.

"Which means...?" Rory prodded her.

It took a minute before Nan reacted to his question. She looked at Rory, "That means we're getting infection within hours and death maybe in less than a day with this strain. That's incredibly fast."

Rory looked at her for a few moments, "So even if we *do* go down there and tell them what happened, what then? If this is a totally different strain, as you thought it would be, didn't you already tell me you doubted modern-day drugs would be effective against it? "

Nan's eyes blinked several times as she looked at Rory, "Y-yes...but that doesn't mean we do nothing...."

"I'm not saying we do nothing. You're a researcher. Wouldn't it be better to try to figure out a cure for it? To find some way to stop it?" Rory asked her. "To me - that seems to me a more important line of pursuit for us right now."

It took a moment, but Nan's eyes finally took on a small glow of hope as she followed his line of thought. She headed quickly to the bedroom and returned with the backpack over her good shoulder, "Let's go to the NYU Genetics Laboratory. We can open up this urn under controlled circumstances. Once we find out what we're dealing with, we can find a line of treatment."

Rory nodded and they headed out the door. Once outside, they hailed a cab and jumped in, heading for the laboratory. Rory pulled his cell phone and called Professor Leonard Bonifay. He informed him that Nan was now safe and they were headed for the laboratory to work on the plague down in Harlem. Not long after, the cab dropped them off in front of the laboratory and they ran into the building.

Bonifay was rushing down from his office and met them inside the door, "Nan dear. I'm so glad you're safe." He threw his arms around her, hugging her tightly.

"Thank you, Professor Bonifay," Nan said. "We need to hurry though. We don't have much time."

"Of course, of course" Bonifay replied, "how can we help you?"

Nan Bacon slipped the backpack off her shoulder, "I have the urn in here, with the same strain of the plague that is down in Harlem. We need to –"

"What!" Bonifay exclaimed as he pulled back in horror. "You're carrying around a deadly strain of plague in a backpack! I thought you were better than that. I can't believe you would be that irresponsible."

"You don't understand. We need to get this up to the laboratory. Right now!" Nan said. She moved towards the elevator.

Bonifay quickly moved in front of her to block access to the elevator. "I'm afraid I *can't* allow that to happen," Professor Bonifay said in a loud voice.

"What are you talking about?" Nan replied as she stood there in shock, looking at him.

"I have to think about the safety of this University and the people in it," Bonifay replied sternly. "As well as the entire city of New York. You obviously aren't thinking about any of them!"

"People are already dying Professor," Rory said. "We need to figure out what we're up against–"

"I *know* people are dying, Mr. Steele!" Bonifay yelled. "And I know that we're up against the deadliest disease known to mankind. And now you're telling me Ms. Bacon here carries it around in a backpack, in a city of more than 8 million people!"

He turned abruptly and began yelling for the University security guards.

Rory quickly retreated, pulling Nan Bacon with him.

Security guards ran into the foyer and Professor Bonifay instructed them to detain Rory and Nan. But both were out the front doors quickly as the security guards ran for them.

Rory and Nan quickly weaved in and out of the crowd on the sidewalk, soon losing sight of the security guards. They crossed First Avenue in the middle of traffic and headed across a small grassy area and through a stand of trees towards Kip Bay Towers. They walked out the other side of the block to 2nd Avenue and turned right towards East 34th Street.

Nan's face was filled with anguish, "I can't believe he wouldn't let me use the laboratory. I know what I'm doing. He knows that."

"He's scared, Nan," Rory told her, "and I don't blame him. We've been carrying that urn around like it's a picnic lunch. How do we know it won't contaminate us?"

"Because we'd be dead by now," Nan said. "And the plane carrying your sister back with it would've plunged into the ocean long before she got here."

Rory's blood ran cold when he realized how fortunate they had been to this point. Trusting that a terracotta urn, buried for thousands of years, wouldn't break apart had been foolhardy. And the fact that Nan Bacon was so casual about it worried him as well. Had she been so insulated within her academic realm that she failed to see the implications of her actions in the real world? Maybe they needed someone else to talk to, some older scientist who could impress upon Nan the seriousness of the situation. And to help to keep them alive. Bonifay was out, that was for sure. Maybe this Tamburri could help.

"What are we going to do now?" Nan asked. She looked back to see if any of the University security guards were still following them.

"Maybe we can try your original idea and head down to the Apollo Theater in Central Harlem," Rory said. "We're not far from Grand Central Terminal. Once we take care of something, we can take the train down to Central Harlem and talk to the CDC. Maybe we can still find some way to stop what the Postigan family has started."

Chapter 22

CENTRAL HARLEM, NEW York City

RORY AND NAN took the train from Grand Central Terminal to Harlem. They sat in silence as they watched the buildings in Midtown Center and then the Upper East Side pass by. As the train neared the Marcus Garvey Park area, there was a lot of commotion over on the right side of the train. Through the car window, they could see dense smoke rising over the skyline in the west.

"Harlem is burning," a woman said to passengers around her, "my sister just called me and said it's on CNN."

Rory and Nan just looked at each other in silence as the passengers around them speculated and argued about what was happening. The train pulled into the station at East 125th Street and Rory and Nan jumped off. They headed up East 125th Street towards the Apollo Theater. Traffic was at a standstill. Some people were headed in the same direction as they were, but a lot more were moving rapidly past them. These people were getting *away* from Harlem in a panic and were encouraging others to join them. Rory and Nan struggled against the sea of people moving away from the smoke rising to the west. The weather over the city had created an inversion layer and it was keeping the smoke smell down, making it evident even at this distance.

They crossed Lennox Avenue and continued up West 125th Street against the flow of bodies. The smell of smoke was becoming stronger and more acrid. As they approached West 125th Street and 7th Avenue they realized people on the sidewalk here were staring in shock at the block to the west.

Rory and Nan squeezed through the people and finally saw what they were looking at. It was a shock to them as well. There was an 18-foot high chain link fence directly ahead of them. It was riveted into the pavement and ran all the way down to 7th. High over top of the chain link fence, they saw flames, pulsating in deep reds, ambers, and blacks, leaping from a number of the buildings. The smells of burning wires, rubber, charred wood, drywall, and roasting metal were strong and heavy. Nan wrinkled her nose, wiping at it and then turned to a woman standing nearby, asking her what was happening with the fire and the reason for the fence.

The woman's face was a mask of agony. "It's terrible," the woman told Nan. "Everything is burning from here down three blocks to West 122nd Street. Somebody started a fire to kill the plague. Some people are blaming the city officials for setting the fires, but I don't know." She pointed ahead, "The Army is putting up that barricade to quarantine the area off. I've got family in there, you know. I got family."

"The Army? The United States Army?" Nan asked her. "Are you sure?"

"I saw it with my own eyes," the woman answered. Her eyes were filling with tears. "The police are still here, but the Army showed up and began putting up that chain fence. It looks like the doctors can't do nothing. People are dying everywhere in there. They are ripping their clothes off and screaming." The woman crossed herself and spoke in a fearful voice, "Lord have mercy on our souls. We're all going to die"

Rory leaned over, bringing his head closer to Nan and asked her in a low voice, "*Why* would they be screaming and taking their clothes off? Is that how the plague–"

"No," Nan said firmly. "She must be wrong. I've never read about plague victims reacting like that. It's just foolish fears added to baseless rumors."

Rory took a deep breath and let it out with a bit of relief, "Okay. Okay. Why don't we move on to the Apollo and see if you can help stop this thing." He led Nan away from the woman and towards the theater. And just as the woman had said, squads of soldiers were working feverishly off to their left to erect the high steel barricade, taking it straight down the middle of the street. He could already see a number of completed sections, half a block down on his right.

"What do they think they're doing?" Nan asked in an indignant huff.

Rory didn't bother answering her. There wasn't time. He could see soldiers bringing sections fence towards the spot where they were standing. It wouldn't be long before the path to the Apollo would be blocked off. He took Nan's hand and led her through the crowd and towards the gap.

But before they could get through, they were stopped and pushed back by a combination of police and soldiers. They tried to reason with them, telling them why they needed to get through to the Apollo Theater. But everything was too chaotic and too many other people were wanting through the gap as well.

Rory and Nan were just two more hysterical people in a rapidly growing population of hysterical, desperate people.

Rory pulled Nan over to the side of the gap, hoping to try from that spot, but there were still denied. Nan yelled at the soldiers and police, trying to get them to understand, but she could barely be heard above the yelling, shouting and sirens around them.

Yelling as well, Rory realized it was useless. And he sensed things were beginning to get worse if that was possible. A number of police cars were being maneuvered into position to prevent people from passing through until the barrier could be completed. Despite what Tamburri had said, *nobody* was being let through to the Apollo. Something had changed in a short amount of time.

And beyond the barricade already set in place, firemen worked feverishly, hoses on burning buildings as well as those that hadn't caught fire yet. Water was soon flowing down the street in a wide red river, reflecting the flames in a macabre dance. The scene was chaotic and filled with people in full panic.

Rory made a decision, took Nan's hand and began heading north to West 126th Street, sloshing with her through the water running in the street.

"What are we doing?" Nan asked him in desperation. She yanked her hand out of Rory's and started moving back down the street. "We need to find some way to get in back there and help," she yelled back over her shoulder.

"I know, but they won't let us," Rory said as he ran after her and took her by the elbow.

Nan ripped her arm away, "I'm going back. You don't have to if you're afraid." She continued moving down the block.

Rory caught up to her again, "Nan, listen to me–"

"No! I have to help. It's my fault. Don't you see that? It's all my fault!"

Rory took her by the arm firmly and turned her around to face him, "Look. I know how you feel. But we can't get through back there–"

"But–"

"Just listen to me. It looks like they haven't erected the barricade completely on the other side yet. Maybe, if we go around the block, we can reach the Apollo Theater from the other side before they have it closed off completely. Trust me, I'll get you in there, okay?"

Nan looked at him, her face screwed up in agony, wanting to get through the gap and afraid they would lose the opportunity if they moved away. Finally, she licked her lips, "Okay. How...?"

"This way." Rory placed his hand on her back and guided her up the street. It was difficult walking among the mass of people. Turning west, once they reached West 126th Street, they found the streets were crowded here as well. People were crying and screaming. More sirens could be heard heading for Central Harlem. Water was running in heavy streams down the roadway and over the sidewalks now.

Rory and Nan finally reached 8th Avenue and they turned south, heading back towards the Apollo. They could hear as well as see the flames now. They were roaring and leaping around and over the tops of the buildings. Heavy black smoke was being pushed to the west and the burning smell was harsh. Ash was floating in the air and beginning to coat the street and sidewalks in spots where the running water wasn't pushing it away. The crowd was becoming louder, more chaotic and frightening. And far down the street, Rory could see another high barricade being erected.

As they neared West 126th Street again, Rory and Nan stopped dead in their tracks. They could see a young black woman in the distance, running up 8th Avenue in their direction. She was screaming at the top of her lungs and ripping her clothes off. Two men in hazmat suits were running after her.

Rory put Nan behind him to shield her, not sure if the men would be able to catch the woman.

Nan struggled to get by Rory, trying to shake his hands away, "Let me go."

"It's too dangerous, "Rory said as he blocked her attempts to get by. "Let the men do their job."

Nan tried to push by again but Rory kept his arms out, blocking her. Nan stumbled back a couple of steps, "Y-you don't understand–"

But Rory couldn't let her headstrong nature and self-blame put her in contact with the woman without protective clothing.

By the time the young woman ran across the intersection, she was nearly naked, her skin glistening with sweat. The two men in hazmat suits finally caught her and wrestled her to the ground, now not more than ten feet from Rory and Nan.

The young woman screamed and fought the hazmat team, reaching out in Rory's direction with her hands.

Rory felt an ache in his throat as he watched her suffering.

A moment later, a black man came running across the intersection, tearing away his shirt and screaming in agony. His body with dripping with sweat, just like the young woman.

One of the men in a hazmat suit jumped up and tackled the screaming man around the waist. They both crashed hard to the pavement. Three other men wearing hazmat suits came running to help.

Rory stayed on high alert, watching the struggle in the street as he started walking again. He needed to get Nan to the Apollo Theater so she could help – his heart raced when he realized Nan wasn't beside him. He spun around, looking for her.

Nan had collapsed to her knees on the sidewalk. She was rocking back and forth and crying, watching the man and woman being dragged away by the hazmat team.

The woman was still screaming as she was taken away and her hands were clawing the air in Nan's direction.

Rory ran back and knelt beside Nan, "Are you all right? What's wrong?"

Nan's mouth moved but she couldn't say anything in her anguish. Tears streamed down her face as she looked across the intersection at where the man and woman were being dragged away.

Rory put his arm around her and gently held her, "I know it was hard to see that–"

"It was Bella," Nan cried. "And her husband. She recognized me and was asking for help. I did that to them, I did that. I can't believe what I've done. I did that." Her shoulders curled over her chest and her body shook with sobs.

It took Rory a few moments before he recognized who she was talking about. The woman in the street, now being dragged away, was Bella Atkinson, the granddaughter of Cordell Bacon's receptionist.

Cordell had told him how Nan and Bella had grown up together. Seeing her like that must've been incredibly painful for

Nan. All Rory could do was try to comfort her and hold her as she cried.

Chapter 23

THE SCENE AROUND THEM was becoming more chaotic. Flames and thick smoke climbed higher over the tops of the buildings across the street. The ash attacked their lungs. Rory was positive he could smell burning flesh. He had experienced it a few times on an army mission and you could never forget it.

As he squatted next to Nan, trying to comfort her, he could see the squads of armed soldiers coming closer, working feverishly to put up the 18-foot high barrier to cordon off this side of the block. They were riveting section after section of fence into the pavement and welding them together. It wouldn't be long before the entire area was sealed off and impenetrable. Time was running out.

Rory spoke gently to Nan, "Do you want to go back to the genetics laboratory? Or do you want to try to get into the Apollo Theater and help? We don't have much time before the Army completes the fence and we can't get in."

Nan wiped her hand across her nose and spoke in a voice sore from crying, "I want to go in. Maybe I can still help Bella and Ronnie. Maybe I can help the others." She wiped away her tears with her hands. Her eyes were red-rimmed and puffy. With Rory's help, she got to her feet. She did her best to compose herself as they started moving down the street towards the Apollo Theater again.

The crowds of people they passed through were a mix of soldiers, police, nurses, paramedics and men, women and children. All of them moved in a chaotic dance of determination, fear, sobbing, shouting and praying. A haze of smoke from the burning structures was blanketing everyone, a potential death shroud touching their shoulders.

Rory led Nan past a large tent, in a vacant lot on the left, just before the Apollo Theater. The billing on the Apollo Theater just ahead of them read: 'Ronnie Mattis and Family All Week'. Rory wondered if those entertainers were also part of the dead right now. The whole situation was surreal.

Rory and Nan entered the front of the Apollo Theater. It was chaos inside here as well. People were crying, screaming and yelling for someone to help their families inside the quarantined zone. Others were sitting in the theater seats like patients in a giant hospital waiting room.

A young woman who had CDC credentials around her neck was rushing up the aisle.

Rory grabbed her arm, stopping her. He yelled above the din, "Is Dr. Simon Tamburri of the CDC here?"

The young woman gave him a look of anger at being stopped from her assigned task and gave him a curt answer, "He's here somewhere. Try further back in the theater. I'm sorry, I have to go." She pulled her arm roughly away from Rory and headed out the front door in a hurry.

Rory led Nan further into the theater, trying to pick out a doctor among the frantic mass of people, "Keep your eyes peeled for Tamburri."

Nan nodded as she wiped more tears from her eyes. They moved deeper into the chaos of the theater. Closer to the front, After a few more minutes of searching in the turmoil and noise, Nan pointed, "There, I think that's him."

Stretching his neck, Rory spotted the side of a face that did look like the doctor. He was talking to three other men in white smocks. Rory pushed his way through the mass of people, leading Nan toward the man with wire-rimmed spectacles. He called out, "Dr. Simon Tamburri?"

The man turned his head. He looked frazzled, like he hadn't slept for weeks. Not sure who had called him, the doctor turned back to his conversation.

Finally reaching him, Rory put a hand on the man's shoulder, "Dr. Tamburri–"

The man turned like he had been touched by a hot poker.

Rory held a hand up, "Sorry. My name is Rory Steele. I've brought Dr. Nanette Bacon from the New York University Genetics Laboratory to see you."

Nan was already holding out her NYU photo identification card to Dr. Tamburri.

The man took a look at the card and then looked at Nan, "Yes, I've heard of you, Dr. Bacon. But I'm afraid I don't have any time to talk–"

"I understand that," Nan replied loudly over the din. "I'm here to try and help if I can." She wiped away more tears and sniffled.

Dr. Tamburri nodded, "All right. We can use all the help we can get."

Nan gestured over her shoulder, "We saw...we saw people running and screaming outside. Can you tell me what's happening to them?"

Tamburri took a deep breath, "Come on, I'll take you next door and show you what's happening. It's hard to believe until you actually see it." Nana and Rory followed back him to the front of the Apollo Theater. Once outside, Dr. Tamburri led them down the sidewalk to the large tent in the vacant lot they had passed earlier. He stepped through a cordon of police officers and inside the large tent. Everything was chaotic in here as well. There were several makeshift quarantine rooms set up around the tent and Dr. Tamburri led them to the observation window of the closest one.

Rory and Nan stepped up to the window and peered inside. A number of individuals in hazmat suits were working over a naked man and a naked woman. There were remnants of clothing dangling from each patient. Both were strapped to cots and were screaming in sheer agony. Next to them was another woman, lying prone in a long tub and covered with ice. It obviously wasn't working as she was screaming and fighting with the two individuals trying to hold her down.

"The incubation period seems to take just a few hours," Dr. Tamburri said as they watched the mad scene. "Everything is happening so quickly that we haven't been able to save a single person. Death is no more than 24 hours after contracting the disease. In the final hour, blood is pouring from every opening in their body, because their cellular structure inside is being completely destroyed. From what we understand so far, the disease causes the body's heat mechanism to go into overdrive. Body temperatures are soaring over 120°F. That's why people are ripping their clothes off. They're in sheer agony and they are literally burning to death from the inside out."

Nan seemed to stagger a little and Rory held her by the shoulders from behind. He knew she was probably thinking of Bella. "Are you going to be okay?" he whispered.

Looking up at him, Nan's eyes filled with tears, "That must be why it's called the Fire Plague."

Tamburri overheard Nan and looked startled, "How do you know that?"

Nan ignored the question as she wiped tears from her eyes, "Are any of the known plague drugs working on the bacterium? Streptomycin, Chloramphenicol, Doxycycline–?"

"No," Tamburri interjected forcefully. He narrowed his eyes and looked at her closely. "*Nothing* seems to work so far, Dr. Bacon. We're not sure if it's because we can't catch it in time or because they're not effective. We're not even sure what it is we're fighting. It seems similar to the enterobacteria Yersinia Pestis but it's much, much more powerful. It seems to be a combination of the Plague and the Ebola virus. But that doesn't make any sense to any of us–"

Nan looked at Rory, "I doubt there was any time for Lillian to make any modifications. That should make it easier to zero on a cure for the original bacterium–"

Tamburri took a step, confronting Nan, his countenance hard, "Dr. Bacon, do you know something I should know?"

"Why is the Army here?" Nan asked him, again ignoring his question.

"The President ordered them in here the minute we told him we couldn't stop the progression of this disease," Dr. Tamburri answered. "In a few hours, they'll have that barrier set up and contain everybody infected inside–"

Nan protested loudly, "But you can't do that! You can't let the military take over. We need to maintain control–"

"And what exactly do we do?" Dr. Tamburri yelled back at her. "We can't stop it. And there are 8 million people at risk. Some of the dead were the first responders. The first responders! What do we tell their families? They died at the hospital, along with the people they took there. Which means this disease may *already* be outside the quarantined area, for all we know. I have no time for the standard academic rant against the military, Dr. Bacon!"

Nan stood frozen to the spot against his tirade.

"Freeze!" a voice yelled.

Rory and Nan looked behind them.

Detective Ainsworth was standing behind them with his gun drawn. There were three other NYPD officers beside him, all with their guns drawn as well. And every single weapon was pointed at Rory and Nan.

Rory turned slightly to talk to them. A gun was placed against his temple.

"Don't even move, dirt-bag!" It was Detective Crenshaw. "Cuff them!" he yelled.

Several other NYPD officers moved in quickly and they handcuffed Rory and Nan with their hands behind their back.

"Didn't I tell you these two would show up here?" Ainsworth stated.

Crenshaw nodded his head as he holstered his weapon, "They always return to the scene of the crime."

"What are you doing?" Nan cried, "I'm here to help. You need my help. People are dying –"

"No thanks to you two nut bags," Detective Ainsworth spat. He put his weapon back into his shoulder holster. "Take them right to Rikers," he ordered the officer beside him. "And don't let them talk to anybody, understand? *No one talks to them!* We'll be right behind you."

Rory and Nan were led out of the tent and passed the Apollo Theater, with their hands cuffed behind them. They could see flames leaping into the air over top of the buildings across the street. They were put into the back of a police cruiser and it pulled away. As the cruiser approached 125th Street and 7th Avenue, it stopped at the nearly completed barricade, waiting to be let through.

Rory was on the right side of the back seat. Looking out the window, he saw a white woman come out of the building on the right, screaming and tearing her clothes off.

The nearly naked plague victim rushed at the barricade, her face a mask of torture, her eyes wild and frantic, looking for relief, looking for a way to escape the horror.

Gunshots rang out.

Several policemen had cut her down; afraid she would get outside the quarantined area.

Rory shook his head in horror as he looked at the naked, bloody corpse lying in the water and the ash.

The Postigan's plan may have targeted blacks, but they were killing all races.

The cruiser drove them away from the carnage as Harlem burned and people died in terrible agony.

Chapter 24

RIKERS ISLAND, NEW York

RORY SPENT A SLEEPLESS NIGHT in his cell. It wasn't the heat. Or the smell of urine. Or the coughing and yelling of nearby inmates. Or the hollow, clanking sounds of prison doors opening and closing. It was Nan Bacon. He worried about her. He wondered how she would cope with being hand-cuffed and put into a jail cell. And he was worried about the Postigans. How many more people were being infected and how many more would die through the night in Harlem. And even worse. He worried about what Lillian Postigan and her father were planning next.

The next morning, Rory was placed in wrist and ankle shackles and shuffled out of his cell. He was taken to an interview room, one that smelled of more urine, where Detective Ainsworth and Detective Crenshaw were waiting for him. When he sat down at the table on the opposite side of the Detectives, a policeman bent down and secured his foot shackles to a ring bolted to the floor.

"Isn't this a little extreme?" Rory asked.

"Not for a mass murderer and terrorist," Detective Ainsworth said firmly.

"And who would that be?" Rory asked calmly.

Ainsworth's face was a mask of anger as he shifted forward. "I wouldn't be so cavalier, son. You're in a lot of trouble. A lot of people are dead because of you and your little girlfriend."

"She's not my girlfriend," Rory replied quietly.

Crenshaw, thumped the table with a finger, "If you come clean on this whole thing, we can try to help you. If you don't...." Crenshaw made a show of pressing a phantom needle into his arm.

"That's right," Detective Ainsworth said, "the Attorney General is willing to take the death penalty off the table if you are willing to cooperate. So let's start talking, okay?"

"You don't have any evidence to prove that either one of us had anything to do with this," Rory countered.

"Oh yeah!" Ainsworth said as he leaned forward, "I *personally* took a report from you when you first came into the precinct. We talked about diseases, didn't we? Do you remember that, Steele?"

"It was just speculation," Rory said.

"We were both present when you and your little girlfriend came in and talked about the Black Plague," Crenshaw added. "And what do we have? The Plague in Harlem, New York. And that's not speculation dirt bag, that's fact!"

"We checked for police reports on other nut jobs, making similar, wild claims. You and your little girlfriend were the *only* ones to mention the Plague, let alone any other disease," Ainsworth said sternly.

Rory looked across the table at Ainsworth and Crenshaw. What they were talking about was flimsy circumstantial evidence. But the two detectives looked too confident. There had to be more.

Crenshaw picked up a brown folder and flipped it open, "It's very interesting how unrelated cases pop up on our desks, simply because *your* name is associated with it, Steele. Ever hear of the Guimonti Collection?"

That question surprised Rory. How did they find out about that?

Tapping the report inside the brown folder, Crenshaw said, "For some unknown reason, someone breaks into the New York City public library and steals the entire collection. A collection no one but *you* has ever shown any interest in. Then the hard drive and the memory were taken from the supercomputer and the rest of it is burned. You know anything about that?"

Rory didn't know what to say and his mind raced, trying to fit the pieces together. This had to be Lillian and her father tying up loose ends. What else had they done or said that–

"According to a Dr. Gonzalez you were very interested in the Guimonti Collection. Especially about the part on *biological warfare and the Plague*? Is that where you and your friends got your information to use in attacking New York City?"

Rory was stunned at the news. Everything was being manipulated to point right back at him. He had to admit this was beginning to look bad. Real bad. Long prison term bad. Or death row bad.

"Come on, Steele, do yourself a favor and cooperate with us. You were the last one to use the collection and the supercomputer before the break-in that night–"

"Lillian Safford was there too," Rory interjected in a quiet voice. That fact had to count for something.

"Oh right," Ainsworth said, with a slow nod of his head, "the young lady you reported *kidnapped*. The same one who said she *wasn't* kidnapped! The same one you kept hitting on? When we *first* talked to her, she told us you had an abnormal interest in the Black Plague."

That comment caught Rory off guard. He hadn't seen it coming. But what he did see was a cocky grin appear on Ainsworth's lips.

"A little fact we kept back when I talked to you. Surprise, surprise," Ainsworth said. "She said she felt afraid of you. That she was afraid to object when you insisted on her going to the library and helping you out. You told her that you needed her scientific expertise in diseases."

Rory just sat there, feeling numb. And dumb. He had been too busy looking at Lillian's legs and panties to see this coming.

"Look, Steele," Crenshaw said in a soothing voice, intended to get Rory to believe he was trying to help him. "Give us the collection and the hardware from the supercomputer, so we can undo the damage that's been done. That's all you need to do."

His head was racing with all the implications of what had happened and Rory shook his head, "No. You don't understand. I don't have it. But I would bet Lillian does—"

"You have some kind of hatred for this woman, Steele?" Ainsworth bellowed. "You can't stand being rejected by a woman? You want to screw her but she don't want anything to do with you?"

Rory couldn't believe where this was going. "Just check her place. She's the one who unleashed this plague."

"She couldn't have had anything to do with it, Steele," Ainsworth bellowed again. "She has an alibi for the entire time. She told us about it the first time we talked to her. After she was able to dump you, she went to dinner with Dr. Gonzalez. In fact, they spent the entire night together in his apartment."

Stunned, Rory could only blink dumbly.

Ainsworth smiled, "Yeah, that's right. Dr. Gonzalez confirms it. The building security saw them go up together in the evening and come down together after breakfast in the morning. She don't want to screw you but she did do the doc."

His shoulders slumped as Rory chastised himself. He had been such an idiot, allowed himself to be set up and his circumstances were going from bad to worse.

"Where were *you* after you left the library, Steele?" Crenshaw asked him. "I suppose you're going to tell us you were all alone...all night...right?"

Rory's head moved lower. He wished he could sink right through the table and through the floor and hide. Stupid, stupid, stupid.

"Your story is falling apart, isn't it Steele?" Ainsworth said with a smile. "The evidence is starting to stack up and that needle in your arm is coming closer and closer, isn't it?"

Rory just looked up at Ainsworth, wondering how he could get out of this one.

Crenshaw opened another file, "And then we get another case. We have you and your little girlfriend on tape at JFK airport, shooting up the terminal."

He had almost forgotten about the airport incident. Rory wagged a finger at Crenshaw, "No, no. You know that's not the truth. We didn't shoot up the airport. We didn't have any guns. All you saw was us defending ourselves–"

"Against who? And *what* was in that backpack that everybody was fighting over? Is that the agent that you used to infect the city?"

Rory stayed silent. He didn't dare say anything right now until he could think this whole thing through.

Crenshaw leaned over and spoke in a soft voice to Rory, "Maybe you were trying to help, right? Is that how it went down? You and your little girlfriend were part of a terrorist group that was going to attack New York City. You two had a change of heart and tried to do the right thing. You take whatever it was they were going to use and run for it. They find out and they follow you. They attack you at the airport, trying to get it back. But they don't get it. You're a hero, Steele. You're the hero here. We'll make sure the Attorney General sees it that way. All you have to do is give us the backpack."

When Rory stayed silent, Detective Ainsworth banged his fists down on the table, making it jump, "C'mon Steele! Talk to us. Where is the backpack? Where are your friends? Where is your headquarters? Give us something, jackass!"

The room went silent as the two detectives waited for Rory Mack Steele to answer.

After a few moments, Crenshaw leaned over and changed tactics. He spoke to Rory in a soft voice, "Look, Steele. We're trying to work with you. Help us out here."

"Why should we work with him!" Ainsworth yelled at Crenshaw, "the man's a scumbag." Ainsworth got up with a scowl on his face and walked over to the corner of the room.

"Work with me here, Steele," Crenshaw pleaded. "If the CDC can find out what you were using, they say they might be able to figure out how to end this. I'm sure you don't want to see more people dying. I promise you, there will be no death penalty –"

"I just say we let them fry his ass," Ainsworth barked from the corner. He had crossed his arms and looked sullen.

"Just tell us where you got the disease from," Crenshaw pleaded, "and this can be all over. Just work with me here Steele, please."

Rory didn't look up as he said calmly, "The good cop, bad cop routine is not going to work with me." While they were talking, he was trying to think of a way out of this. But he couldn't see it.

Detective Ainsworth strode back over to the desk and sat down. "You do realize, once Homeland Security gets here, they can whisk you off to some foreign country or Guantánamo Bay and bury you. No one will *ever* find you again, Steele. And once they start water boarding you, you'll wish you talked to us. But it'll be too late by that time. Take the opportunity we're giving you. Either you start working with us or we turn you over to them."

Rory shook his head softly, "I told you who was involved–"

"Okay, Steele, time for the truth." Ainsworth said. "We know everything. Your little girlfriend already gave you up. She spilled her guts earlier. She's blamed everything on *you*. We just wanted to give you a chance to cooperate with us."

Crenshaw's voice was hard, "You're going to go down, Steele! Once the jury hears the story from that sweet-faced young lady, you're going to fry. Don't let her do that to you, Steele. Get yourself out from under this before she buries you."

Rory couldn't help himself and a smile creased his lips.

"This is not a game, Steele!" Ainsworth yelled. He banged his fist down on the table again, "There is not *one* thing funny about any of this! People are suffering agonizing deaths."

"You're right," Rory replied as the smile left his face. "There is *nothing* funny about what is happening. But Nanette Bacon would never give me up or sell me out as you imply. She would rather die before she told you a lie. And knowing her, you can't even interview her. She's crying, she's broken down, she can't understand why she's here. She's one of those people who believes only bad people ever get arrested by the authorities. Her whole world is shattered and upside down because she believes that *anyone* who tells the truth would never end up in a place like this. But we all know better than that, don't we Detectives?"

Detective Ainsworth and Detective Crenshaw just looked at each other.

Chapter 25

RIKERS ISLAND, NEW York

Day 2

NANETTE BACON SAT at the interview table again across from Ainsworth and Crenshaw. She was handcuffed and her legs were shackled to a ring in the floor. She had spent the night in the infirmary under doctor's care. When the guards first brought her into the interview room, she had been crying. Now she was just rocking back and forth and staring into space. Ainsworth and Crenshaw looked up at the doctor, who was standing off to the side in the corner. He just shrugged.

Detective Ainsworth pulled his chair a little closer to the table and spoke in a low voice. "Ms. Bacon, we know Rory Mack Steele put you up to this. If you work with us, you can go home. He'll never bother you again. I can promise you that. He'll never see the light of day again."

"All you have to do is tell us what he made you take from the University lab," Crenshaw added in a gentle tone. "The CDC will know what they're working against and people will be safe again. Please help us out here. People are dying and we need answers."

Nanette Bacon just continued her staring and rocking back and forth. She was totally unresponsive to any words or movements around her.

"Ms. Bacon, we understand how difficult this has been for you," Detective Ainsworth said, "just talk to us and this will be all over in a moment." He shoved a pencil and yellow notepad towards her, "Just write down what he made you do and you'll never have to see him again. I promise you, you'll be safe."

"Stop talking to my client," a firm voice said from behind them. "This interview is over."

The two detectives turned to see one of the guards unlocking the cell door to the interview room. As the door started opening, Rory Mack Steele moved quickly into the room and around the interview table to Nan Bacon. "Take off her chains and cuffs," he said to the guard.

Detective Ainsworth stood up, barking, "What's going on here?"

A tall, round gentlemen, with curly white hair and wearing a dark pinstriped suit, walked inside the room, "As I said, detectives, this interview is over. Or don't you understand English? Oh! I'm sure you know Mr. Paiser, the Attorney General," he said as he indicated a gentleman walking in behind him.

The two detectives were speechless when they saw it *was* Neil Paiser, the Attorney General himself, who was behind the white-haired gentleman.

Paiser nodded solemnly at Detective Ainsworth once. Paiser also told the guard, "Uncuff her. She is free to go."

The guard moved around Rory and began unlocking Nan Bacon's handcuffs and leg irons. She stopped rocking back and forth and looked up at Rory.

"Are you okay?" Rory asked her gently. He put a hand on her shoulder.

Nan Bacon nodded slowly, her voice low and anguished, "They wouldn't believe me. Why wouldn't they believe me?"

"You can take her home, Mr. Steele," the tall, round gentlemen said, "I'll make sure they don't bother you again." He passed a sheaf of legal paperwork to Ainsworth, who still stood there, stunned at the turn of events.

Nan Bacon looked up. In a small voice, she said, "Dad?"

Cordell Bacon gave his daughter a small, concerned smile, "Hello, sweetheart." He put a finger to his lips and then said to the Attorney General, "Can you give us the room, please?"

The Attorney General nodded at Bacon and then stepped out of the room, followed by a silent Ainsworth and Crenshaw. But as the three disappeared down the hallway, the two detectives began an onslaught of harsh, whispered protests and questions that echoed off the walls. Carrying the chains, the guard slipped out as well, leaving the door wide open as he left.

As soon as they were all gone and out of sight, Cordell Bacon stepped up to the table. He wasn't carrying a briefcase, he was carrying something else. "You're going to need this," he said. He placed a backpack on the table in front of his daughter.

Nan looked at the backpack in astonishment. She put her hands on it and pulled it closer. She looked up at Rory, "I thought we left it in a locker at Grand Central Station?"

"We did," Rory replied. "Do you remember the bike courier I talked to? I sent the locker key and a note explaining everything down to your father. He went to the station and secured it for us."

From the corner of her eye, Nan glanced to her father.

Cordell Bacon gave her a nod of assurance, "You're safe now. They can't hold you here any longer. You can go with Mr. Steele and do what you do best."

Rory urged her to get up, "Come on, Nan. We have some work to do. We have to help those people in Harlem."

Nan Bacon stood up on shaky legs. She looked like a broken, frail doll as she stared wide-eyed at her father.

A moment later, Cordell Bacon turned and walked out of the cell, "Take care of her, Mr. Steele."

"He hates me," Nan said in a weak voice.

"No," Rory replied, "he loves you very much."

Tears filled her eyes. "But all those years, all those things I said to him...."

"About only guilty people being arrested? If he held that against you, he wouldn't be here. He went to work on our case as soon as I called him. He's the *only* reason why we're free and not stuck in some black hole in the Guantanamo Bay detention camp with other terrorists. He called in favors he had built over the years." He put a hand on her shoulder. "Go after him, Nan."

Nan hesitated. When Rory gave her a reassuring nod, she handed him the backpack and ran out the door.

Rory stepped out of the room and watched as she ran past the two police detectives and the Attorney General, who were still discussing the situation in heated animation.

Nan called to her father, who was further down the hallway. He turned.

Rushing to him, Nan was folded into her father's open arms.

Rory walked to the detectives, interrupting them, "I know it still sounds crazy, but you need to check out the Postigan family and a laboratory they have–"

"We did check it out," Crenshaw snapped. "Do you think we're stupid? They have a pharmaceutical factory, complete with a research laboratory, down near the Coney Island Wastewater Treatment Plant. They were quite willing to allow us to search it...*without a warrant*...and there's nothing there. The general manager talks to Mr. Postigan once a month and he hasn't seen him in three weeks. And he's *never* seen this woman you're so obsessed with."

That confused Rory, "But–"

"We still have squad cars, sitting front and back down there, and there's nothing happening beyond the day-to-day activities," Crenshaw continued.

Detective Ainsworth jabbed a hard finger at Rory, "We still think *you're* the guilty one, Steele. I just think your buddies out there continued on with the plan."

That comment surprised Rory. "What do you mean by that?"

The two detectives and the Attorney General just looked at each other in silence. Then the Attorney General spoke directly to Rory, "If I could prove you *are* part of some conspiracy, Mr. Steele, you would *never* see the light of day again. However - while you and Ms. Bacon were being held in custody here on Rikers Island - someone else released the Plague into Spanish Harlem. More people are dying as we speak."

Chapter 26

A LIMOUSINE WAS WAITING for Rory and Nan outside the main jail complex, courtesy of Cordell Bacon. They soon were crossing Rikers Island Bridge and headed for Grand Central Parkway. The sun was brilliant and high in the cloudless blue sky.

"My father said Professor Bonifay has agreed to help us," Nan said. She looked tired but sounded buoyant.

"And that's where we're going right," Rory confirmed. "Your father's a very persuasive man."

"I can't believe how badly I treated him over the years," Nan said as she shook her head. Her eyes misted over, "Just more of the same arrogance that got me into this trouble in the first place."

"Once this is all over, you can sit down and talk with your father. But right now we have work to do, Bacon."

Nan wiped a tear from her cheek with a finger and nodded, a smile crossing her lips at the use of her last name.

He held his cell phone out, "Why don't you call Bonifay and tell him what you're going to need when we get there."

Taking a small breath and letting it out, Nan handed Rory the backpack. She took the cell phone and punched in the numbers for the genetics laboratory. As she put the phone to her ear, she cleared her throat, clearly trying to compose herself.

As she went over her plan of attack with Bonifay, Rory wondered how many people would end up dying before they could find a solution. His mind flashed back to Lillian and how she had manipulated him. His jaw clenched as he looked out at the passing buildings. He couldn't wait to catch up to her.

Once the limousine reached the NYU Genetics Laboratory, Nan was out the door and bounding up the stairway.

Rory followed behind her, carrying the backpack. He had convinced Nan that it would be better for him to carry it than her since he could guard it better. Nan admitted it was hard for her to give up any kind of control but had reluctantly agreed. She said she was 'trying to do better'. Rory wondered how long that would last.

Bonifay was waiting for them inside the entrance. "Nanette," he said as he rushed to her. "I'm so sorry. If you could see a way to forgive me–"

"Only if you forgive me, Professor," Nan replied as she clasped his hands. "You were right to be cautious. I've spent so much time in academic settings that I forgot about the realities of how people around me can be affected by what I do. I'll forgive you if you can forgive me."

Professor Bonifay smiled at her, "Why don't we just go up to the laboratory and start helping all those poor people. I have a number of our staff and students up there, ready to help."

Nan nodded and they all headed for the elevators.

Bonifay turned as they walked and held out something to Rory, "Mr. Steele, here is a temporary identification card and your password for the keypads. You'll be able to enter and exit the entire laboratory, just like everyone else."

"Thank you," Rory said as he took the card and password in hand. He slipped the card around his neck as they entered the elevator and then looked at the password, memorizing it on the way up.

When they left the elevator, Cora-Anne Junkins and other members of the laboratory staff were waiting for Nan. They had the lab door wide open and were ready to go.

Rory followed them inside, carrying the backpack in his right hand now.

After a brief reunion of hugs and tears, the group marched down the glass hallway and into the lab area. Several students were there and Nan accepted their hugs and tears as well as she kept moving with the group to the far side of the lab where the group moved through a doorway.

Rory followed them into a long room. Dead ahead was a large stainless steel door with a large wheeled handle in the center that he assumed was some kind of airlock. He watched as one of the staff spun the handle.

"I'll take that now."

Nan hand her hands out to him and Rory gave her the backpack, The stainless steel door swung open and everyone began moving inside, Nan right behind them.

Bonifay turned to Rory, "That door leads to our BSL-4 biosafety room. It has special engineering and design features to prevent microorganisms from being disseminated into the environment. Which is important since we're going to examine the container and its contents."

Rory nodded in understanding, "Right."

"We'll pull the door closed and lock it, then get into positive-pressure personnel suits to protect us as well." Bonifay moved forward to follow the others in. He put his hands on an internal wheel and looked back at Rory, "We'll lock it from the inside as I said. But if we turn into zombies, there is a mechanism on the outside that you can lock to prevent us from escaping and taking over the world."

Rory felt his eyebrows raise, "I'll bet you guys are the life of a party."

Bonifay grinned, "We're scientists and academics, Mr. Steele. We're usually described as the *death* of a party." He gestured to Rory's left, "There is observation glass for the change room and the laboratory and you can watch everything that we do from outside."

Rory nodded, quite happy to stay on the outside while they did their thing with a dangerous disease. As the door was pulled shut and he could hear it lock, he walked over to the glass observation area and looked in.

The entire staff donned positive-pressure personnel suits, protective white suits, gloves, booties, and enclosed masks, complete with respirators, used to protect against infection. Once dressed in the protective gear, they all moved through another airlock and into the large biosafety room itself. It was filled with a wide range of fancy scientific equipment. But the first thing the group did was gather around a white table just ahead of where Rory now stood, looking in. One of them reached out and flipped a toggle switch - from speakers in the ceiling over his head, Rory could now hear everything they were saying on the other side of the glass.

Nan carefully set the backpack on the white table.

The staff inside stood silent, watching as Nan carefully pulled the thermos shell out of the backpack.

Rory could see the tension in the body language of everyone inside the room.

Nan passed the backpack over to the staff member beside her and then began to carefully unscrew the thermos shell.

One of the things that struck Rory was how carefully and purposefully Nan handled the thermos now. It was far different from the carefree attitude she had taken when they were carrying the backpack around and running for their life. Either she now understood the full implications of what they were doing, or the professionals around her made her act more professional.

Someone asked Nan a question that he couldn't hear and she nodded her head. Now she carefully pulled away the top piece of the thermos to reveal the upper half of the ancient urn. Nan set the upper piece of the thermos down and someone moved it to another table.

Rory could now see the complaint ancient urn as Nan pulled it free from the bottom half of the thermos shell.

Everyone inside the laboratory was speechless as Nan held the urn in her hands, turning it slowly and examining the pictures again.

Professor Bonifay leaned over and began to look at all the different carvings on the urn, "Amazing. The figures look like they're going through the agony we're witnessing in Central Harlem and Spanish Harlem!"

Nan nodded, "You're right. I looked at them before but didn't fully appreciate the message of the figures." Her eyes flicked to Bonifay, aware she was admitting she had done that *without* the safety protocols they were now following.

Bonifay's body language had stiffened but his face visibly showed he was trying to push past it and he gave her a nod.

A few of the others though, including Cora-Anne Junkins, were exchanging glances, their faces showing disbelief.

Nan took a small breath, letting it out as she returned to examining the figures, "An artist must have carved these figures from what he saw happening to plague victims a few thousand years ago." She shook her head softly, "It must have affected him very deeply." She looked at the staff around her, "The ancient document that led us to this urn described what it contained as...the Fire Plague."

That comment seemed to affect everyone and there was a lot of murmuring and low talk as they squeezed closer to take a look. Nan took the time to allow each staff member to step beside her and look closer.

When it was Cora-Anne's turn to stand beside Nan, she lightly passed her gloved fingers over the carvings, "Professor Bonifay said this came from China?"

"That's right," Nan said. "It was buried with one of the 6,000 terracotta figures at the Terracotta Army Museum in Xi'an, China. This is probably the original plague bacterium that later plagues derived from."

"Do you really believe there could be the *original* strain in there?" asked one of the staff.

Nan shrugged, "Let's find out." She turned and stepped across the room where she placed the urn on a work table.

"We should record the figures for others to study before we do that," Bonifay said.

Nan turned to him, nodding her head, "Yes, of course, Professor. I'm sorry. One step at a time."

"Yes, right, one step at a time," Bonifay said with a nod.

A couple of other lab personnel retrieved digital cameras and began taking pictures of the figures as Nan rotated the urn.

After a few moments, Professor Bonifay gave Nan the go-ahead to try and open the urn.

Nan picked up a sharp instrument and began to examine the lid area at the top. "It's hermetically sealed with what looks like amber," she reported to the others. She slowly began carved away the substance.

"Cora-Anne," Professor Bonifay said, "would you please examine the amber before we proceed?"

Picking up a glass plate, Cora-Anne stood next to Nan, holding it out.

Nan carefully placed each piece of the material she removed on the plate.

When all the amber was removed, Cora-Anne took it over to a piece of equipment, labeled as a Pyrolysis-Gas chromatography-Mass spectrometry, where she began to examine the material.

Everyone watched her silently as she looked at various readings.

"It *is* amber but...it doesn't fit into any present-day categories," Cora-Anne said finally. "I see n-alkyl compounds, so the closest fit would be a Class V resin. Those are produced by pine trees or close relatives of the pine. But I would say it's probably from a tree that doesn't exist anymore. For something that's been buried for centuries, the amber remains amazingly pliable."

Professor Bonifay spoke up again, "Okay, place the material in a labeled container. And let's go ahead and take the lid off."

Rory took a deep breath as he watched. This was *definitely* one time he was glad he wasn't in the middle of the action.

Chapter 27

TO RORY, the 'dead air' smell in the air-scrubbed laboratory seemed even deader as he watched them working with the deadly Fire Plague strain on the other side of the glass. With so many people already dead from the plague in the city, you couldn't help but wonder what could happen to those working with the urn.

On the other side of the glass, even with everyone encased in those positive-pressure, personnel suits, the tension was very visible in the body language. In both how they moved and how they simply stood stock still, their attention laser-focused on Nan Bacon and the ancient urn.

Nan slowly and carefully removed the lid. Then, cradling it in two hands, she carefully passed it over to one of the other staff, who received it with an awestruck look in his eyes. He slowly turned and put the lid inside a padded box.

Nan leaned over and looked inside the urn

Everyone in the room seemed to be holding their breath, waiting for her to describe what she was looking at.

"I see something...like a long stick inserted in the urn...it's about three inches around...orange and shiny," she reported.

After a brief moment, Nan beckoned with her hand without looking up, "Can we get a camera over here and take a look down inside? That will let everyone see."

Two of the team immediately reacted and swung a camera boom, holding a high definition video camera, over top of the urn. They worked carefully to lower the video camera towards the container and focus the lens.

Everyone else looked up at a large LCD screen to see the camera output. The end of a shiny, orange object inside of the urn slowly came into focus. Whispered questions, conjectures and theories filled the room.

"Okay, Nan," Bonifay said. "Why don't you bring the object *out* for us to see closer?"

Using her fingers, Nan reached into the urn, grasped the object, and slowly pulled it out.

Cora-Anne moved in for a closer look as Nan held the object steady. It was a translucent, orange material and it contained something white in the center. Cora-Anne gently moved her hand over the orange material, "It definitely is more amber, just like the material sealing the lid." Cora-Anne retrieved a scalpel and passed it over to Nan.

Nan carefully laid the long, orange object on its side on the table and began to deftly slice through the material. Everyone seemed to hold their breath as Nan freed the object from the center of the translucent, orange material. She set down the scalpel and pulled the object out very carefully. "It's a piece of bone," Nan whispered. She held it in position under the camera. As the camera zoomed in, Nan slowly rotated the bone and allowed them to take pictures from every angle. Once that was completed, Nan picked up the scalpel again. Working carefully, she took a scraping from the end of the bone.

Now taking a slide in hand, Cora-Anne held it out, allowing Nan to place the sample on the slide.

Nan set the bone and scalpel down as Cora-Anne headed over to a huge microscope that was connected to the monitors as well.

Cora-Anne set the slide in place, everyone looked up at the monitor as she brought the substance on the slide into focus.

"It's *live* bacterium," Cora-Anne said in awe as she stared down through the microscope.

Despite the protective gear, Rory could see the astonished reaction in the demeanor of the scientists on the other side of the glass. They weren't expecting that at all.

Nan's eyes were wide open and one hand covered her mouth, "It stayed alive inside the internal honeycomb of the bone. I don't know of *any* scientist living today who would've thought that was possible. But there it is."

"I hate to say this, but...that looks like human bone as well," someone said in a hushed tone.

Professor Bonifay stepped closer to look at the image on the monitor, "You're right. It's probably an early plague victim. I imagine this is how they harvested the plague. They collected a dead body, cut the person up and sealed this piece of bone inside the amber."

Nan's voice was low as she said, "The ancient document that led us to this urn, discusses the military use of disease...in warfare...."

One of the staff put a hand to her mask, her voice raspy, "They cut someone up to use them as - as a weapon?"

Everyone just stood around, the shock evident on their faces.

Bonifay looked around at his colleagues and said in a voice barely above a whisper, "I wonder if more plague samples are buried...that we don't know about?"

On the other side of the glass, Rory knew all this information was fine, that it was necessary in the long run, but there was something more important they had to get to right now, "Can you tell if modern day drugs will work against that strain?"

That question seemed to get the staff moving again, recognizing why they were actually doing this.

"Difficult to say at this point," Nan replied as she looked up at the image. "But to be honest, I've never seen anything like it. Like the CDC said, it looks like a strain we've never seen before. Which means...." Her voice trailed off, the full implications evident to everyone.

Cora-Anne moved across to a drawer, took another slide out and then placed it beside the first, "This is a sample the CDC sent up to us from one of the victims down at Harlem. We can check to see if we're dealing with the same strain."

Everyone looked up at the screen to compare the two samples.

"It...it looks a little different," Cora-Anne said.

"Oh, god," Nan whispered.

Everyone in the room looked at her.

"What is it, Nan?" Bonifay asked her.

Nan spoke in a hushed tone, "They look different, but only in one aspect. Someone crossed this strain of the plague...with a salmonella strain at the genetic level."

Rory shook his head as he looked at the monitor from the other side of the glass, "Why would someone do that?"

"It's an attempt to modify the strain to be resistant to the drugs we use today to treat the plague," Nan replied. "But they didn't have to do that, because this Fire Plague is already different from anything we've seen. That means someone was in a hurry to get it out there. They didn't study it very well beforehand–"

"Are there any other modifications?" Rory asked.

Nan turned to look at Rory through the glass, "What you mean?"

"The Postigan plan was to attack specific races," Rory explained. "No doubt, that's why they attacked Harlem because they wanted to kill African-Americans. Were there any attempts to modify the Fire Plague to do that?"

"Not that I can see. And I doubt it *can* be done. I told Lillian that, but she wouldn't listen. Her racist beliefs have colored her understanding of race. African-Americans are a higher risk group to get lung cancer. But that doesn't mean other races don't get lung cancer. European Americans are a high-risk group for coronary artery disease, but that doesn't mean blacks can't have it. And 22% of cardiovascular deaths in China are from coronary heart disease. You can't attack skin color."

"That explains why I saw white people dying in Harlem," Rory said.

"And more white people will die," Nan replied. "And more blacks...along with people with yellow or red skin. Or purple skin for that matter. They can't modify it to do what they want and they can't control it like they think they can."

"Which is why every one of us and our families are at risk," Professor Bonifay said. "So let's start working to see what we can do to *counter* this plague that is killing so many people in our city. Every minute that passes, we lose somebody else."

Rory watched as everyone went to work on solving the problem. Not have anything to do on his side of the glass, he took a deep breath and wandered away. He needed a break and time to think. A sandwich and a coffee, away from the biosafety room for now, was in order. Leaving the lab area, he stepped into the elevator and punched the button for the cafeteria on the main floor. As the elevator descended, he pulled his cell phone and called his office. He asked them to send a few things over to him in the cafeteria while he was there.

Chapter 28

IN THE CAFETERIA, Rory paid for a couple of chicken salad sandwiches and wolfed them down with a couple of cups of coffee. The buzz of conversation around him was focused on what was happening in Harlem and now Spanish Harlem, and the horrific deaths and the mounting count body count. They were obviously unaware of what was happening on one of the floors above them, and he wondered just how fast the panic would clear this place out, if they knew.

One of the office assistants arrived with his Baby Eagle 9915RL Polymer 9mm handgun, along with a shoulder holster and a light blue windbreaker to hide it. Once he had his trusty handgun under the windbreaker, he bought the largest cup of coffee he could find and headed back to the elevator. Rory took a look over at the building directory and noted there was a small laboratory dedicated to animal genetics on the second floor. He remembered Bonifay saying they no longer had animals on the premises and he decided to pay a quick visit to see what they were doing. He exited the elevator on the second floor and wandered down the hallway. A young woman was just coming out of the door marked NYU Pet Genetics Research. There was the same dead air smell coming from the other side.

Rory approached the young woman casually, "Hi, can you tell me what's in there? Professor Bonifay told me you no longer had animals here at the University."

The young woman glanced at the card around his neck, obviously wondering who he was. She shook her head, "No. We stopped doing that."

"So, how do you do your research then?"

Hesitating for a moment, the woman said, "We do have genetic samples from the various breeds of dogs and cats, but any research done here is through computer models. This lab was set up after a request from a patron whose wife was saved by a medical team on floor three. He gave us two very large gifts, one was for heart research and the other was for animal research. He was an animal lover and wanted us to do genetic research for pets like we do for humans."

That made sense. Rory remembered Bonifay telling him Nan had been doing research on crops as well. "So you don't work with live animals?"

"Actually we do, but not for live experiments," the young woman replied. "Most laboratories are moving away from that because of the ethics. But veterinarians around the city bring in seriously sick animals and we work to help them. We've been able to make a number of breakthroughs. Due to our research here, some animals have lived quite a bit longer than expected, with a good quality of life."

"I see," Rory said. He had an idea and wondered if she could...or would help. He looked at her name tag; Nysa Gagarin. "Ms. Gagarin. My name is Rory Mack Steele. I'm an investigator, working with Professor Bonifay on something very important.

This might seem like a strange request...but would you mind doing me a favor?"

SEVEN HOURS LATER, when Nan Bacon came out of the secure biosafety room and removed her safety gear for a break, Rory and Nysa Gagarin were waiting for her. Rory approached Nan and gave her a hug. "How is it going in there? Making any progress?"

"We're working hard is all I can say," Nan said, "I have some ideas on modifying present-day drugs, but it may take some time before we can replicate enough to cure everyone. *If* it does work. And that's a very big if right now."

"Well, more fires are burning in Central Harlem and Spanish Harlem," Rory told her. "Entire blocks are on fire. I'm just hoping the flames destroy the disease the Postigans released down there. In the meantime, I know you haven't had much sleep. And I know you're not going to give up. So I asked Nysa here to give us each a B12 shot to keep us going."

Nan raised her eyebrows as she looked at Gagarin, who held a couple of hypodermic needles in her hand, "I thought you worked down in Pet Genetics Research?"

"She does," Rory said, "but she can still handle a simple needle. Now let's go, Bacon." Rory was rolling up his sleeve and he let Nysa Gagarin give him an injection.

Nan shook her head but indulged Rory and rolled her sleeve up as well.

Nysa Gagarin held Nan's elbow and placed the hypodermic needle against her upper arm.

"Ow!" Nan complained as Gagarin plunged the needle into her arm. "That hurts."

"Don't be such a big baby," Rory teased her. He put his arm around her shoulder and drew her close, giving her a big hug.

"And it's a little lumpy," Nan added as she ran her hand over the injection site.

Nysa Gagarin and Rory exchanged satisfied glances.

Chapter 29

RORY AWOKE with a start. He had fallen asleep in the laboratory's lounge area in a big easy chair in front of the television. He looked up to see Nanette Bacon standing beside him holding two cups of coffee.

"You look like you could use this," Nan said as she held out one of the coffees to him.

Rory sat up a little straighter. He was very groggy. "Thanks," he said as he took the cup. "Is it morning already?"

"Actually it's noon. We decided to break to get something to eat," said Nan. She flopped down in the big easy chair beside him.

"I can't believe it's that late," Rory said as he took a sip of coffee. He looked over at Nan. There were dark circles under her eyes. "You look beat," he said.

"I missed my beauty sleep," Nan replied as she yawned, "Sorry. We worked 18 hours straight."

Rory shook his head. He looked around the room. It smelled of stale coffee and there were dozens of cups, stained with coffee, sitting on the counter next to the small sink. Old sandwich and sub wrappers were stuffed into the garbage container, not even allowing the swinging lid to close.

Nan looked up at the television. The sound was off but there was no mistaking what was happening. CNN was showing the present scene in Central Harlem from a helicopter that was circling the area. Dense smoke was rising from buildings over several blocks. And more dense smoke could be seen to the east, in Spanish Harlem.

"It doesn't look much better," Nan said in a quiet voice.

"No," Rory agreed. "When we were down there, they were trying to contain it by putting that chain fence down 7th and 8th Avenues, across East 125th and down at West 122nd. But it didn't work. By 3 AM last night, the fire plague had spread a block west, over to Manhattan Ave, and a block east to Lennox. It also spread south four more blocks, all the way down to West 118th."

Nan just shook her head in disbelief. "It looks like someone set fire in Spanish Harlem as well."

"People are scared and I don't blame them for trying to burn out the disease. The army was putting up a chain fence in Spanish Harlem last night as well," Rory said. "So far they've blocked off the area from 5th Avenue, across to 3rd Avenue, and from East 108th Street, all the way down to 99th Street. Between Spanish Harlem and Central Harlem, there are a total of 58 blocks in New York City that are contained and quarantined."

Rory could tell Nan was shaken by the events that had unfolded while she was working in the lab. He was almost afraid to ask, "Make any progress on beating this thing?"

"No," was all she said. There were tears in her eyes.

Rory stayed silent. He didn't imagine a pep talk would do any good right now.

Professor Bonifay leaned into the doorway. He had dark circles under his eyes as well and he was unshaven, "Nan, sorry to bother you. I'm told Dr. Simon Tamburri of the CDC has been trying to get reach you all morning."

Nan looked over in surprise, "Dr. Tamburri...?"

Bonifay nodded, "Yes. I talked with Tamburri late yesterday and I told him what we were doing, what you brought us."

Swallowing, Nan just looked back at the television screen. It was now showing dense smoke rising against the New York skyline.

"Do you want me to call him for you?" Bonifay asked her as he took a step into the lounge. "I can tell him–"

"No," Nan Bacon said softly. "It's up to me to talk to him. It's my failure–"

"That's not true," Bonifay said forcefully. He stepped to the side of Nan's chair. "Every member of this team, including you, has worked as hard as possible to stop this thing. It's not on any one individual's shoulders."

"Except for the fact that I'm the one that kept digging," Nan said forcefully. She was obviously mad at herself. "I'm the one responsible for allowing them to get this thing and kill all those people–"

Rory interrupted them forcefully, "Actually, I'm the one that's responsible since I solved the puzzle and gave it to Ms. Safford." He reached into his windbreaker and pulled out his Baby Eagle 9mm handgun. Setting it down on Nan Bacon's lap, with the butt towards her, he said, "So, why don't you just shoot me right now, so you two can get on with whatever you need to do."

Nan looked down at the gun in shock and then over at Rory.

Professor Bonifay's eyes were wide open for a moment. He looked at the gun and then at Rory in disbelief. Then a look of embarrassment crossed his face. He clasped his hands behind his back and said in a low voice, "Perhaps I should do it, Nan. I've actually shot a gun, so I probably won't miss."

Nan looked up at him in surprise. She saw the hint of a smile playing on his lips and she finally realized what he was trying to do. A look of embarrassment crossed her face as well. "The great Bonifay and the great Bacon perform their public flagellation," she said.

Bonifay held a finger up in the air and twirled it with a flourish. "Two members of Opus Dei."

"Can you two eggheads speak English," Rory grumbled.

"What he means is, we get your point," Nan replied. She picked up the handgun gingerly.

"Oh. Good," Rory said as he reached over and retrieved his handgun. He slipped it back into his jacket and into the shoulder holster. "I was afraid you might only wound me and leave me in agony."

Nan Bacon leaned over and hit him with a small fist on the shoulder.

Bonifay held a fist against his mouth, snickering with relief.

Nan took a deep breath, let it out and then stood up, "But I don't think a phone call is the right way. I think it's best if I go down to the Apollo Theater again. Tamburri might as well hear it from me face-to-face."

"Do you want me to go?" Bonifay offered. "You can stay here and work with the others. That would seem to be the more important use of your time."

"Thanks, but I need to do this," Nan replied. "Besides, maybe I can still learn something by seeing this thing first-hand again. We were arrested before I could study it closer the first time, to see what actually happens in the progression of the Fire Plague. There might be some clues there to help us."

Bonifay agreed with a nod of his head, "Okay, that makes sense. We can continue to study the bacterium in the laboratory until you get back."

"I'll call us a cab," Rory said as he rose from the easy chair.

"No need," Bonifay told him as he pulled out a cell phone. "When I talked with Tamburri about what we were doing, he sent a police car, in case we came up with something. It's waiting downstairs I'll call the CDC reporting center to let them know that you need to go down there to get a first-hand look at the victims. Then I'll go down to the policeman to make sure there's no delay in getting you there."

Nan began taking off her lab coat in a hurry.

Bonifay put a hand on her arm, "Just do me a favor? Before you two leave, grab a sandwich from the refrigerator. I brought them in so we could continue to work. Even if you eat it on the way down there, it will help to keep your strength up. Okay?"

He received a nod from Nan and then started speaking into the cell phone. He turned and hurried out of the room.

Chapter 30

A LARGE, BLACK PANEL VAN, with no license plates and no way to identify it, entered the back ramp of the NYU Genetics Laboratory with a bump. A second nondescript van followed closely behind it. Both drove down into the basement parking area and slowly made their way across to the bank of elevators. The basement garage was nearly empty because of the early morning hours. The driver in the lead panel van stopped just in front of the elevator doors and seven men in dark clothing and black ski masks quietly slipped out the sliding side-door of the panel van. One man stayed inside the back of the van, to operate jamming equipment.

One of the seven men spray-painted the video camera inside the elevator with black paint before they all entered. One man pressed the open button and held it down to keep the elevator doors open

The second van pulled to a stop behind the first and nine more men in ski masks slipped out through the side door. One joined the others in the elevator, seven others headed for a back stairway, while one man headed for the building's terminal equipment room.

The two vans pulled forward and parked side by side in an open spot.

The gunmen holding the doors open now pressed the seventh-floor button with a gloved finger. As the doors closed and the elevator began rising, all eight men pulled out a handgun equipped with a silencer.

BONIFAY WAS LOOKING at the cell phone as the laboratory door closed behind him. The call had cut out for some reason. He hit the redial button, turned and head for the elevator, wondering–

The cold steel of a gun was pressed against his forehead.

Bonifay was frozen in fear as he looked into the dead eyes peering at him from behind the black ski mask. The gun was pressed harder against his forehead and he was slowly pushed backward until he stood beside the keypad.

"Open the lab door," the lead gunman instructed calmly.

Despite being terrified, Bonifay shook his head no. His whisper was stained with fear, "I won't do that, no matter what you–"

The hooded gunman pressed the gun harder into his forehead.

Bonifay grimaced with pain and his body shook with fear, but he held firm. He closed his eyes, waiting for the inevitable.

A ding sounded and the elevator door opened. A young female student in a lab coat hurried out into the hallway, her head down as she headed towards the lab.

One of the other gunmen clamped a gloved hand over her mouth and dragged her over to Bonifay. He held his gun against her head. "Open it or she dies," the gunman said.

Looking into the eyes of the petrified student, Bonifay gave her a small nod of assurance that everything would be all right. He slowly turned as the gun was pulled away from his forehead but remained pointed at his head. He swiped his card and punched in the code. The laboratory door was opened by one of the gunmen and Bonifay and the young student were pushed through the open doorway.

The lead gunman led the way down the long, glass hallway passing the empty offices on the right.

Bonifay and the young student were wide eyed as they were herded down the hallway behind the man in black.

Putting a fist up over his shoulder, the lead gunman brought the rest of the gunmen to a stop. After a moment, the lead gunman walked several more feet down the hallway, looking through the glass wall into the open lab and assessing the situation.

There were dozens of staff members and students working at desks or tables throughout the large laboratory. Several people in positive-pressure personnel suits were entering the biosafety rooms on the far side. Not one person noticed the gunmen or the hostages on the other side of the glass. They continued working on their projects, oblivious of the danger.

The gunman took a few more steps down the hallway and looked over the office area on the right-hand side. People could be seen working away at computers on their desks, but again, everyone was oblivious of the danger just on the other side of the glass wall. The gunman turned around and walked back to Bonifay, "Where is Dr. Bacon and the urn?"

Bonifay's face turned white when he realized what they were looking for. He closed his eyes, gathering strength. Then he looked directly into the gunman's eyes, "S-she's not here. And I don't know what you're–"

The man raised his handgun and aimed directly between Bonifay's eyes.

Shaking uncontrollably, the professor took his eyes from the gun and gave the man a small shake of his head. He was going to remain firm–

The weapon swung away from Bonifay - a muffled shot rang out.

The young female student dropped to the ground, a bloody bullet hole in her forehead.

RORY WAS JUST CLOSING the refrigerator when he heard the muffled sound. He knew instantly what it was.

Nan was already going out the door, "What was that?" she asked as she stepped into the laboratory area–

Moved through the doorway with urgency, Rory grabbed her arm, stopping her from walking any further. He scanned the large laboratory area, looking for the source of the muffled shot.

"What's wrong?"

Rory didn't answer. He still wasn't sure. Until he looked towards the glass wall - and he saw them. Eight hooded men - Bonifay with them - on the other side of the glass. He watched as the gunmen in the lead marched down the hallway to the arched entranceway to the laboratory, his weapon casually at his side. Another gunman had Bonifay by the collar and he pushed the professor down the hallway and into the archway, where he put his gun against the Bonifay's head.

The lead gunmen spoke in a loud, authoritative voice, "Listen to me carefully. We want Dr. Bacon *and the urn* or this man dies."

Everyone in the lab - staff and students - just froze on the spot. They didn't know how to react to masked gunmen issuing death threats. Nan stood rooted to her spot as well, staring at the gunmen.

Rory knew they were in trouble. His mind began to race, looking for a way to fight back or to flee.

Not getting the response he wanted, the lead gunmen gestured to another one of his team.

One of the hooded gunmen stepped into an office and grabbed a woman hiding behind a desk. He pulled her into the hallway and made a show of placing his gun against her temple.

It was Cora-Anne Junkins.

The lead gunman called out again, "Where - is - Doctor - Bacon?"

Cora-Anne just stood there shaking, the weapon against her temple.

Nan took a step forward but Rory reached out and grabbed her arm, holding her back from doing something stupid.

After a moment of silence, the lead gunman looked at his companion and nodded.

The gunman fired.

The bullet passed through Cora-Anne's skull and drilled a spidery hole through the glass wall as her dead body fell to the floor.

Everybody in the laboratory began screaming, including Nan.

The lead gunman yelled again, "Dr. Bacon? Don't make us kill more people. We know you don't want that."

Rory began pulling Nan away but she resisted, screaming for Cora-Anne Junkins and trying to go to her body.

The lead gunman waited for a few more moments and then nodded to the gunmen holding Bonifay. Then he yelled, "This is on you, Dr. Bacon." The gunman holding the professor pushed him face first against the glass wall at the edge of the archway, raised his weapon and shot the professor in the back of the head. Bone, brain, and blood splattered the glass wall.

The screaming mass in the lab now scrambled in every direction, looking for escape or cover from the crazed killers.

Rory pulled Nan over behind one of the larger laboratory desks and pushed her down to her knees as he dropped behind the cover as well.

Nan whirled around and sat with her back against the desk, hugging her knees to her chest, shaking and looking petrified.

The lead gunman looked at the other men, "You know what she looks like. Go find her - and the urn."

Chapter 31

THE SMELL OF GUNPOWDER hung heavy on the air as the gunmen moved through the glass archway and into the laboratory. They spread out, looking for Nan. When they found someone who wasn't her, silenced shots punched the air.

Rory pulled a cell phone and dialed 911...but it didn't go through. He took a peek over to the next desk, to see other people trying the same thing, without success. That meant someone was jamming the cell phone signal. That wasn't good. He exchanged the cell phone for his Baby Eagle and peered over the top of the desk, lifting his weapon in position to fire.

Nan grabbed Rory's gun hand, "You can't shoot."

Rory looked at her in complete bewilderment, "Nan, they're going to kill us, unless we kill them first—"

"The urn and the biological materials are in a sealed container on the table between us and them," Nan said, "If you hit it..."

The news shocked Rory. He took a quick peek up over the desk again. He saw a white table about twenty feet away. And on top of the table, he saw a red container that looked like a picnic basket. She was right, he couldn't afford to shoot. Even if he managed to miss the container himself, he couldn't control the return fire from the gunmen. He slipped the Baby Eagle back into his shoulder holster. His voice was harsh as he whispered, "Why is it even there?"

"Professor Bonifay and I decided to move it downstairs, to another secure lab facility, in case someone tried to steal it," Nan explained. Then her body sagged a bit, "And now he's dead because of me....and Cora-Anne...and now more in here will die now...."

Rory's jaw clenched hard, "Why didn't you tell me?" He waved his hand, "Never mind. It's too late now." He let out a sharp, frustrated breath, shook his head and asked, "Is there another way out of here?"

But Nan didn't answer. She was too busy pounding her small fist against her knee in self-recrimination.

Rory had to shake her arm to get her to answer, "Nan. Are you listening?"

A scream. A silenced gunshot. The scream was cut off.

"Nan?"

Nan had a totally dazed look on her face as she finally looked at him, "What?"

"Is there another way out of here?"

"There...there's a fire exit...back there somewhere...." she finally answered.

Rory clenched his teeth, "Somewhere?" He looked back at the long, frosted, glass wall, with archways leading into another section of the lab. Shaking his head, he turned and looked over the desk, checking to see where the gunmen were.

Two of the hooded gunmen were getting close to them on the left. They were maybe twenty feet away, looking behind and under the desks.

A young man, hiding behind a large desk, jumped up and ran towards the back of the laboratory as they approached his position. A bullet in the back cut him down.

The gunmen back at the arched entranceway called out, "That one is on you, Dr. Bacon. And more people are going to die unless you come out."

More silenced gunshots rang out. Glass was shattered. People screamed.

Rory sat with his back against the desk and tried to figure a way out. He looked over at Nan, "Do you see any flammable liquids near us?"

Nan didn't respond again. She was crying and shaking, telling herself in an anguished voice at how stupid and guilty she was for what was happening.

Rory shifted around on the floor and held her head gently in his hands as he looked into her eyes, "Nan, you have to get a hold of yourself. We can't let them get the other urn."

Nan looked into Rory's eyes and slowly focused.

"Do you see any flammable liquids near us?" Rory repeated.

Nan wiped tears away and started looking around their position. Her head was shaking as she nodded. Her voice quivered as she spoke and pointed, "Yes. That jug is Isopropyl Alcohol. It's used in DNA extraction. The flashpoint is 11.7°C. Autoignition temperature is 399°C...."

Rory looked at a shelf, four feet behind them, and saw the jug, as Nan babbled on about the properties, "Okay, that's a lot more information than I need, but it will do." He peeked around the edge of the desk and saw the gunmen standing still.

One man was turned, looking back, while the other looked off to the left.

That gave Rory his chance and he reacted quickly. He moved on his hands and knees to the shelf, where he pulled down the jug, along with two, large, glass beakers, two stoppers and a portable Bunsen burner. He poured the Isopropyl Alcohol into the beakers and put a stopper in each. He moved everything back to the desk beside Nan. "Do you have something to start the Bunsen burner?"

"It has a built in flint igniter," Nan said. She reached down with a shaking hand and pressed a button several times until a yellow flame appeared.

"Okay, I should have paid more attention in school. Make it as hot as possible."

Nan adjusted the flame from yellow to blue to a roaring-blue flame.

Rory peeked back around the desk.

The gunmen had started moving again, and one was only ten feet away now.

Rory set the flaming burner on the floor against the back of the desk and then turned to Nan, "When I tell you, I want you to run for the back and find the exit. Stay low. I'll go and get the container with the urn and be right behind you. Okay?"

"I don't know if I can," Nan said. Her body was shaking and her hands were pulled tight against her shoulders.

"There are a lot more people who will die if you don't," Rory told her.

Nan closed her eyes and nodded.

Rory peeked back around the desk.

The gunman was six feet away now and looking to his right. He raised his arm and fired a silenced shot at someone.

Rory lobbed one of the glass beakers containing Isopropyl Alcohol over the desk.

It landed at the gunman's feet. The glass shattered and splashed on the gunman's shoes and soaked the lower parts of his pant legs. The gunman was startled and looked down, cursing.

Pushing the flaming Bunsen burner out from behind the desk, Rory sent it sliding along the floor to the gunman's feet.

The gunman looked puzzled as the sliding object with the blue flame hit his shoe and tipped over. A moment later, his shoes and pant legs burst into flames. The gunman tried to back away from the flames, swatting at them with his hand.

Rory stood up and threw the other beaker hard.

The beaker broke against the gunman's chest and his entire body burst into flames.

As the gunman began screaming, Rory looked to Nan, "Run for the fire exit while I get the urn. Stay low." As she took off, Rory pulled his gun and moved to his right, went around the desk, and ran low for the container. He grabbed it just as the other gunman reached his burning companion, now flailing madly and screaming in pain. Rory fired one shot into the second gunman's chest.

The hooded gunmen fell backward to the floor, next to his partner who continued flailing and screaming.

Rory turned on his heels and ran low, heading for the back of the lab and the exit. But before he got there he was dismayed to see Nan trying to get others out of hiding, instead of doing what she was told. He scooted across the floor to where she was. "Nan, we have to go."

"I don't want anyone else dying because of me," she yelled. She tried to pull a young female student out from underneath a desk.

Another muffled shot and a beaker on the desk exploded in a million fragments.

Rory pulled Nan hard to the floor and dropped the container.

Another muffled shot and the screaming gunman went silent.

Rory looked around the desk to see one of the gunmen with his weapon pointing down at the one in flames, now on the floor. He fired once more to end the man's agony.

More screams. More muffled shots sounded.

Slipping his Baby Eagle into the holster, Rory grabbed the container and then dragged a protesting Nan by the arm toward a back archway in the frosted glass wall.

Nan fought him, "We can't just leave them." She hit at him with her fists, trying to break away and get to her friends and students.

Rory's voice was low but hard as he dragged her towards the archway, "Do you want them to catch you? You know what happens if they do...."

Nan was torn between the thought of abandoning everyone and getting captured by the gunmen. And what it would mean if they forced her to work on the plague.

"There she is!"

A muffled gunshot sounded and a bullet tore a groove in the desk, right beside Rory's hand.

Nan screamed.

Rory dropped to his knees and looked back. The men were headed in their direction. "Nan. They know where we are. If we get out of here, they're going to follow us and leave the others alone. Right?"

Nan's frightened eyes looked up into Rory's and she struggled to nod her head in understanding.

Handing her the container, Rory said, "Go! Lead them away from here."

"What about you?"

"I'm going to slow them down first and then I'll be right behind you. Go, go, go."

Nan stumbled several times as she struggled to get to her feet, nearly losing her grip on the container. She cursed under her breath, found her footing and took off at a low run.

Rory pulled his baby Eagle handgun, aimed and fired one - two - three shots. He hit three beakers that exploded in a shower of glass, causing the men to duck for cover. He then turned and ran back through the archway, turning right. He followed the glass wall, keeping a line of desks to his right to maintain some cover. He hoped to get a bead on any one of the gunmen chasing them, to slow them down, allowing Nan to escape.

Several muffled shots rang out in a slow, deliberate manner.

Rory heard bullets penetrating the frosted glass wall in a symphony that followed his footsteps. They were aiming for him, which was good since they were leaving Nan alone. But it was also bad because he didn't want to be shot. And he was too exposed like this. Rory ducked through the next archway and ran by pieces of laboratory equipment that took direct hits from bullets meant for him. He could see an exit sign now, high on the wall and directly ahead. He saw Nan, with the backpack in her hand, come from the left and head for the exit ahead of him.

Muffled gunshots.

Bullets whizzed angrily by Rory's head.

A number of large, glass containers beside Nan explode in a shower of glass and liquids as bullets tore through them.

The liquids came together on the floor and a massive explosion ripped across the laboratory.

Rory was knocked off his feet and everything went black.

Chapter 32

RORY SAT UP WITH A START. His entire body was sore and he groaned. Flames and smoke were everywhere. Loud fire alarms filled the air. The windows on the far side of the laboratory were blown out and flames danced through the jagged opening into the air outside. A wisp of smoke cleared and he spotted Nan's foot. She was lying on the floor, between two desks that were overturned. Rolling over onto his knees to see where the gunmen were, Rory groaned with the effort. The frosted glass wall was blackened and charred and he didn't see anyone. His weapon was right there on the floor, partially covered with debris from the explosion. He pulled it free, turned and crawled towards Nan. As soon as he touched her foot, she stirred. "Are you okay?" he said. His throat hurt.

Nan slowly pulled a leg in and tried to get a hand underneath herself to get up. "Yeah...I think so," she said in a low, sore voice.

Rory looked back for the gunmen again. Flames blocked his view of the archway–

"Where's the container?"

Rory looked at Nan. Her eyes were wild as she looked around. Rory looked around, trying to locate the container holding the ancient urn.

Nan screamed and ran towards flames.

Rory had to move quickly before she was burned - he missed her and fell on his face.

"Get through. Get her." That voice was a man, somewhere behind them, on the other side of the blacked glass wall.

Scrambling to his knees, Rory looked in the direction of the voices.

Someone was trying to beat out the flames on the other side of an archway.

Between the licking flames, Rory could two men in ski masks, trying to beat a path through the flames to get on this side. A third gunman stood just behind them, weapon at his shoulder as he tried to catch a glimpse of their prey on the other side of the roaring flames.

Nan cried out in pain.

Rory turned and quickly rose to a crouch, moving across the floor. On the other side of a wall of flames, he could see Nan, bent low. He held his hands up to shield his face as he jumped through. Pain licked at the back of his hands and his neck and he landing hard on his knees on the other side.

Nan was just ahead, on her knees, reaching forward and desperately trying to grasp the container. It was on fire, in the middle of the burning liquid on the floor. Nan pulled her hand back and cried, "The urn...."

Rory crawled towards her and saw she already had burns on her hands, "Nan, don't. It's too late."

"No," Nan protested as she tried to reach into the roaring flames again. "We have to get it. As long as we have the original strain on hand, we can find a cure. We can see what modifications Lillian might make—"

A muffled shot sounded through the roaring flames and a bullet ricocheted off a piece of equipment, just past Rory.

Rory ducked. That bullet had narrowly missed his head. They had to go. They might not miss the next time.

Nan tried to reach into the flames again and pulled back in pain, crying out.

"We have to go," Rory said urgently as he tried to get her moving towards the exit again.

Nan pushed his hands away, trying to reach into the flames again.

The container was turning black and pieces of it melted away. The ancient urn itself was on fire and one end began to crumble as the flames ate their way inside. The figures in agony on the outside of the ancient urn began to disappear, one by one, in the searing flames.

"No," Nan cried. She tried to reach it again, only to be pushed back by the heat and the hungry, licking beast of the fire.

Placing his arm around her shoulders, Rory held her back and put his lips next to her ear. "It's too late. We have to go. If they capture you...."

Tears streamed down her face as Nan nodded her head.

Rory pulled her away from the burning urn and looked for a pathway through the flames to the exit.

Another muffled shot ripped through the flames and a bullet ricocheted off a piece of equipment. Someone yelled hurry.

Rory could see the partially melted exit sign through the flames and he worked his way around several pieces of lab equipment to where he could see the door. "Run for the door. Keep low," he told Nan. As soon as she took off, he turned and fired off two shots.

Actually, one shot and one empty click. He quickly patted his pockets, looking for his second clip. Finding it, he dropped the empty clip and inserted the new one. He fired off two more shots at shadows he could see through the flames across the lab. The shadows ducked and Rory ran for the exit door.

Nan was waiting for him and as he approached, she hit the emergency bar hard with both hands and pushed the door wide open, running for her life.

Rory was right behind her. He found himself in a stairwell.

Nan was already running down the stairs and he followed. They went down two flights of stairs and started down the third when Nan stopped dead in her tracks.

Rory stopped beside her and realized why. Footsteps were pounding upwards, towards them. Friend or foe? He peered over the railing and saw a man in a ski mask looking up. He barely got out of the way as a muffled shot rang out and a bullet ricocheted against the railing somewhere overhead.

Nan screamed and fell back against the wall the stairwell.

Rory realized they were trapped. If they went up the stairs, they would run into the gunmen. And they couldn't go down. Now what?

Chapter 33

RORY WISHED THE stupid alarm bells would stop ringing so he could think. Then it came to him. They had come down two flights of stairs and they had passed an exit door on the way down. He looked at Nan, gesturing, "The door we passed up there. It needs a key card and a password. Will yours work?"

Nan was leaning back against the wall, her chest heaving, her eyes wild.

Rory reached out to her and shook her arm, "Nan, did you hear me...?"

Licking her lips, Nan nodded woodenly.

"*Can* you get in?"

Her head shook with fright as she nodded, "Y-yes...that's where...we were going to put–"

Rory thrust his hand over the railing and fired a shot downward to slow the men.

The shot echoed loudly off the stairwell walls and Nan screamed

Grabbing her wrist, Rory pulled her up the stairs.

Muffled shots rang out from below. Bullets ricocheted off the steel railings.

As they reached the exit door they had passed on the way down, they heard the exit door bang open above them.

Rory thrust Nan towards the door, "Open it." He leaned over the railing and fired a shot upward.

Nan screamed, the sound fighting with the echo of the gunshot.

Turning, Rory fired downward.

Opening her mouth, Nan cringed but held the scream in. Her whole body was shaking as she hurriedly swiped her card in the keypad and punched a key code in. The small light turned red and Nan cursed. She had to swipe her card and punch in the key code a second time.

Rory shot upward again, making sure the bullet gouged into the concrete wall, sending a message to the gunmen above. Then he looked at Nan, "Take your time to get it right."

Muffled gunshots rang out. From both above and below.

Pulling back, Rory waited for a lull. But it didn't come. Instead, the gunmen orchestrated a series of shots from above and below, keeping him pinned back. And now, even with the fire alarm bells going off, they could hear footsteps echo off the stairway walls, headed downward...and upward.

Now it was Rory's turn to curse.

The light on the keypad flashed red again and Nan emitted a small cry.

Muffled shots. And the twin echoes of footsteps coming closer.

Nan succeeded on the third try and she pulled the door open.

Rory moved in behind her and closed the door as quietly as possible, but there was still an audible click that echoed in the stairwell despite the alarm bells.

"This way," Nan said as she sprinted off into semidarkness.

Rory followed her. There was just enough light to see where Nan was and where they were going. Rory could make out lockers and locked cabinets.

Rory saw a land-line telephone on a desk. "Hold on," he said to Nan.

Nan stopped running and looked back, "What's wrong?"

"Maybe we can get through to the police and get a swat team here." Rory holstered his weapon and he went over to the phone. Picking up the handset, he punching the line one button. He couldn't hear a dial tone. Sticking a finger in one ear to make sure it just wasn't just the fire alarm bells drowning out the dial tone, he tried several of the lines without success. All dead. He slammed the phone down.

A small explosion sounded behind them and echoed through the room.

Rory realized what was happening. "They've used plastic explosives to blow the door. Run."

Nan took off and Rory followed her through the semidarkness.

The exit door slammed back against the wall behind them and someone said, "Go, go, go."

Nan reached a door and began to pull it open, "We can get out this way."

Rory quickly caught up and placed a hand against the door, whispering, "Hold on, you don't know what's out there."

Her voice tight and shaky Nan pulled back, "Oh, right."

Moving Nan behind him, Rory opened the door a crack, peering out into the hallway.

Footsteps pounded closer from behind, as the gunmen moved swiftly, looking for their prey.

The way out looked clear to Rory, "Which way to an elevator?"

"To the left. It's not far," Nan said above the alarm bells.

Rory nodded. He slipped his weapon out of the shoulder holster and led Nan into the hallway. Rory heard a sound to his right and turned quickly to see a hooded gunman entering the hallway at the far end.

The gunman raised his weapon.

Rory did the same.

Two gunshots echoed, one muffled, one loud, one after the other.

But it was the gunmen who fell backward, a bullet in his chest.

"Run," Rory yelled and they both sprinted left for the elevator.

Once they reached the elevator, Nan began jabbing the down button over and over again.

Above the constantly ringing fire bells, Rory heard a noise down the hallway again. He turned to look.

Two more masked gunmen stepped into the hallway.

Out of the corner of his eye, Rory could see the elevator doors begin to open. He pushed Nan roughly through the widening crack. She stumbled and hit the back of the elevator and Rory dove in behind her.

Nan spun around and jumped for the elevator buttons, pushing the one for the main floor.

Rory got around on his knees and held his weapon out to-wards the open doors.

Several muffled gunshots rang out and bullets ricocheted off the still-open elevator doors and buried themselves in the back wall of the elevator car.

"Stay low against the wall and hit the close button," Rory said.

Nan knelt against the wall in front of the elevator keypad and reached up to the close button. She pounded it over and over.

Rory got down on his back, with his weapon aimed towards the wide open elevator doors.

The doors began closing. Slowly.

Rory heard footsteps echoing down the hallway.

Nan continued to punch away at the close button, hoping to get the doors to react faster. They seem to be taking forever to close.

Two men suddenly appeared. One of them slammed a palm against the inside of the elevator door as both of them fired into the elevator. The bullets buried themselves in the sides and back of the elevator wall as the elevator doors began opening again.

Nan screamed and threw her arms over her head.

Rory fired from the floor. He pumped two shots into the chest of the first man and then two into the other.

Both men dropped to the hallway floor.

"Nan. The doors," Rory yelled, staying in place on his back, in case more men appeared.

Nan kept one arm over her head as she reached up and start-ed to pound the close button again.

As the elevator doors began closing again, Nan punched the button for the main floor.

Once the elevator started dropping, Rory got to his feet and got Nan to her feet as well. He stood with her against the wall as the elevator slowly dropped. When the car stopped on the main floor, Rory was prepared for anything. They both held their breath as the elevator doors opened slowly.

There were no hooded gunmen waiting for them.

Rory took Nan's hand, holstered his Baby Eagle and stepped out into the lobby.

People were streaming out the front door as the fire alarm bells continued to ring.

Nan and Rory joined them. They stepped aside as a team of firefighters passed them and ran into the building.

The sidewalk was pandemonium, as more people poured from the building, joining the crowd or early evacuees, onlookers, police, and firemen. The air was already thick with the smell of the fire.

Rory pulled his cell phone and found it was working out here. He made a 911 call to alert the police as he and Nan continued moving away from the building. His head was on a swivel as he watched for more gunmen. He had no doubt they would attack, even out here in the open, to get Nan. He finished the call as they reached the edge of the road near two fire engines. Turning and looking back, he could see flames leaping from the windows on the seventh floor. Thick, black smoke hid the upper floors from his view. Small explosions of chemicals shook the air.

"I can't believe we lost it," Nan whispered. Her arms were crossed and she shook her head slowly, her body still shaking from the attack.

Rory understood how she felt, but he was far happier they had lost the container and not their lives. At least they could live to fight another day. Although that day might see them die from the Fire Plague.

Chapter 34

LILLIAN POSTIGAN STRODE down the hallway towards her father's office, her red, high-heeled shoes clicking out a steady rhythm. She wore a white lab coat over a white blouse and red skirt. She raised an eyebrow as one of the men she passed kept his eyes glued to her long, shapely legs. She resisted the temptation to scold him. For now. You never knew when you needed to use your assets, in combination with someone's weaknesses, as leverage. Opening the office door, she paused briefly to give him a few more moments to caress her legs with his eyes and then she stepped inside.

Helmer Postigan was sitting back in his plush office chair, his brow furrowed with concern. He swirled a drink in his hand, the ice clinking against the glass as he focused internally.

"You wanted to see me?"

It took a moment before Postigan looked up, nodding solemnly, "Yes. I just received word from Eberstark that he was unable to secure either Ms. Bacon or the other urn."

Lillian slipped her hands into the side pockets of the lab coat and clenched her jaw, "That man keeps failing–"

"I know," Postigan snapped. He set the drink down, the amber liquid splashing onto the desk, "I'll deal with him later. For now, I've told him to keep searching. All those dolts managed to do was set fire to the place. They could've easily destroyed the urn–"

Lillian cocked her head, "What do you mean?"

Postigan looked up at his daughter, "Apparently the gunfire between them and this Steele character caused a chemical explosion that caught fire."

"How bad is it?

"According to news reports, the entire NYU Genetics Laboratory is engulfed in flames, along with several of the upper floors."

Lillian narrowed her eyes as she thought about the news. After a moment, she said, "That's good. That's very good."

"It is? Why?"

Taking a deep breath of satisfaction, Lillian had a devious smile on her lips, "Because that makes it nearly impossible for them to counter the disease, at least in the short term. The only other laboratory equipped to handle the situation, beyond our own here, is across the continent in Los Angeles."

Postigan drummed his fingers on the desk for a moment - then nodded - a little happier with the results of his men's attack than he was a few minutes before, "You are right. That is good."

"And that should help us with Nanette Bacon as well."

Now it was her father's turn to cock his head, "How so?"

"Because of her Achilles' heel. Nanette Bacon *needs* to work on an exotic disease like this. It's her holy grail. *Before* she could always turn up her nose at working with us because she always had that precious laboratory that she could return to. *Now* she has no choice if she wants to work with this ancient disease, to live it, to breathe it. She'll be driven into our arms. Especially...if we have a few pieces of equipment destroyed at UCLA...."

Her father caught her meaning, "That is a very good idea. I'll have that taken care of." He held a finger up, " *And* I know a perfect way to put a little extra leverage into our negotiations with Ms. Bacon."

"Good," Lillian said, now fully convinced it was only a matter of time before her old friend was back working with her.

Her father narrowed his eyes, "Now...have you been able to modify the disease in any significant way to accomplish our goals? And have you been able to increase the quantity of the virus so we don't run out of our weapon?"

Lillian gave her father a smug grin, "Oh, we won't run out. All we need are a few modern, positive-pressure personnel suits and a page out of the ancient Chinese book of war - and we can send an unlimited supply of the disease into the midst of our target populations."

Her father sat forward in his chair, his eyes gleaming, "Are you sure?"

"Positive. All we need to do is get a crew of men back down to Harlem with the proper credentials...and the harvest begins."

Postigan looked at his daughter for a moment and then an evil smile slowly creased the corners of his mouth. He knew exactly what she was planning and it was ingenious. He reached for his phone, "I'll have someone take care of the lab in Los Angeles. Then I'll have the men head for Harlem and begin the harvest."

Lillian nodded, baring her white teeth, "I would also suggest renting a cargo plane and putting the proper containers onboard. Have it ready to fly at a moment's notice. Once the men are back from Harlem, I'll begin the work for a full-scale implementation of our plans."

Chapter 35

RORY AND NAN STOOD in the crowd across the street, watching the firefighters battle the blaze that threatened to engulf the entire University. SWAT teams had done what they could to clear the building and help firefighters rescue the wounded. Now they formed a loose perimeter, still trying to figure out what exactly they were dealing with.

Nan Bacon had been silent for some time now, her eyes filled with tears, as he watched her beloved laboratory go up in flames. But more importantly, she also was watching her perceived redemption at overcoming a deadly disease and the wicked plan she felt totally responsible for.

"What do you want to do now?" Rory asked her gently.

She spat the words out like they were poison, "There's nothing we can do."

"You can't just give up–"

"I'm not giving up," she said harshly, "they took it away from me. There's nothing else I can do. Except watch people die. And all because of me."

"But you said earlier if you studied the disease to see what actually happens in the progression of the Fire Plague–"

"That was when we had the original disease in our hands. Now - if Lillian *does* change something at the genetic level - there isn't any way to know. We have nothing to compare it to. She's beaten us."

People around them turned to look at her. A few members of the SWAT teams nearby also turned, looking suspiciously in her direction.

Rory knew they couldn't just give up. But how could he reach her? He thought back over all the events that happened and decided there was only one other thing that might spur her back into action. "You know, your father freed us from Rikers Island because he had faith in your ability to overcome this disease. And because he loves you."

Nan blinked as more tears filled her eyes.

"Do what you can for him," Rory added. "At least you can tell him you tried."

Nan wiped tears from her cheeks and then cleared her throat like she was trying to clear away her own doubts. She finally glanced at Rory, giving him a small nod.

Rory took a deep breath and let it out. Now all he had to do...was find some way to get them down to the Apollo theater again. He considered asking members of the police, maybe even one of the SWAT teams to help them get across town. That's when his eyes went back to an NYPD squad car, sitting just down the street, on the other side. A police officer had been standing beside the vehicle, looking up at the building through the entire episode. Rory pointed at it, "Is that the squad car the professor said would take you to the CDC reporting center?"

Nan looked at where he was pointing and shrugged, "I have no idea. I just assumed when we came down here, there would be one police car waiting for us, not the entire force."

Rory took her arm and walked her through the crowd and down the street, before crossing over and approaching the officer, "Excuse me, officer. Professor Bonifay of the University said there was a police car standing by down here on behalf of the CDC. Is that you?"

The officer became alert, "Yes sir. I was told to stay put until further orders. And you are...?"

Nan still had her credentials around her neck and she stepped forward to let him examine them, "Professor Bonifay said you would take me down to the reporting center. I'm Dr. Nanette Bacon and I'm working on the plague."

"Let me check," the officer said as he reached up to his shoulder microphone.

Nan looked back of the building, still obviously shaken with everything that had happened.

Rory didn't say anything. He just put an arm around her shoulder to comfort her. At least they were moving ahead again.

"Okay folks," the officer said, "I received the green light to take you."

Rory watched from the backseat of the squad car as flames broke through the roof of the University and reached for the sky.

Nan turned her head away, closed her eyes, and lay her head back against the seat as the cruiser drove away.

HARLEM, NEW YORK

The police car didn't take them to the Apollo Theater. They drove west up East 125th and then turned south down 5th Avenue, skirting around to the western side of Marcus Garvey Park. The streets here were filled with people and the NYPD police car had to sound its siren off and on to get people to let them pass through. People were crying or yelling and screaming for someone to help their family or their friends. It was utter chaos. They passed through a police barricade and stopped at 122nd Street, in front of the Pelham Fritz Recreation Center.

"Why are we stopping here?" Rory asked the officer.

The police officer turned, looking back over the seat, "Didn't you want to go the CDC center of operations?"

"Yes," Nan said, "but it's at the Apollo–"

"They had to move it, that's all I know," the officer said. "You'll find that Doctor Tamburri and his team inside."

Nan slipped out of the police car and met Rory on the sidewalk, "If they had to move the center of operations over here, the plague must be spreading even more than we thought–" Someone banged the lid of a dumpster shut and she jumped, putting a hand to her chest.

Rory realized her nerves were wound tight, still affected by her ordeal at the genetics laboratory. And he couldn't blame her. He found himself watching around them as he led her to the front of the recreation center.

Two police officers were on guard outside the doors. One of them stepped forward as Rory and Nan approached the door, "Hi, folks. Do you either of you have any weapons on you?"

"Yes, I have a carry permit," Rory said.

"I'm afraid you'll have to leave it here with us," the officer told him.

Rory was about to object but the officer was anticipating that.

The officer raised his hands, "I know. But we can't let *anybody* inside with a weapon. We've already had a few desperate people trying to take doctors away at gunpoint to help their families. If you can't leave your weapon with us, you can't go inside. Simple as that." The officer gazed firmly at Rory and his partner took a step to the side, as if they had already experienced the physical objections of others, and were ready for anything.

"Of course," Rory said as he held his hands where they could see them. Then he carefully pulled out his Baby Eagle handgun and handed it to the officer.

"Thank you, sir," the officer said. He placed the weapon inside a plastic bag and zipped it shut. "We're holding any weapons in the trunk of our cruiser and you can pick it up on the way out." He pointed to one of the police cruisers pulled up near the doors.

RORY AND NAN COULD hear the hectic turmoil going on inside as soon as they opened the front doors. Everything looked like organized chaos once they were inside and the humid room smelled of sweat, stale coffee, and fear.

"Dr. Bacon," someone called out. They turned to see an obviously tired Dr. Simon Tamburri approaching them, "I had been trying to get you all last night and again all morning."

"I know, Professor Bonifay told me. I'm sorry but I was working all night and through the morning," Nan replied.

"I was hoping you could tell me you've had success with the samples I sent you," Tamburri stated with a hopeful look "Were you able to find some way of battling this disease?"

Nan looked at Rory for a moment, then turned back to Tamburri. "I'm afraid I don't have any good news for you at this point Dr. Tamburri. We spent over 18 hours in the laboratory, looking at your sample and the one we retrieved from China. We haven't been able to find anything that works to stop this."

The news seemed to crush Tamburri. "I'm afraid that's the same answer I got from the CDC in Atlanta," he said. "I'm at my wits end here." He cocked his head, "Did you notice what looked like salmonella within the bacterium in our sample...?"

"Yes," Nan said. "Someone added the salmonella strain at the genetic level, in an attempt to circumvent any drugs we use for the cases of the plague we see these days."

Dr. Tamburri, nodded, his Adam's-Apple bobbing as he swallowed. "That's what we thought as well."

"The thing is, they didn't need to do it," Nan said. "This plague is resistant to everything we use today. And even if we can figure out an antidote to keep people from dying now or to act as a preventive agent, it would still take months to create enough serum to do us any good. By the time production is sufficient, millions of people will be dead."

"We feel the same way," Tamburri said, with obvious reluctance, "So far, everyone who has contracted the disease has died. At this point, we have no answers. Maybe if the CDC and your laboratory keep working on this−"

"My laboratory won't be working on it," Nan said. Tears filled her eyes.

"What? Why not?" a confused Tamburri asked. "You can't just give up—"

Rory shook his head, "She's not. Someone just murdered a number of staff members at the genetics laboratory - including Dr. Bonifay."

"What! Why would they do that? Why—?" Tamburri seemed to stagger at the news.

Rory reached out and steadied the man, "They were trying to get the rest of the plague samples as well as kidnap Dr. Bacon."

Tamburri shook his head, trying to understand everything that was happening.

Nan's voice was low and tortured, "And - we lost the original sample we had - it was destroyed, along with the entire laboratory in a fire that resulted from the gunfire."

Tamburri took off his glasses and placed his hand over his forehead and his eyes, trying to regain his composure, "B-but how can we tell if they modify it again?"

Shaking her head slowly, tears filled her eyes as she said, "We can't."

Clenching his jaw, Tamburri whispered in horror as he realized the full extent of the situation, "Which means...even if we do come up with an antidote...they could change it again...and it would take us months every single time...."

Nan silently watched the doctor go through the same pain and anguish she had felt.

After a few moments Tamburri took a deep breath and put his glasses back on, "Follow me, please. We have a small makeshift office we're using as our headquarters. There is someone I want to include in the rest of our discussion." He led Rory and Nan over to a small room and shut the door behind them. Inside the stuffy and humid room, a tall man in an army uniform stood up from one of the small desks. Rory noted there were a number of maps of New York City on the walls. The areas of infection by the plague were marked in red. Rory noted two other areas, beyond the present two plague zones he was aware of.

"This is General Slater," Tamburri said to Nan and Rory. "General Slater, this is Rory Mack Steele and this is Dr. Bacon, the top geneticist I was telling you about."

They all shook hands.

Tamburri took a deep breath and let it out harshly, "I had been *hoping* for some good news. But Dr. Bacon has the same news as the CDC. We have nothing to use to beat this thing right now. And we lost the original sample we had in a fire. Along with the entire NYU Genetics Laboratory."

"I see," the General said in a deep voice. He looked as dejected as Tamburri did.

"I wish we had better news, I'm sorry," Nan said.

Rory watched them all look at each other in awkward silence.

The General looked at Nan, "Did you lose all the bodies in the fire as well?"

Rory looked at Nan. That was a strange question about the staff back at the University and she looked as confused as he was.

Nan rubbed her forehead as tears filled her eyes, obviously not sure how to reply.

"What do the bodies of the staff members have to do with any of this?" Rory asked in a low voice. He was hoping the General would understand the callousness of the situation, considering he was talking about Nan's friends.

The general just gave a slight shake of his head, "I wasn't talking about the staff. I was talking about the victims."

Nan and Rory exchanged glances again, still not sure what the general was talking about.

"What...victims?" asked Rory.

The general look at Rory, at Nan and then back to Rory, "The victims from Harlem. The ones your staff took to examine."

Nan and Rory exchanged confused glances again.

Dr. Tamburri spoke this time, "Yes. Staff members from the University showed up and transported at least twelve of the plague victims back to the NYU genetics laboratory. They said you were going to do autopsies and–"

Nan brought a shaky hand to her forehead and then her legs gave way.

Rory caught her before she collapsed to the floor.

The general took a bottle of water and offered it to Rory for Nan to drink.

But Nan pushed it away, her hands shaking.

"Is it the plague?" General Slater asked anxiously as he looked to Tamburri.

But Tamburri wasn't sure what it was. He placed a hand on Nan's elbow.

"No bodies ever showed up at the laboratory while I was there," Rory told him.

"No. Because we never sent for them," Nan whispered in horror.

Tamburri frowned, "But...?"

"It had to be Lillian," Nan said in a strained voice.

Shaking his head softly Tamburri, said, "Is this the woman you mentioned at the Apollo? Why would anyone...?"

"The ancient urn we brought back from China, contained a piece of bone, cut from a plague victim thousands of years in the past," Nan said in a low voice. "That means Lillian is going to..." Her voice faded away in anguish and fear.

Rory understood what she was talking about now. He looked at the Doctor and then the General, "That means they're going to harvest more of the Fire Plague...like the ancient Chinese did...cutting up the bones of the victims and leaving them wherever they want to spread the disease."

Chapter 36

GENERAL SLATER STOOD looking down at his desk. He tapped the pencil in his hand a few times on the top of the desk, "I could send a squad of soldiers to recover those bodies...hell...I'd send a whole division...*if* we knew where they were."

Rory understood how he felt. Everything was going from bad to worse. From death in one city to many deaths across the world in a very short amount of time.

"I'll have the police look through any video feeds that are available for the area," Tamburri said. "Maybe we can see them loading the bodies. Once we know which vehicle to look for, we can search video feeds on the surrounding streets, to tell us where they went."

The General shook his head slowly in frustration, "*That* is going to take some time. And right now...we have to figure out how we solve the problem we have at hand." He looked at his watch, "In fact, I'm due to talk to the President about the situation. But I'm not sure *what* to tell the President." He looked up at everyone, "Is there anything we can do, beyond the stopgap measures we've applied so far?"

Rory watched Nan and Tamburri look at each other. Neither looked like they had anything to say. They were obviously out of ideas at this point. Rory had thought long and hard about the situation himself and he had come up with a possible solution.

The General looked at his watch and then tapped it with a finger, "Times up, folks. What do we tell the President? Anyone?"

Nan and Tamburri both looked extremely uncomfortable.

Rory decided it was time to figure out of his solution really *was* a solution. "I noticed when I was watching the news feeds that you've created a buffer zone around the plague areas. Is that correct?"

"Yes," Dr. Tamburri replied as he stepped over to one of the maps. He traced the red areas with his finger. "We evacuated everyone at least a block away all around the infected zones in both Central Harlem and in Spanish Harlem. Unfortunately, we've also had to do the same thing around Harlem Hospital Center. That's where the first victims were taken. The paramedics and medical teams that took care of them have all died as well. The same thing happened at Mount Sinai. Overall, we have thousands of dead and thousands more infected. The buffer zone you talk about has so far allowed us to contain the disease within those blocks. But eventually, we're afraid that rats or maybe birds will spread the disease outside our buffer zone. It may even get airborne. Once it does, all bets are off."

"We put up the wire fences to not only contain the disease but the people as well," the General added. "And it also serves to keep people *out* of the infected zones. People are desperately trying to get inside the quarantined zones, to help their families or to take them out. As you can understand, we can't let that happen. If they did, there's no telling how far this thing would spread."

Rory looked at Nan for a moment. "Gentlemen, could you give us a moment? I'd like to talk to Dr. Bacon for a minute outside."

Nan's eyebrows were knitted together in worry and confusion as Rory led her outside the office and closed the door behind them.

Rory took a deep breath to gather himself as he looked at the organized chaos going on inside the recreation center.

"What's wrong?" Nan asked him.

Chewing on his lower lip, Rory wondered how he should approach this. He cleared his throat and looked at Nan, "Do you remember what that puzzle you found said? About what you should do *after* you use the Fire Plague to kill your enemy?"

Nan looked at him, he eyebrows pushing together, not sure where he was going with this.

"It said - burn everything after to occupy your enemies land."

Nan nodded in agreement, "Yes but–" She placed her hands over her mouth when she realized the only solution Rory was referring to. She shook her head no.

Rory just continued to look at her in silence, emphasizing they had little choice.

Nan crossed her arms and turned away from him. Now it was her turn watch all the chaos in the room, thinking about what it meant, about the death and the desperation everyone was feeling...and experiencing. After a few moments, her shoulders slumped. She turned around again but didn't look up at Rory. Her chin trembled slightly.

Rory knew exactly how she felt. "Unless you have a better idea right now, I don't think we have much choice," he said.

After a few more agonizing moments, Nan nodded her head in agreement.

Rory opened the door and they walked back inside the office, closing the door behind them. Rory took another deep breath to prepare himself. "Dr. Tamburri, General Slater, I'm afraid there is only one solution left. There is only one answer that you can give to the President. You need to burn *everything* from the buffer zone inward to the center of each infected zone."

Tamburri's head pulled back in shock, "Are you crazy? We just can't go in and burn everything down. No one is going to allow that."

Rory and Nan looked at each other.

It was Nan who spoke up, her voice filled with agony, but firm, "Dr. Tamburri...what Mr. Steele says is true. It's the *only* way we have to stop this thing in its tracks."

"Are you *both* crazy!" Dr. Tamburri shouted. "We can't do that. There has to be another way. There *has* to be."

"There is no other way unless we wait months and let millions die," Nan stated with conviction. "I wish there was another way. But I can tell you that the people who started this outbreak, the people who released this plague, found it through an old treatise on biological warfare from thousands of years ago. The only way they could destroy it back then was by fire. We may be in a highly advanced society, but we need to revert to the past. At this point, we have no other choice. Both of us know the time-line on something like this. Even if I had a drug this minute, that could cure and prevent this thing 100%, both of us know the truth. By the time we ramped up production and produced enough of the drug, we could have another European Black Plague scenario where we lose 60% of New York City. Maybe we even lose 60%

or more of *North America* before we can stop it! In the Chinese provinces, where this thing they called the Fire Plague came from, there are reports that showed they lost up to 90% of the population."

"Good Lord," the General said in a quiet, shocked voice.

"And the people who started this whole thing, now have bodies filled with the plague, that they can use to spread this thing beyond New York, beyond the U.S. borders," Rory stated. "We need to find out *now* if this is going to work. Otherwise...."

There was a long silence in the room before anyone spoke. "I can't believe this is happening," Dr. Tamburri said. He rubbed his hand over his head several times. The future of the entire worlds was hanging in the balance, on their decision...or indecision.

General Slater clenched his jaw and the cords in his neck stood out, "How in the world do I tell the President he has to burn one of his own cities...on purpose...?"

"I would also suggest you even take an extra block outside your original buffer zone," Rory added. "If rats have already started to spread it, or if it has started to get airborne, then it may already be outside your buffer zone."

General Slater squeezed his eyes shut for the moment, realizing Rory was right.

Dr. Tamburri leaned against the General's desk and then pounded the side of his fist on top of the desk, making everything jump, "I can't believe we have to burn Central Harlem and Spanish Harlem. I just can't imagine doing that. And Harlem Hospital Center and Mount Sinai? There has to be some other way. There just has to be." He whirled away from the desk, his hands clenched into fists.

Rory stayed silent as he watched the two men come to grips with the horror of what they were dealing with. But Rory knew there was one other thing he had to bring up. Especially in light of what Lillian had done. He glanced at Nan and then asked, "Dr. Tamburri, where are all the dead bodies?"

Tamburri had a puzzled look on his face as he considered Rory's question. "Some are still in their homes. We haven't had time to move them. Others are in our quarantine tents. Some are in quarantine at the hospitals, where they were first taken when this thing broke out. Why are you asking?"

"You need to make sure *every single body* is inside your buffer zone as well. You have to bring them all back inside, you have to - cremate - all the dead bodies as well. *Everything* needs to be burned."

"No!" a stunned Dr. Tamburri said. "Families would never allow that. I'm not even sure we could enforce that." He looked to General Slater.

"I'm not even sure if the President himself could order that among the civilian population," General Slater admitted.

"He has to figure out a way to make it happen," Rory said. "Dr. Tamburri, do you know the point of origin for the plague?"

Tamburri rubbed his jawline, "I believe the original site was in Harlem. And specifically, the first infected victims of this plague strain were in The Harlem Flophouse."

Rory shook his head, "That figures."

"What do you mean?"

"If I remember correctly, that's a beautiful, old brownstone that was turned into a hotel. The racist people who unleashed this disease in Harlem, probably thought it was a real flophouse, frequented by blacks." He looked at General Slater, "You can tell the President that's the kind of people we're dealing with."

Slater grimaced, "Still...."

Tamburri spoke in a quiet, disbelieving voice. "The point of origin for Spanish Harlem was in the El Museo Del Barrio. It's a museum devoted to Caribbean and Latin American art and culture."

"More racial profiling by madmen," Rory added. "What do we wait for next? Manhattan Chinatown? Little Manila? It could be even Little Italy for all we know. These people are nut jobs. In their racial hatred, they'll stop at nothing. They even kidnapped Dr. Bacon, to try to get her to modify the disease to take out specific races. We're all fortunate she got away. And not long ago, they shot up the NYU Genetics Laboratory, killing many of the staff members and students, trying to get their hands on more of the plague samples—"

"But we've had other racist events resulting in deaths in North America before," Tamburri said. "To burn down large parts of a major city—"

"But here's my bigger point," Rory said. "Up to now, these people had a *limited* supply of the Fire Plague. That meant they had a limited supply of biological agent to infect their targets. But now...they have at least twelve bodies they can harvest. If they hear news reports on the locations where they can find other bodies to steal and harvest...."

"Maybe we can ask the families to cremate their loved ones right away," Tamburri suggested.

"Do you think we really have time for that, to track down the next of kin for each plague victim?"

Tamburri shook his head in frustration, "I don't know...."

"These people are fanatics," Rory stated. "They've already shown a willingness to do whatever it takes to win. The question for us is: are we?"

"I agree with you, Mr. Steele," General Slater said with conviction. "We have to do everything in our power to counter whatever it is they do, no matter how distasteful the actions are. I'm going to send soldiers up to the hospitals to protect the bodies to start with. And then...I'll have to convince the President to declare martial law to start with."

"I guess I have to agree with what you're saying," Dr. Tamburri said finally. "But it's hard to imagine having to burn a city down to save it. And to have a mass cremation, that's almost unthinkable. I'm not even sure how easily we could do it—"

"Military flamethrowers," General Slater said as he reached for the phone on the desk. He picked it up and barked an order, "Get me the President!"

Chapter 37

AFTER A LONG, AGONIZING HOUR, Rory and Nan walked out the front door of the Pelham Fritz Recreation Center. Both were a little dazed at how events had unfolded over the last few days. They walked down to the curb and stood side by side, looking straight up West 122 Street. Thick, dense smoke could be seen rising several blocks away and they could smell it in the dense humid air, even from this distance. And they now knew there was going to be a lot more smoke and a lot more fire before too long.

Nan shook her head, "I can't believe we just talked to the President of the United States."

"I can't believe we just convinced him to burn down parts of New York City."

"That, too," Nan said.

Rory stood there for a moment and then realized they hadn't passed the police officers when they came out of the building, the ones who had been guarding the front doors earlier. He turned and looked again. They were definitely gone. And the only police car in sight was just down the block to their left. *Maybe they have my handgun in their trunk?*

Just then a police officer came out of a building, opposite the police vehicle. He had a hand up near his shoulder, obviously talking into his shoulder microphone. A moment later, he jogged across the street, heading for the vehicle.

"Wait here," Rory said to Nan and set off at a jog down the street, calling out to the officer.

The officer stopped beside the patrol car, turning to look at Rory warily, his hand automatically going to the holstered weapon at his hip.

Rory halted on the sidewalk, ten feet away from the officer and held his hands out where he could see them, "All I want is my handgun back. The officers at the door of the Center took it and said they would put it in the trunk—"

"Sorry buddy, but everybody's been pulled out of here to go over to Harlem. You can probably pick your gun up at the nearest precinct later," the officer said. With that said the officer pulled the door open and got into the patrol car.

Rory watched him pull away. He turned, walking back to Nan—

But Nan wasn't there.

Jogging back now, Rory scanned the front of the recreation center. Nothing. When he reached the spot where he had left her, Rory turned in circles, wondering where she had gone. Something caught his eye to the right of the recreation center.

Two men were carrying something up near a baseball diamond, heading for the trees of Marcus Garvey Park....something that was struggling. When the figure kicked out, Rory realized it was Nan! He took off at a run, leaping over the small iron railing in one bound. He ran along the fence of the baseball diamond, chasing the men as they moved uphill into the trees.

Nan was struggling hard and that was slowing them down.

Rory's running footsteps caught the ear of the men.

The one carrying Nan's legs looked back. He said something to the other man and dropped Nan's legs. He reached into his jacket, pulling a gun.

Holding firmly onto Nan, the other man continued to drag her into the trees.

Rory tackled the man before he could level the weapon. The gun flew in the air as Rory and the man landed hard on the grass and rocks.

The man flipped Rory to the side, rolled and picked up a rock. He jumped to his feet and attacked.

Rory spun around to his knees and shot a straight hand with stiffened fingers upwards into the man's throat.

The man dropped the rock and clutched at his throat, trying to breathe as he fell to his knees.

Rory was up and running after the man carrying Nan.

She was dragging her feet now and that allowed Rory to make up ground.

As the second man reached the crest of the hill he stopped.

Nan slapped at him, trying to free herself.

The man grabbed a handful of her blouse with his left hand and smashed her across the face with his right.

Nan dropped to the ground.

The man turned on Rory, pulling a handgun.

Rory was still twenty feet away from the man as he leveled the weapon, dead center now on his chest.

The man grinned and cocked the hammer.

Rory waited to feel the bullet enter his heart as he continued running forward.

A broken tree limb smashed down savagely on the man's arm. The handgun discharged with a loud clap.

The bullet entered the ground at Rory's feet.

Nan Bacon screamed and chopped the tree limb down on the man's shoulder. He fell to the ground and Nan continued to attack, hacking away as he lifted his hands to deflect the savage blows. It was futile.

By the time Rory reached Nan, she had clubbed the man another five times and he now lay in a bloody heap. Rory grabbed the tree limb with his left and put his right arm around her, "It's okay, it's okay. I think he got the point. Don't kidnap Nan Bacon. It's over."

But Nan said fearfully clutched at Rory's sleeve, "No it's not. It's not over."

Rory opened his mouth to calm her down—

"I heard them talking about my father," she said frantically. "We *need* to get to him. I'm afraid they'll hurt him to force me to work for Postigan."

Rory dropped the bloody tree limb, "We need to find a taxi or a bus—"

"Or steal a car," Nan said frantically.

"Okay, that'll work too," Rory agreed. "The closest street is that way." He grabbed Nan's hand and they ran together over the hill and through the trees. They hit the sidewalk at a run, looking up and down the street for some kind of transportation.

Rory took note of a police car, sitting in the middle of the street with its lights flashing. There was no one inside. The officer was on the sidewalk on the other side of the street, talking to a group of people. Grabbing Nan's sleeve, Rory pulled her into the street to the cruiser. With one eye on the officer, Rory looked in the driver's side. The keys were still in it. "Go and get in the other side. Hurry.

Nan hesitated for a minute, looking at Rory like he was crazy.

"Hey, it was your suggestion to steal a car."

"But a police car?" Nan threw her hands up and ran around the vehicle for the passenger side.

Rory jumped in and started the cruiser.

Nan was barely in when Rory floored the gas. The passenger side door was thrown shut with a bang and the tires squealed loudly as they shot down the street.

In the rear-view mirror, Rory could see the officer running after them, trying to keep up as he weaved in and out of traffic. "I have an idea Ainsworth and Crenshaw are going to have a field day with this stunt."

"If we don't get shot by 50 cops chasing his first," Nan said. Her hands were shaking as she struggled to get her seatbelt on.

Rory got the siren working and they flashed through the streets. He barely slowed at intersections and even took to the sidewalks a few times to get around other vehicles.

Chapter 38

UPPER WEST SIDE, MANHATTAN, New York

IT WAS A HAIR-RAISING RIDE but Rory finally jammed the brakes on and the stolen police cruiser screeched to a sliding stop in front of Cordell Bacon's old brownstone building. Above the six steps, the front door leading to his office was wide open.

Nan was struggling to get out of the cruiser before it even came to rest, forgetting she still had the seatbelt on. She finally unbuckled herself and jumped out, running around the front of the cruiser.

Rory left the driver's side door wide open and ran for the stairs. Reaching for his weapon, he cursed. The police still had it. He took the steps to the front door two at a time.

Nan was just running up the steps as Rory ran through the doorway.

As soon as he ran inside, Rory knew something was wrong. He could see the back of a woman's head and her shoulders, lying on the floor, behind the desk. Rory ran around the other side and saw it was the elderly lady who had greeted him the first time he was here to see Bacon. There was a bullet hole in her forehead.

Nan rushed in behind him and screamed, "Grandma Denelle!"

Rory knelt down to check the woman's pulse, but he knew there was nothing they could do.

Nan knelt beside the body as well, hands to her face and sobbing.

Looking around, Rory saw the door leading to Cordell Bacon's office was wide open.

Nan saw it as well and she went rushing through it, calling for her father, before Rory could stop her.

Rory followed behind her quickly, ready for a fight as soon as he stepped through the doorway. The room was a mess. It was obvious a struggle had occurred in here. The door on the right, leading up to Cordell Bacon's living area, was also wide open.

Nan saw it as well and got to her feet, heading for it.

Rory caught her arm and stopped her, "Hold on–"

"Something has happened to my father!" Nan yelled. She ripped her arm away from Rory and started for the door again.

Rory grabbed her again, "It could be a trap–"

"Let me go!" Nan struggled to free herself and she banged her fist against his arm,

Rory ignored her pounding as he looked through the door, "Nan, calm down." He didn't see anyone in the office.

"But my father–"

"I don't see him–"

"Maybe he's hurt upstairs," she said frantically.

Rory remembered Bacon coming from a door to the right. He stuck his head further in. That door was wide open as well. "Okay," he said. "Let me take a quick look upstairs while you wait here. We can't let them capture you again. Right?"

Nan stopped pounding against his arm, "Okay...okay...you're right. But hurry. Don't let them hurt him." Her eyes were filled with frantic fear.

Rory nodded as he released her and stepped through the doorway and across the room. There was a short hallway on the other side of the doorway and then a flight of stairs. He reached for his handgun and silently cursed again. *Stupid. Stupid. Stupid.* He pushed the door right back against the wall, to make sure no one was behind it. Then he quickly moved down the short hallway and stood at the bottom of the stairs, listening. He placed a foot on the first step and it squeaked. He went up the next step and then the next. He moved slowly and cautiously up to the top of the stairs.

A loud, piercing scream sounded from the office downstairs.

It was Nan!

Rory ran back down the stairs quickly. He ran down the short hallway and burst into Cordell Bacon's office.

Nan wasn't there.

The door leading out to the reception area was closed.

Rory ran for it. But the door wouldn't open.

Another loud, frantic scream sounded on the other side of the door.

Rory ran for the window, looking out onto the street in front of the building.

Nan Bacon was being thrown into the same black van they had used for the fake kidnapping of Lillian Safford.

He tried to open the window but it was one piece of glass, with only two small slides that opened for air at the bottom. Rory cursed.

The van doors were being slammed shut out in the street.

Rory ran back to the locked door and began kicking at it.

A loud explosion erupted out in the street.

The building shook, nearly knocking Rory off his feet.

Tires screeched loudly out in the street as a vehicle pulled away from the brownstone building.

Rory kicked at the door harder and harder, but it was useless. He looked frantically around the room and then ran around behind Bacon's desk, where he picked up the large office chair. Taking a run at the front window, Rory heaved the chair with all his strength. It struck the window hard, shattering the glass. Rory kicked out the pieces still stuck in the frame and then he climbed out, jumped to the ground and ran into the street

The black van was rapidly disappearing down the street.

Rory turned to the police cruiser - it was a gutted, burning wreck. He could smell tar and gasoline, which meant the men had used C4 and gas to destroy the cruiser. But all that was just useless information and he cursed. The more important piece of information was that he had lost Nan Bacon. And probably her father as well. No doubt they were going to use Cordell Bacon to convince his daughter to work for them. If she refused to modify the disease, her father would be tortured. If it still didn't work, he would be killed. And then Nan herself. There would be no reason to keep either one alive if Nan didn't cooperate.

And all for nothing really...because Lillian and her father could still go ahead with their plans, causing untold numbers to die horrible deaths from the original, unmodified Fire Plague. And he couldn't do a damn thing about it.

Chapter 39

RORY TURNED IN A TIGHT CIRCLE beside the burning police cruiser, anxiously looking for some way to pursue the black van. There were no taxis or any other car he could stop. All he saw up ahead was a long line of parked cars on both sides of the street. This was no time for niceties. He ran for the first one and yanked on the door handle. It was locked. He went to the next one and the next....all locked. Same with the next one and he banged his fist on the roof of the car in frustration. He crossed the street to try his luck on the other side. He was surprised when he pulled open the passenger door on the first car...he put a knee on the passenger seat and looked inside...no keys. This was getting serious. He slammed the door shut hard and contemplated calling the police. But the dead body inside Bacon's office would probably mean time at the police station. He had to keep trying, but every minute that went by meant it would be harder to catch up with the black van.

Rory ran up the street and crossed over to the next line of cars. One car stood out and he ran for it. A 1967 Shelby Mustang GT500, the number one classic muscle car of all time. He pulled open the driver's side door and cursed. No keys. But just as he was about to close the door, he noticed the end of a keychain hanging from the visor. He reached out and flipped the visor down...a set of keys dropped to the seat. Rory grabbed them and quickly got in. He sorted through the keys, looking for the key to start the car—

"Hey!"

Rory's head snapped to the right. He hadn't noticed the white guy standing on the steps of a brownstone. But there he was. A *big* white guy with a goatee and muscles...lots and lots of muscles. That figured...a muscle car owner with lots of muscle.

Rory returned to sorting through the keys. He glanced over again.

"Step out of the car, bro," Mr. Muscles growled. He was already down the steps.

Turned his attention back to the keys, Rory found the right one.

Mr. Muscles was near the passenger door.

Rory inserted the key and the engine roared to life.

"You deaf?" Mr. Muscles growled as he reached for the handle on the passenger side.

Rory reached across and hit the lock button.

When he heard the sound, Mr. Muscle's banged his fist down on the roof, "Hey."

Rory cranked hard left and stomped down on the accelerator. The 428-cubic-inch, Police Interceptor engine howled with power and the muscle car squealed out into the street. He kept the pedal down and black smoke erupted from the racing tires as the car accelerated away. Rory looked into the rearview mirror.

Mr. Muscles was running up the street after him. The last thing Rory saw of Mr. Muscles was him standing in the street, gesturing wildly as he talked into a cell phone.

Rory realized this was an either/or situation.

Either he found Nan and her father...or he got shot to death for driving a stolen car under martial law.

Rory took out his cell phone and hit speed dial. His only hope right now was the long-shot plan he had cooked up back at the NYU Pet Genetics Research laboratory yesterday. Was it yesterday? Time was blurring with all that was happening and he wasn't sure. It was a long agonizing wait as he drove...no answer. C'mom, c'mon, answer, answer–

"Hello."

"Nysa?"

"Yes?"

"It's Rory Mack Steele. They took Nan Bacon again. And this time they have her father."

"Oh, no!"

Rory could tell Nysa Gagarin had put her hand over her mouth in shock. He hoped she wasn't the freaky type. He was going to need someone cool to work with. "Can you get that experimental animal pet tracker working? The one you put under Nan's skin along with that vitamin B12 shot?"

"Uh...uh...."

He could tell she was panicking. "Nysa, I need you to get the tracking program going. The men who took Nan left in a black van and I have no idea where they're going. You're my only hope."

"But...I'm...outside the university...everything is on fire...."

Rory squeezed his eyes shut and a sudden coldness shot through his body. He had forgotten about the fire. The computer to use the GPS tracking software, to find and track the signal from the pet tracker put under Nan's skin, would be burned to a crisp by now. Another failure–

A horn blared loudly.

Rory's eyes shot open and he realized he was driving on the wrong side of the road.

A transport truck was right there. It loomed large and filled the entire view through the windshield of the stolen car.

Rory yanked the steering wheel hard right.

The stolen car protested and shuddered as it slid sideways. The tires squealed in fear.

The transport truck clipped the back end of the stolen car and the metal bumper under the plastic surface was torn away and bounced off several vehicles as it spun down the road.

Rory fought hard to get the car under control as the world around him whirled in a nauseating, blurry spin.

Horns blared and tires squealed.

The back end of the stolen car hit something else.

The spinning view through the windshield exploded in the other direction.

Rory's head was bashed against the driver's side window.

Blackness descended.

Chapter 40

"RORY? RORY?"

He could hear it in the distance. His brain was foggy and he frowned, trying to remember where he was. He rolled his neck, trying to get the kinks out–

"Rory? Are you there?"

It all flooded back to him and Rory's body shot to attention and he immediately groaned in agony. His whole body felt like he had been rolling around in a cement mixer. He realized he was in the middle of a traffic accident...one that had been caused by him. His stolen car was turned sideways in the street, surrounded by several other cars with cracked windshields, dented fenders, crunched side panels and steam rising from popped hoods.

"Rory? Answer me."

His cell phone...where was it? He looked around for the sound...his cell phone was on the floor on the passenger side. Crap, the face was cracked. As he bent over the passenger seat to retrieve it, he had fears she wouldn't be able to hear him. Everything else had gone wrong, why wouldn't this? He groaned as he sat back in his seat and put the phone to his ear, hoping for the best, "C-can you hear me?"

"Yes. Yes. Thank god. I could hear–"

"I know, I'm fine. A little worse for wear but −" His senses went on high alert as he heard Nysa Gagarin breathing hard on the other end of the call, like she was being chased. "Nysa, are you okay?"

"Yeah. Well...as okay as I can be...under the circumstances...."

He had visions of the gunmen chasing her. But how would they know? "Nysa, is someone chasing you? Hang up and call 911 right now−"

"No, no. Nothing like that."

"But it sounds like you're running..."

"I am. I'm heading for my car in the back parking lot. If I can get through, I have a laptop...I should be able to use it to access the tracking software. The University has everything on a cloud server, you know what I mean?"

"Yeah, yeah, that's great." Rory felt a temporary surge of relief. Until he looked into his rearview mirror.

An NYPD police cruiser, with lights flashing, was just coming to a stop between two other wrecked cars just behind him.

"What's wrong?"

Rory realized he had sucked in his breath when he had spotted the police car. "Nothing. Just a sore muscle," he answered quietly. "How much longer to your car?" Rory set the cell phone on speaker and slowly set it down on the passenger seat. He didn't want to make any fast movements to alert the officer.

"I'm not sure...there are fire trucks back here too...I'm going to have to run farther down...."

Rory watched in his rear viewmirror, while he reached slowly for the ignition key. He had to keep calm despite his rising anxiety. He couldn't afford to get arrested now. But would the car start?

The NYPD officer was talking into his radio mic.

Nysa Gagarin cursed under her breath, "I'm going to have to go back...."

A moment later, the police officer opened his door and stepped out. His hand went to his holster as he closed the driver side door. Then he took two cautious steps and leaned a little to see into the driver side of the Shelby Mustang. The officer wasn't just stopping for the traffic accident. He was stopping for the *stolen car* in the accident.

Rory turned the ignition key and the engine roared to life again.

"Shut it down!" yelled the officer as his weapon started to come out.

Rory floored the accelerator and his tires squealed. His car hit the front edge of the vehicle in front, pushing it aside. His tires skidded sideways to the left as he kept the accelerator to the floor, trying to gain traction on the pavement. And that's what saved him.

Crack. Crack.

Two bullets punched spidery holes through the back window and the front windshield, not far from the right side of Rory's head.

Smoke billowed from the tires and the Shelby Mustang rocketed down the street. Kind of. It had a heavy shimmy and vibrated left and right as he gained speed. Rory glanced in the rearview mirror.

The officer was getting back into his cruiser, his weapon still at his side.

"What's that noise? What's happening?" Nysa Gagarin asked him.

"Just a distraction. Are you there yet?"

The police cruiser slipped through the accident scene and rocketed away after Rory.

"I'm just at my car...."

Rory could hear the chirp as Nysa was unlocking her vehicle. His own vehicle was shaking heavily but he kept the gas pedal down, looking for a way out of this police chase while waiting for a direction to start chasing after Nan.

"C'mon...c'mon...."

Rory heard Nysa cursing under her breath again. Now what. Why couldn't it get easier?

The cruiser was slowly getting closer, lights flashing in hot pursuit.

The shake and bake of the Shelby Mustang's body was just enough to keep the 355 horsepower engine from pushing the car at peak speed. Rory knew it wouldn't be much longer before he was caught from behind. Or when other NYPD cruisers joined the chase and cut him off. Or shot him dead at the wheel. So many choices–

"I've got it!"

Rory sat up straighter. "What?" No answer. The silence seemed louder than the growl of the Shelby Mustang's engine. "Nysa?"

"It's working. There they are! They're driving southbound on FDR Drive," Nysa told him.

"Good, good. Keep your eyes on them and let me know if they make any changes."

"Okay. I can do that."

Rory felt a bit of relief. He had a direction. That was good. But he still needed to lose the cruiser. The problem was the Shelby Mustang just wasn't fast enough with the shake and shimmy to outrun the cruiser. And now he spotted another set of flashing lights far to the rear of the cruiser behind him. It closing fast and would be part of the chase within seconds.

Sirens sounded in the distance to the left and right, heading this way as well. Time was running out.

Rory's eyes scanned the roadway ahead, watching for just the right timing of traffic and roadway to use– there it was! And the sidewalk was clear on the other side as well. A risky maneuver but it was time for desperate measure. He slowed the Shelby Mustang, allowing the chasing officer to close the gap rapidly. Hold it...hold it....

The NYPD cruiser shot closer–

Rory made his move – he stamped down on the gas and swung the Shelby Mustang into the opposite lane ...headed directly for a bus.

The cruiser followed him.

The bus driver's eyes were wide open in panic.

Rory swerved left onto the sidewalk at the last minute.

The bus shot past him on the right.

The cruiser followed, barely missing the front of the bus.

Rory cut back hard right, passed behind the bus...cut through the oncoming traffic...cut off a truck and took a side street.

The cruiser hesitated, then tried to time his own cut through traffic...he clipped the back end of a garbage truck and spun out of control.

Rory shot past another NYPD cruiser coming in his direction. In his rear viewmirror, he saw the flashing lights of the cruiser spin around as it tried to change directions and pursue...its back end slammed into the front of another cruiser trying to join the chase from the other direction. Rory drove the stolen Shelby Mustang hard block after block, shaking and shimmying through stop signs, stop lights and weaving in, out and around traffic until he was finally southbound on FDR Drive.

"The signal just disappeared into the Queens Midtown Tunnel," *Nysa yelled.*

"They must be headed for Brooklyn," Rory said. "Helmer Postigan has a pharmaceutical factory with a research laboratory there."

"Who?" Nysa asked.

"Doesn't matter," Rory said, "just keep an eye out for any change of direction."

"Okay."

The shake and shimmy of the Shelby Mustang was getting worse. Rory gripped the steering wheel harder, determined to keep his speed up

"The signal is out of the tunnel and now they're headed down *Long Island Expressway now."*

It wasn't long before Rory was approaching the Queens Midtown Tunnel Toll plaza himself.

This was no time to stop.

There were no cars in the right lane.

Rory accelerated harder and crashed through the barrier. He was into the garish yellow light of the tunnel in an instant. He passed as many cars as he could, waiting for the next set of directions.

The sounds of a police cruiser siren now echoed in the tunnel behind him.

"What's that?" Nysa asked. "Is that a siren? Oh my God, you're *being chased by the police! Are they going to come here? Are they–"*

"Nysa, I need you stay calm," Rory said. "People's lives are depending on it, you know that." He could hear her frantic breathing but there was no answer, "Nysa?"

"Uh...okay... okay," she said finally, "I'm okay, I'm okay."

"Where is the signal now Nysa?" The wait for an answer seemed agonizingly long. He could see the pursuing cruiser, only a number of cars back now.

"The signal is now heading down Brooklyn Queens Expressway," Nysa said finally.

Rory shot out of the tunnel and headed onto the Long Island Expressway himself. He pressed the accelerator down harder, fighting the increased shimmy as he moved in and out of the traffic.

The cruiser was moving in and out of the cars behind him as well, moving closer.

Rory took a few extra chances to stay ahead.

The cruiser was being more cautious but still stayed on his tail, just falling back behind a few more cars.

Rory had to time his next move perfectly or he would be caught.

Cars started peeling away, realizing they were in the middle of a chase. The cruiser was only three cars back now.

Rory hit the brake hard.

The drivers behind him reacted by slamming on their brakes and skidding sideways.

The cruiser tried to go around but hit the back fender of the car in front and spun out.

Rory accelerated again and cut hard between two cars, taking the exit to the Brooklyn Queens Expressway. He cut off two cars as he entered the expressway and a cacophony of blaring horns protested...he accelerated and wove in and out of traffic.

"Now the signal is going across the Williamsburg Bridge," Nysa Gagarin reported.

Rory wondered what was going on. They were heading away from Brooklyn. Were they backtracking? Rory kept the stolen car driving hard, wondering what they were doing. And why was he beginning to catch up? Then he realized they wouldn't be traveling as fast as he was. They couldn't afford to catch the attention of the police. Then again, Rory couldn't afford more police attention either...but he had no choice. He kept the stolen car shaking at top speed.

"Hold on," Nysa Gagarin said.

The wait for more details was agonizing.

"The signal is headed back across the Brooklyn Bridge," Nysa Gagarin said. *"That doesn't make any sense...."*

Rory agreed. That didn't make any sense at all. "Are we following the right signal?" he asked her.

"Yes, I'm positive," Nysa said. *"At least...."*

Rory's heart sank for a moment. Then he realized what they were doing, "They're trying to see if anybody is following them. That's what they're doing."

"Okay," Nysa said, *"that makes sense. I guess."*

Rory's spirits rose for the first time since they had taken Nan and her father. This should help him to catch up to them. Rory kept his foot pressed on the accelerator as he waited for more directions.

"It looks like your assumption is right," Nysa Gagarin said, *"they're headed south down Brooklyn Queens Expressway again."*

Rory drove on as he waited. He wondered what he would do if he did catch up to them. He no longer had his Baby Eagle and there was no time to stop and get a weapon now. Whatever happened, he would have to take his chances. He owed that to Nan.

"The signal is off the expressway now," Nysa Gagarin told him.*"It's near the old Brooklyn Navy yards...."*

"Are you sure?" Rory shook his head as he drove and waited.

"Y-yeah...it looks like they're on Washington Avenue," she said *after a moment.*

Rory wondered if it was another ruse - if they were checking to see if they were being followed–

"It's stopped."

"What?"

"The signal has stopped. At the old Brooklyn Navy yards...."

Rory looked out the windshield, trying to visualize what they were doing. "Why would they be there?"

"I...I don't know...."

It didn't make any sense. According to Detective Crenshaw, the pharmaceutical factory with the research laboratory was down near the Coney Island Wastewater Treatment Plant. But that was far to the south-east. "Do you know of any laboratories near there, Nysa?"

There was a long period of silence as Rory drove on. He could hear Nysa typing on her laptop.

"No. I don't see any laboratories listed there. There's nothing like that in the entire area," Nysa told him.

"What *is* down there? Can you tell me that? I mean, it sounds like an old navy base, but...."He was getting worried. Had they lost them?

"The only thing on the Brooklyn Navy Yard grounds is an old naval hospital. But it looks like it was there before the Civil War. I don't think it's been in use for a long, long time...."

"You're sure it's in that area...?"

"Yes, that's basically where the signal is stopped," Nysa Gagarin said. *"It's not moving at all right now."*

Rory took a deep breath and let it out, trying to relieve the tension that was building. Either that *was* their destination...or they had cut the tracker out of Nan's arm and left it behind. "Okay. Can you send a link to my phone for a Google map of the area?" Rory asked her. "And I need something that gives me the layout of that building."

"All right. I can send a map of the area. It looks like the grounds are around 20 acres in size. But I don't see anything with the layout of the old 60,000 square foot hospital itself. It looks like there's the hospital...and an old, large house...nothing else that I can see. I hope you can find her in one of those two buildings."

"So do I," Rory said, "so do I."

Chapter 41

IT WAS ALL DOWN to an experimental animal tracker under Nan's skin. Rory prayed they had followed the right signal. He finally exited the expressway, heading for the old Brooklyn Navy Yard. After driving across a couple of streets in the area, he parked beside some old buildings. Picking up his cell phone, he brought up the Google map Nysa Gagarin had sent him. With the help of the nearby street signs, Rory finally figured out where he was. He started driving again until he came to the edge of the 20-acre site Nysa had talked about.

The grounds had a brand new, 8 foot high, perimeter chain link fence around it. And the property wasn't overgrown with tall grass and weeds. Despite what Nysa had said, that meant someone *was* using the site. That was good. There were a number of trees on the other side of the fence and he could see a large, old building in the distance. It looked like the front of the building faced to the right and overlooked a small parking area. It was a long shot but Rory made a decision. He turned off his iPhone and slipped it into his pocket. He had to get inside the grounds and check out that building.

Rory drove the stolen Shelby Mustang back a couple of blocks to those old buildings and he parked the car behind one of them. He picked up a small plastic lighter from the center console and an old newspaper from the back seat. Pressing the button to pop open the gas lid, he got out and walked to the back of the car, where he took the gas cap off. Rolling up the newspaper, he carefully inserted it down the filler tube. Then he lit the end of the newspaper and jogged away to the edge of the building.

It only took a few moments for the fire to burn down to the fuel and the gas tank exploded.

Rory raised his arm to shield his face. It was a bigger bang then he had expected and would probably bring police to the area very soon. But he wasn't about to leave behind fingerprints or DNA in a stolen car. That would only give Crenshaw and Ainsworth more ammunition to add to their screwed up theories...and put him away for life.

Rory left the burning car behind and sprinted back across the blocks to the chain link fence. He climbed quickly, jumped to the ground on the other side and ran low through the trees. Crouching behind a large tree, Rory realized he would have to run several hundred yards across open ground to reach the old building. That wasn't good. He couldn't afford to take any chance in broad daylight and get captured...or shot. Looking into the sky, he estimated darkness would start in a little over an hour. As much as he hated to wait, he had no choice.

Rory sat down and kept watch around him. But his eyes kept going back to the old building. Anger was building inside of him. He hoped he would meet up with Lillian Postigan and her panties again. He just might suffocate her with them.

IT WAS FINALLY DARK enough, but Rory started to worry. There were no lights apparent on this side the building. This didn't look good. Maybe he had the wrong place after all. He readied himself and then ran low across the open grass field, towards the old hospital. No one came out of the dark at him and there were no gunshots. So far so good.

Reaching the old building, he settled with his back against the wall and listened for any sound or movement.

Everything was quiet.

Rory decided to head to the back of the building. He crouched low and took off at a run. Reaching the edge of the building, he peered around the corner.

There were still no lights visible and no evidence Nan was being held in this building.

Rory cursed silently, wondering if his plan had failed. Edging around the corner, he ran low along the wall, looking for evidence of someone being inside. There wasn't a single light anywhere. Moving away from the building at an angle now, he looked up, hoping to see lights at the far end of the large building or higher up – there!

It was on the second floor on the far side of the building. One-third of the entire floor was lit up. That was good.

Rory scanned along the back of the building, looking for a way in. He saw a door for an old coal chute, going down into the basement. He moved over to it quickly....it was locked. Rory cursed. He had no choice...gripping the door handles firmly, he set himself...and a strong yank on the hinges pulled them out of the old wood with a loud bang. The smell of old coal dust swirled around his head. He stayed in position for a moment, holding the door as a makeshift shield, wondering if anyone had heard the noise. After a long, tense moment, Rory lay the doors aside and slipped down into the dark basement.

Rory pulled the lighter from his pocket and lit it. Everything he could see in the small area of light was covered with dust and cobwebs. It smelled damp and musty. He moved slowly across the floor, cautious not to fall over anything and cause any noise. He found a set of worn, wooden stairs leading upwards. He put a foot on the first step and slowly applied his weight. The board creaked but felt solid enough to walk on. He looked up. Twenty steps to the top.

Closing the lighter, he slowly moved his foot to the next step in the dark. It creaked in a low protest. He placed his foot closer to the edge of the frame and the creak disappeared. Moving up to the next step, he hesitated and listened...then the next...then the next...finally he reached the top of the stairs, grasped the doorknob and slowly turned it. When there was no reaction, he slowly pushed the door wide open.

The room on the other side was not as dark as the basement, but it was dark enough that Rory couldn't see if anybody was hiding inside. All he could see was the outline of a door over on the left-hand side. The room smelled old, damp and musty, just like below. Rory took a deep breath and took a step. He moved inside the room, closing the door softly behind him. He took another step into the room and heard a faint whisper of sound behind him.

A shadow descended from above his head. Someone was trying to garrote him from behind!

Rory barely got his right hand up in time against his throat and he felt a wire bite into the palm of his hand.

The attacker grunted with effort as he pulled the wire against the intruder's throat He had no idea Rory's hand was in the way.

Pushed back with his feet, Rory tried to slam the attacker back against the wall.

But the attacker was smart and he stepped back in a circle, negating Rory's efforts while maintaining a strong pull on the wire.

Rory knew he had to act fast or he was dead. He sensed the attacker's head near his left shoulder. He brought the thumb of his free hand up and back over his shoulder, jabbing it into the assailant's eye.

The attacker howled and released his pressure on the wire.

Rory pushed the garrote away enough to allow himself to drop down and whirl around in a defensive posture.

The attacker kicked at Rory's head.

Blocking it, Rory then swept his right leg out, taking the attacker off his feet.

The man cursed as he landed on his back.

Rory moved forward to attack.

The man got his legs up in time and tossed Rory back over his head.

Rory landed hard on a wooden table. The breath was knocked out of his lungs as the table collapsed under his weight. Shattered wood flew everywhere. Rory barely got his eyes open in time to glimpse a wooden table leg descending towards his head. He rolled away and the table leg bounced off broken wood on the floor. Rory fought to regain his breath as he got up into a defensive crouch again.

The man swung the table leg like a baseball bat.

Rory jumped back and the table leg brushed his shirt across the stomach.

The man advanced quickly.

Moving away from the attack, Rory bumped into something. It was a wooden chair. Rory reached down and grabbed one of the chair legs with his right hand. He flipped the chair under-handed towards his attacker.

The chair struck the man on the shoulder and head before the man could get his hands up. The man staggered back, dropping the table leg.

Jumping forward, Rory bent over and reached for the table leg.

But his attacker stepped on it, preventing Rory from picking up the makeshift weapon.

His brain told him it was a dumb move. He was bent over and susceptible to an attack. Rory's brain told him that - but his muscles didn't react fast enough.

The attacker brought both hands down on Rory's lower back.

The pain in his kidneys was excruciating and Rory barely stayed on his feet as he staggered back.

The man bull rushed him.

Rory could only sidestep and use the man's momentum to push him past.

There was the sound of breaking glass.

Turning in a staggered step, Rory brought his hands up, try-ing to be ready for the next attack.

But it didn't come.

Staggering another step before he steadied himself, Rory now realized the man's form was hanging through a window. He moved forward cautiously. There was a large piece of dirty glass embedded in the man's neck. Rory checked the pulse in the man's neck. He was dead. Rory's body was aching but there was no time stop and recuperate. Holding a hand on his lower back, he staggered over to the door and slowly opened it. It led into a dark, wide hallway. He wondered how many other guards were in the building.

Chapter 42

RORY HELD HIS BREATH and stepped out of the room into the wide hallway, fully expecting to be attacked again. He slowly released his breath when nothing happened. On his right was a small staircase. That was good. The light had been on the second floor. Rory walked over to the stairway as silently as possible and walked slowly up to the second floor, listening for anyone else on guard. At the top of the landing, he paused in front of a pair of double, swinging doors. Everything was quiet.

Then the doors burst open and two large men knocked him back against the railing. When the two men realized he was there - they stepped back quickly - looking at Rory with fear in their eyes.

Rory took advantage of the situation and attacked, swinging, like a man possessed. If they captured or killed him here, people would die. He couldn't let that happen, he'd already made enough mistakes.

The two men began pummeling him back, knocking him to the floor. But in the tight space they were in each other's way, giving Rory a small advantage.

Rory rolled towards the wall, spun around and pushed with both legs against one of the attackers.

The man staggered back. But in the small landing, he didn't have anywhere to go. Except over the railing. A glint of light flashed off the bottom of the man's shoes as he flipped over backward. The man didn't stop screaming until he hit the floor, twenty feet below.

His partner attacked, driving a hard right into Rory's jaw.

Rory was stunned by the blow and he fought against blacking out as he threw punches wildly. He received another hard crack to the side of his head. Rory kicked and threw more wild punches. He felt something soft against his knuckles as he threw a hard left. He heard the man gag. He must have hit him in the throat. Rory reacted quickly, getting his feet under him and driving up against the attacker with a shoulder.

The man staggered backward from the blow.

Rory saw the brief flash of surprise on the man's face as his left foot found only air.

His arms windmilling, the man tumbled back and down the stairs.

Scrambling to his feet, Rory moved down the stairs to continue the fight.

But the man was lying on the staircase just above the first landing, his neck cocked at a deadly angle.

Taking a quick look over the banister, Rory saw the other man lying at the bottom of the stairs. There was no movement. Rory listened intently. He didn't hear any footsteps or shouting, so that must mean no one had heard the fight. He had to get moving again. He quickly ran back up to the second-floor landing and pushed one of the swinging doors open a crack. Not seeing anyone, Rory slipped into the hallway and began moving towards the end of the building where he had seen the lights.

He constantly checked behind himself, making sure no one was sneaking up from behind. He passed several cross hallways but didn't see anyone. He finally came to another set of old double doors. He opened one side of the doors and light spilled out. Not seeing anyone in the hallway on the other side, Rory quickly passed through and let the door close behind him.

This hallway was cleaner and Rory could smell fresh paint. Everything was white with gray or brown overtones and it re-minded Rory of the NYU Genetics Laboratory. He wondered if the decorating was part of Lillian's twisted sense of humor. This was probably the building where the Postigan's had set up a sec-ond laboratory to work on their mad plans in secret. At least, he hoped it was.

Rory moved quickly down the hallway, feeling exposed and vulnerable to more attacks. He stopped as he spotted an open doorway on the right-hand side. Hugging the wall, he crept silently towards the open doorway. Now he held his breath as he peered inside.

It was empty of people. There was a large table in the center of the room, surrounded by a number of chairs. But the chairs were all pushed back and away from the table. There was an ash-tray, in the middle of the table, with smoke rising from it. Ro-ry could see two cigarettes were still burning in the ashtray. It looked like everyone in this room had cleared out quickly.

Rory glanced back behind him. He had to assume they were all out looking for him and he decided he had to move quickly now. There was simply no choice if everyone had been alerted to his presence in the building. He walked fast down the wide hall-way now with an increased sense of urgency, if that was possible.

Rory noticed a couple of other doors were wide open. He didn't see anyone inside the rooms, but it looked like people had cleared out quickly here as well. Moving further down the wide hallway, Rory noticed a large door on the left that looked like a modern, industrial door. Farther down he could see another one just like it. Rory walked quickly to the first one and pressed his ear against the door, listening for any sound on the other side. He couldn't hear anything. He reached down to the large doorknob and slowly twisted it. To his surprise, it wasn't locked.

Was it a trap?

He would know soon enough.

Rory slowly opened the door, ready for trouble.

It didn't come.

Slipping inside, Rory closed the door softly behind him.

He was in a long, white room with a large desk on the left and a long line of cabinets. The wall on the right had four doors. And in between each door was a large window that ran from waist height to the ceiling. It reminded him of the biosafety level 4 rooms back at the University. He detected the same 'dead air' smell that he had experienced at the NYU Genetics Laboratory. That meant air scrubbers were at work here as well. Someone was definitely engaged in working with dangerous substances here. He didn't like the looks of this. He moved to the right wall and approached the first door. He was going to try and open it and thought better of it. Better to see who...and what...was inside. He tiptoed to the edge of the window and peered inside...and his blood ran cold.

RORY TOOK AN UNSTEADY step forward to get a better view. The room had four stainless steel autopsy tables, with all the requisite equipment. Blood stains ran down the table to a stainless steel container at the end. And on top of each table was a body. Or parts of a body. The arms and legs were gone from the bodies on the first three table. The fourth had one arm left from the elbow up. It looked like the rest of the arm was in three-inch long, bloody pieces, lying on the table. A bloody bone saw lay on the table just below the stump. On the floor sat an open, stainless steel box that looked to be overflowing with bloody pieces of flesh. The room inside looked like a human slaughterhouse.

Rory threw all caution to the wind and ran to the next window. All the bodies in this room were missing their arms and legs. The same with the next two rooms.

Rory staggered back a step. Lillian had already harvested pieces of plague-infested bone from the bodies. Taking them from the arms and legs first had allowed her to work fast. He was too late. Rory leaned his forehead against the window, squeezed his eyes shut and felt another failure course through his veins. More people were about to die. Chinatown? And which one? Chinatown, Manhattan? Little Fuzhou? Chinatown, Flushing? Chinatown, Brooklyn? Or how about the place some called Curry Row in the East Village, Manhattan? He realized it didn't matter which one - it would be all of them eventually if he didn't stop them. Rory turned his back to the observation window, thinking. Creating a manifest to ship the Fire Plague was ridiculous, of course, but he assumed it would be faster to use courier and trucking firms. He looked at the row of filing cabinets and then at the desk. He ran for the desk and began looking for a possible clue as to where she might send the harvest.

A set of papers on the desk gave him hope.

He pulled out his iPhone, turned it on and hit speed dial.

"Are you all right–?"

"Skye, where are you?"

"I'm at the office. What do you need me for now?" Her voice was on full alert.

"I'm at the Brooklyn Navy Yards–"

"I'm on my way–"

"No, no. I need you to do something else. These nut-jobs have cut up pieces of plague victims."

"What!"

"That's what was in that urn that you brought back from China. A plague infested piece of bone from an ancient plague victim. Listen carefully, I found a bill of sale for a special, biosafety level four vehicle used for transporting infectious persons. They must have used it to pick up the twelve dead plague victims from Harlem–"

"You have to be kidding me!"

"I wish I was, Skye. Lillian cut them up and I think I know where they're going. I also found a copy of an email confirming a Global Express XRS cargo plane is fueled and ready to go at Floyd Bennett Field–"

"That's in southeast Brooklyn. But it's a park area now–"

"With a usable airfield away from prying eyes. They can't go through customs with this stuff, so an abandoned air field fits in with their needs. And since it's near their other lab, they'd know all about it. I bet that's how they brought the other urn into the country–"

"You're right, it makes sense. The Global Express XRS is an ultra long range aircraft that can fly 13 hours without refueling. They

probably used it to bring the plague this way...and now they're going to send more back the other way. What do you need me to do?"

"I need you to stop them from getting the body parts on that plane. They *can't* get that plane off the ground, Skye. They *can't*. While you're doing that, I'll finish up here."

"Okay. Anything else before I go?"

"Yeah. Just one thing...."

Chapter 43

SKYE STEELE PRESSED her foot down hard on the accelerator and the 1200 horsepower engine of the Bugatti Veyron 16.5 Super Sport reacted in a heartbeat. She hit 267 mph and the few cars still on the Belt Parkway were just a blur as she flew past them. Her nerves were on high alert. Killing someone in an accident wasn't in the plan but she had no choice. She had to reach those body parts. Assuming they were headed to Floyd Bennett Field. She agreed with Rory, it made sense. But if they were wrong a lot of people would die.

She roared past a police cruiser and saw the lights go on as the pursuit started. And ended just as quickly as far as she was concerned. The cruiser disappeared in her rearview mirror in the blink of an eye. Hopefully, there wouldn't be time for them to put a road spike belt out in front of her on the road. If they did, she wondered if she would end up embedded in a building on the left - or sinking into the water on the right. Skye Steele kept her foot down and her speed up. Lives depended on it.

The turnoff was fast approaching and Skye slowed the Bugatti. Now it felt like she was going through everything in slow motion as she navigated onto Flatbush Ave. But that only lasted a few more seconds until she applied the gas again and roared down the straightaway. She slowed for the left turn on to Aviation and then rocketed to the next left turn and headed for the airfield. Skye applied full power and kept the tachometer in the red, watching for a big truck. That's all she knew. A big truck. Even at 267 mph, time slowed down as she felt her anxiety levels rise. There wasn't *any* vehicle in sight, let alone a big truck.

Then she saw lights. Lights from high towers that shone down on the airfield, far off to the right. And under the lights was a large plane with swept-back wings. That *had* to be the Global Express XRS.

Skye cut to the right, dropped her speed and swooped across the flat field of grass between the landing strips. As soon as her wheels touched the next tarmac, she floored the Bugatti again. Skye could now see a large, square, stainless-steel truck, parked thirty feet off to the left of the plane.

Six men, dressed in heavy white suits, were around the back of the truck. One of them was reaching for the handle for the back door...which meant she had caught them before they had started unloading their deadly cargo.

The men turned as they heard the roar of a turbocharged engine approaching fast across the landing strip behind them.

Skye was close enough to see a large XRS on the plane's tail. Bingo.

Three men came running from the plane in her direction while the men in the heavy white suits scrambled for the front of the truck.

In an instant, Skye's brain registered the Ruger MP9 19 mm submachine guns being pointed in her direction by the three men and she cut to the right.

Bullets tore up the tarmac just behind the Bugatti.

Skye kept the wheel cranked and took a wide circle on the landing strip, her tires squealing and smoking.

The three gunmen tried to track the speeding vehicle but their bullets just continued to rip up lines of tarmac.

Driving one handed, Skye lowered the window, switched hands on the steering wheel to grab her Sig Sauer P238 pistol from the cup holder and brought it back across her body. Her red hair was whipping straight back as she set the barrel pistol on the lower window frame. When her circular turn cut back across in front of the men - she fired. The sound of her first shot was hidden under the loud growl of the Bugatti engine, but there was no mistaking her accuracy. The first bullet went through the throat of the man in the middle and he was down.

The two remaining gunmen stopped firing and changed their aim before they started firing again.

Compensating for their expected move, Skye palmed the steering wheel and spun it hard left - the bullets tore up the tarmac to her right - they adjusted their aim - Skye turned the Bugatti to the right again and pulled the trigger.

The bullet hit the man on the left in the eye. As the body dropped, the third man glanced down when the dead man's arm landed on his boot. He kicked it away and looked up - the speeding Bugatti was coming right at him! He brought his weapon up.

But the glance at his buddy had been his undoing. It had given Skye the time to get her foot on the brake and come to a sideways stop.

The gunman's aim was put off by the sudden stop and he missed his target, his bullets ripping up the tarmac only feet from the Bugatti.

Skye pulled the trigger and blew his knee out.

Falling to one knee, the man stopped firing, grimaced and tried to bring the weapon up.

Skye's next shot hit him between the eyes. As he fell, she turned her attention to the six men who had been dressed in the heavy white suist. They had discarded their suits and one of them was pulling weapons from the front of the truck and passing them to the others. Stomping down on the gas, Skye drove the Bugatti Veyron hard across the tarmac again, and then cut hard to the right, braking to a stop with the plane and the men she had killed on the right and the gunmen and the truck on the left.

The six men were now holding submachine guns and turning in her direction.

Skye was out of the driver's side door, vaulted up onto the roof and rolled over to the other side.

They opened up - trying to track her - ripping the roof of the Bugatti to shreds.

But Skye had already dropped to the tarmac beside the Bugatti, rolled three feet away in the direction of the three dead bodies - she grabbed one of the Ruger MP9 19mm submachine guns - then reached for another.

The six men stopped firing - looking for their target - and began to spread out.

Skye had her chance. With a submachine gun in each hand, she rose swiftly - covered the distance to the front hood of the Bugatti - lay the weapons across it and opened up.

The six men danced in a crazy, bullet driven jitter-bug until Skye stopped firing.

As they were dropping to the ground. Skye whirled around and looked for more danger from the plane.

It was quiet.

Skye propped one submachine gun on a shoulder - kept the other at the ready - and moved quickly but cautiously towards the truck. Skirting the six dead bodies, she checked the front of the truck. It was empty. Still keeping an eye in the direction of the plane, Skye now moved to the back of the truck. She dropped one weapon, undid the latch and opened the wide back door. Inside the back were a number of the same heavy, white suits the men were wearing. Skye climbed into the back of the truck and took a look. And her legs almost went out from under her. Through the transparent headgear, she could see pieces of bloody bone, wrapped inside clear plastic. These idiots were transporting the Fire Plague in what looked like sandwich bags inside biohazard suits. For a fleeting moment, Skye wondered if she would be dead within a day. She pushed that thought out of her head. She had work to do. Lives depended on it.

Skye jumped out of the back of the truck and sprinted across to the passenger side of the Bugatti. In moments she pulled out her next weapon.

Rory had made arrangements for her to stop and see some General. He had given her some quick instructions...and right now Skye wished she hadn't been in such a hurry. She had to do this right.

She slipped the straps of the double tank over her shoulders and then picked up the gun assembly. The General had explained how the liquid-operated flamethrower worked and she tried to remember his instructions as she ran for the back of the truck. The smaller propane tank had two tubes. One expelled the liquid into the napalm tank, to push that to the spot where the 2nd propane tube ignited it. Or something like that. She set herself behind the open doors, pressed the trigger...and was nearly knocked off her feet as the flame exploded from the nozzle.

The contents in the back of the truck burst into flames.

Skye kept the trigger down. She wanted to burn every little atom of plague. She refused to let up and see people die –

Boom!

Skye was knocked on her backside and went for a tumble as the tanks on her back bounced hard off the tarmac from the force. Rolling up on her knees Skye realized the gas tank in the truck had blown up. She had forgotten about that and could have been killed. But she wasn't. She struggled back to her feet, stepped as close as she could and added more flames to the intense fire.

When the flamethrower went empty, Skye discarded the tank and headed for the Bugatti Veyron 16.5 Super Sport. She had borrowed it from Uncle Murdock's collection because of its speed. Grimacing at the damage, she wondered if she could talk Rory into paying for the repairs.

Chapter 44

RORY MOVED TO the next industrial door and turned the doorknob. Unlocked as well. He slowly opened the door and peered inside. He was fully expecting to be attacked at any moment. But everything was deadly quiet. He slipped inside and closed the door behind him, leaning back against it. There was the same 'dead air' smell but Rory's mind added the scent of the bloody corpses he had seen in the other one. He wondered if he would find the same thing in here.

But this laboratory had a different layout. To the left and right lay a line of offices. Rory moved as quickly and quietly to the left first, checking the offices. He didn't see anyone. Moving back the other way, Rory found only empty offices as well. But there was a long hallway on this side of the room. With more office spaces. He checked them out one by one, staying against the right wall as he did. He couldn't afford to be surprised since he had no weapon. Again, only empty rooms–

Rory heard noises up ahead and he froze on the spot for a moment.

Did they know he was in here? Were they coming this way?

He listened carefully and then realized the sound was muffled. But he could tell *someone* was talking loudly in one of the
rooms up ahead.

Rory tiptoed down the hallway. Nearing the end, Rory realized the sound was coming from behind a door on his right. He
wondered if it was Nan trying to get out. He slowly opened the
door just a crack but there was no one on the other side.

And the sound stopped.

He slowly opened the door a little more. He still couldn't see
anyone. Glancing around to make sure no one was sneaking up
behind him, Rory listened carefully - trying to pick up the least
sound of danger - and slipped through, closing the door softly behind him.

Dead ahead was the large observation glass of another
biosafety level 4 room. The others had been used to chop up the
bodies. He wondered if this was the one where they were working
on the plague, trying to modify it to kill specific races they wanted to remove from their new society. If so, the other urn should
be nearby...and probably Nan as well. His hopes rose at the possi-
bility he could rescue Nan *and* steal the urn from them.

But...where were the guards? Shouldn't he be fighting his way
through an army of gunmen, protecting the Postigans and their
lab?

Rory shook his head softly and took a breath to ready himself. He inched closer to the glass, not sure what he would do if he
found Lillian and her staff working inside. He was still unarmed.

More noise. More talking. It was definitely coming from behind the observation glass.

Rory stepped ahead and looked into the secure room. What
he saw stunned him.

Lillian Safford was inside. And she was alone. She turned around to face in his direction. She was totally nude, except for a few remnants of her blouse lying in tatters from her shoulders. As he had imagined, Lillian had a great body. But right now it didn't look so attractive. Lillian's breasts were covered in long, deep scratches - her stomach was gouged with deep lacerations and he was sure he saw a fingernail stuck in the oozing flesh - her long, shapely legs were also covered in deep scratches and running blood.

Rory could see her clothing, including her white biological suit, lying in tattered shreds around the inside of the laboratory. That sent a chill through him.

Throwing her head back, Lillian looked up at the ceiling, and let out a howling scream.

Rory could hear the pain and agony very clearly on this side of the observation glass. He could see her raised fingers and hands, bloody from digging deeply into her own flesh. She had been infected by the Fire Plague!

Lillian brought her hands down, screaming in agony and tearing at her body with her fingernails. She careened around the room as if she was trying to escape the disease inside her.

As she moved closer, Rory could see blood beginning to come from her eyes, her nose, and her mouth. She was in the last stages. She turned and her bloody eyes saw him on the other side of the glass. It sounded like she screamed 'help me' as she staggered towards him. Lillian stood in front of the observation glass on the other side, banging her bloody hands against the glass as their eyes met. Her naked, bloody breasts swayed. She screamed and tried to claw away the glass barrier between them. She turned and staggered off to Rory's right.

Rory leaned his head against the glass, watching her stumble with some purpose towards the wall on the right - she set her hands on a long handle on the wall. He slid his head to the left - wondering what she was doing - but he couldn't get a good enough angle.

Lillian lifted her head and screamed in agony for a moment - then she lowered her shaking head and her hands seem to rotate

Rory heard a clunk in the wall off to his right and then Lillian disappeared. He wondered - a metallic spinning sound came from his right - and he suddenly realized what was happening. His blood ran cold. He ran for the stainless steel door and grabbed the handle. Lillian was trying to leave the secure, biosafety level 4 room. The wheel jerked in his hand. He held it firmly - heard her scream and yell - and the handle jerked. It started turning and his mind whirled with fear. He was fighting against her hysterical strength in a life-and-death situation - he remembered hearing stories of mothers picking up cars to save a child and he wondered if it was true. The wheel turned more despite his resistance - he was fighting against a woman driven by the burning fever from the Fire Plague and the adrenaline rush of her own fear of a horrible death - he was about to find out if those stories were true.

He could hear Lillian yelling and calling for his help. She banged her fists against the door and then returned to turning the wheel.

Holding tight, Rory desperately looked around, looking for some way to blockade the door. There was nothing.

Lillian screamed in rage - and the wheel began turning slowly.

Rory knew he was going to lose the battle - Bonifay's joking came back to him - something about a mechanism or...? What was it? He leaned against the stainless steel door and looked up and down - nothing he could see. He turned the other way - a narrow,one-inch groove in the door caught his attention. He put his finger inside - felt a tab and pushed it sideways. A sliding and clunking sounded inside the door.

"Noooo!" Lillian began banging against the door on the other side, yelling, "No, let me out. Help me." The pounding stopped. The screaming and yelling receded from the door.

Looking at the door and the wheel, Rory realized he must have swung a deadbolt in place and she knew it. The yelling seemed to come from the area of the glass again and Rory cautiously moved across the floor to look - watching the wheel in case it started turning again. A moment later, he looked through the glass to see Lillian staggering around the room again.

She stopped - back to him - swayed and backed up toward the glass. Coming within several feet of where Rory stood, she turned. Seeing him standing there, she screamed his name and lunged for the glass.

Rory flinched and felt his heart pounding. His breathing was ragged - he knew she couldn't get at him but the fear was still there. Was there another way out? Had she messed with the filters and the plague was all around him?

Lillian pounded and scratched at the glass on the other side, looking into his eyes and pleading for his help. Suddenly, Lillian Stafford stopped moving, she leaned forward with her hands braced against the glass. She looked at him with bloody eyes as her stomach heaved.

It heaved again.

Another heave and Lillian Safford projectile vomited blood.

Rory took a step back as her blood splashed against the glass and Lillian disappeared from his view behind a blanket of gory red. Rory was stunned as he watched her clawing fingers create a trail in the massive amount of blood on the glass.

The trail in the blood slowly moved downward as Lillian sank to the floor on the other side of the glass.

Rory felt himself shaking. To be so close to someone who was dying of this Fire Plague, and to see the suffering, was horrendous. But more than that, Lillian Safford had died from the Fire Plague, *despite her biological suit.* That meant the disease had gotten outside of her laboratory's security features. He wondered if he had any chance to survive himself. He had to calm his breathing. He still had to find Nan and her father. Then again, even if he *did* find them and got away, was that only to die a horrible death someplace else in a few hours?

Chapter 45

RORY WENT BACK into the main hallway. He was still shaking as he tried to figure out what to do next. He had no idea where to look for Nan and her father. Choosing a direction, he stayed on full alert as he moved quietly down the hallway, ready for an attack as he searched - something bothered him and he stopped in his tracks. His thoughts went back to the two men who had burst through the doorway at the top of the landing when he had first come in. What was it that bothered him? He closed his eyes - visualizing what had happened.

The two men - they came through the doorway - that wasn't surprise at seeing him on the landing - they had *fear* in their eyes - they had *hesitated* before attacking him.

Why?

Then he thought back to the rooms he had seen, where it looked like people had cleared out quickly.

The men on the landing hadn't been looking for him, they were fleeing. They were running for their life.

They *knew* the Fire Plague had gotten out.

So had the others.

But even if he was wrong, he realized it may not matter.

He had to take chances and he had to act quickly...and faster. Stealth, caution, and safety were out the window. He took in a deep breath, put his hands to his mouth and yelled, "Nan!"

He listened.

No answer.

He moved faster down the hallway, calling her name loudly and listening. The building was fairly big and he wondered how long it would take to find her. He turned a corner in the hallway and began to move towards the front of the building, yelling and listening.

A sound stopped him in his tracks.

Nothing.

Rory moved further down the hallway, stopped and yelled again. His ears perked up. Someone was yelling - it was up ahead somewhere. He moved faster now, trotting down the hallway as he yelled. Finally, he heard a muffled, "in here" behind a door up ahead on the right. He ran to the door and jiggled the knob, "Nan?"

A muffled 'yeah' came from behind the door.

"Stand back," he yelled. He lifted his foot and tried to kick the door in. It shook but didn't break open. He kicked it several more times. Then he backed up and took a run at it, hitting the door with a shoulder. The door broke open and he fell into the room, crashing to the floor.

"Thank goodness you found me," Nan cried as she rushed over to him.

"Where's your father?" Rory asked as he got up from the floor.

"I think he's in the room next to me," Nan said. She rushed into the hallway.

Rory followed behind her.

Nan ran to the next door, jiggling the knob and banging her fist on the door, calling for her father.

Moving her aside, Rory stepped back and took a run at the door with a shoulder. This old door gave way quickly and Rory tumbled into the room, falling on his side. In an instant, Nan ran in and stepped over his prone body, "Dad!"

Cordell Bacon was lying on the floor and Nan dropped to her knees beside him. He was unconscious and she lightly tapped his face, trying to get him alert and awake. "I think they've given him something like they did with me. I'm not sure if I can wake him up without some countermeasure."

Rory knelt beside her, "Okay. What do we need to do?"

Nan looked around, "I don't know." She rocked slightly, "When I was first here - Mr. Postigan had a study somewhere - and someone came out of a door on the left and gave me a shot. They should have something in that room. I hope." She closed her eyes, "When they brought us in here this time...."

"Do you know where it was–?"

Her eyes popped open, "Yeah, I think it was a just few doors down." Nan jumped up and rushed for the open door. She disappeared off to the right in the hallway, yelling back,"Maybe if I find that room next to the study, I'll find something in there."

"Hold on." Rory scrambled to his feet and chased after her. He caught up to her outside another closed door. Holding her arm he said, "Let me go in first. I think everybody has left the building, but we can't take the chance."

"Okay, but please hurry."

Rory checked the doorknob. It was unlocked. Rory opened the door a crack and peered inside. No one attacked him and he couldn't see anyone inside. He opened the door fully and moved inside the room. Nan had been right, this room looked like a small pharmaceutical storeroom.

Nan followed in behind him quickly and began checking labels on vials behind the glass doors. "I think they used a drug in the Benzodiazepines class."

"And...?"

"And I need something like Flumazenil - there it is." She picked up a packaged needle and rushed back down the hallway to her father.

Rory followed behind her, still keeping his eyes open for an attack. But the hallways were eerily empty.

Nan knelt by her father, tore the package apart frantically and filled the needle from the vial. Her hands were shaking as she gave her father a shot in the arm.

Rory kept watching from the open doorway, looking up and down the hallway as she worked to revive her father.

Nan kept talking to him, trying to get him alert.

After a moment, her father began to stir.

Rory moved quickly back into the room and helped Cordell Bacon to his feet. Then, as sleepy father and relieved daughter hugged, Rory looked back out into the hallway. There was no time for a long reunion, "We need to get moving folks."

Cordell Bacon looked over at him - it took a moment - and then nodded once in recognition, his voice still in a fog, "Mr. Steele."

Nan put her father's arm around her shoulder and helped him into the hallway. She asked Rory, "What about Lillian and her father? We still have to do something about them."

"Lillian is dead. I'm not sure where her father is."

"Dead? What happened to her?"

Rory took a deep breath and let it out slowly as he looked up and down the hallway, wondering how the news would go over. He looked at Nan, "It looks to me like she died of the Fire Plague from the urn they brought back from China." He shrugged, "Or maybe from the bones of the victims she stole and cut up–"

"Oh, no! She actually did it...?"

"Yeah. But don't worry about that for now. I sent Skye after them. Anyway, I saw Lillian behind the glass in the laboratory earlier. She had ripped her biological suit off - let's just say, it wasn't pretty."

Nan was stunned. Her voice was hushed, "That means the bacterium is loose."

"I was afraid you'd say that. Do you think we're infected?"

Nan narrowed her eyes as she gave it some thought. She shook her head, "No, I don't think so. My father and I would be dead by now. But we won't have much time."

Nodding with some relief, Rory turned and looked down the hallway, "Okay, I think I can backtrack and find my way out of here. We can have the CDC come back and–"

"Rory?"

The slurred voice was Cordell Bacon's and Rory turned his head.

Bacon was leaning against the wall, but Nan wasn't beside him. Cordell gestured down the hallway and asked in a weak voice."Where is she going? Shouldn't...shouldn't we be leaving...?"

Rory was stunned to see Nan was running back down the hall, away from them.

Cordell Bacon tried to go after her. He staggered a couple of steps down the hallway, "Nan!"

Nan opened a door on the right, passed the one where they had found the drugs, and disappeared.

Rory put his hand on Bacon's shoulders, "Wait here and get your strength back. I'll get her."

Bacon nodded and leaned against the wall, "Please don't let anything happen to her, Mr. Steele."

Taking off at a full run, Rory reached the open doorway and stepped inside the room. It was a large, rich looking study.

Nan was on the far side of the room, standing beside some long drapes that covered the windows. She was flicking something in her hand. It was a lighter.

"What are you doing?" We have to go," Rory said sternly.

"We *have* to burn this place down," Nan yelled. "And I remembered the drapes in this room...."

"Nan, no. This place is too old, it's like a tinderbox– "

The lighter flame appeared and the drapes caught fire quickly.

Nan staggered backwards and dropped the lighter as the flames leapt instantly up to the ceiling.

Rory stepped forward and caught Nan by the shoulders before she fell. Then they both watched in fear as the old ceiling suddenly caught fire.

The smell of old, burning wood burst into the air around them. Before they could move one single step, flames shot across the ceiling over their heads, burned past the door bulkhead and advanced hungrily out into the hallway ceiling.

"Let's go." Rory pulled Nan ran into the hallway and they both stopped in shock, raising their hands against the sudden heat.

Overhead, flames shot down the roof of the hallway in both directions. Hot, roaring flames began to creep down the walls, threatening to envelop Nan and Rory where they stood.

Rory took Nan's elbow and ran with her back to Cordell Bacon - who was now slumped over in the hallway, flames creeping down the walls toward him.

Death by Fire Plague or death by fire, which was it going to be?

Chapter 46

RORY LOOKED IN BOTH DIRECTIONS as they helped Nan's father to his feet. The fire was already starting to burn the floor in both directions. Thick black smoke began to curl in the air - the smell was strong and acrid.

Cursing under his breath, Rory realized the smoke was denser in the direction he had come from earlier. They couldn't go that way. He yelled above the roar of flames, "Let's move away from the smoke. That could kill us before the flames do." He looked at Cordell Bacon, "Can you walk?"

Bacon shrugged, "I think so but I'll need help."

Rory put the man's arm across his shoulders and propped him up. Nan did the same on the other side and they helped her father down the hall, moving away from the billowing smoke.

Nan gestured ahead, "There should be some medical masks inside that small medical room we were just in. It should help with the smoke."

Glancing back, Rory didn't want any delays but they needed every advantage they could get, "Okay. Good idea but we'll have to be fast."

"Understood,"

As soon as they reached the still open doorway, they moved inside the small pharmaceutical room. Rory stayed with her father as Nan began searching. The minutes were long and agonizing but Nan finally came up with three pairs of surgical masks. They each donned two for extra protection against the deadly smoke.

They heard a crackling sound above them.

Everyone looked up to see flames beginning to eat through the ceiling of this room.

Cordell Bacon spoke up, "We're going to have to move faster out there. I'll try to walk on my own–"

Nan looked alarmed, "But what if you fall?"

"Then it pick myself up, dust myself off...."

Smiling, Nan said, "That's the song I used like as a kid."

"Yes, and that's what we have to do right now." He pulled away from Rory, staggered a bit and held his hand out to his daughter.

Nan took his hand and they moved out into the hallway

Rory followed them back out into the wide hallway and looked up and down the hallway again. Then he held out his hand to Nan, "Hold onto your father's hand behind you, and don't let go of his or mine. Do you understand?"

Nodding, Nan gripped Rory's hand and they moved down the hallway linked hand-to-hand.

Nan's father couldn't move very fast and it was slow going.

"Keep an eye out for a stairwell. There has to be something close by," instructed Rory.

Flames were starting to roar over their head and the smoke chased them.

They passed a connecting hallway but Rory continued on, heading for the back corner of the building, He was positive they would find a stairwell there. Flames were starting to lick down the sides of the walls along this hallway.

Rory spotted what looked like the entrance to a stairwell. He moved them towards it. But as they came close, they heard a roar above them. Rory leaped backwards and pushed Nan and her father hard.

All three fell to the floor as the ceiling caved in where they had been standing.

Massive flames filled the hallway, cutting them off from the stairwell.

Cordell Bacon and Nan slapped at the flames that had ignited on Rory's clothing.

Rory rose from the floor, his clothing still smoking, and yelled above the roar of the flames. "We'll have to go back down to that hallway we passed."

The others nodded in agreement and they moved back beneath the flames on the ceiling and turned down the other hallway. The flames and smoke were down here as well. The old wood in the building was feeding the fire at an alarming rate.

Leading the way, they were halfway across the building when Rory felt Nan's hand slip away - he heard her scream and turned around.

Twenty feet away, Cordell Bacon was on his back on the floor and looked to be dazed, holding the side of his head.

A man had his arm around Nan Bacon's neck, held a gun to her head and was backing away.

Rory saw an open door behind them. The gunman must've been hiding and jumped out when they came by.

"My, my, my," the man said to Nan, "trying to get away from us again, are you?"

Rory realized this must be Helmer Postigan, Lillian's father.

Nan ripped her masks off and yelled, "I told you before, I won't help you with your dirty work. I'll die first."

"Now, now, Ms. Bacon," Postigan replied, "Lillian says she still needs your help. I told you what would happen if you continued to defy us." He removed the gun from Nan's head and pointed it down at her father.

Nan screamed 'no' but Postigan calmly pulled the trigger.

Blood erupted from Cordell Bacon's right thigh and he screamed in agony.

Rory ripped his own masks off and advanced, "Your daughter is *dead*, Postigan!"

Swinging the gun towards Rory, Postigan scowled, "You're lying." He cocked the hammer of the gun.

Before he could fire, Nan Bacon bit down hard on his arm.

Postigan screamed in pain, the gun jerked upwards and he fired a bullet just over Rory's head into the burning ceiling.

Nan slipped out from under his arm and dropped to the floor.

Rory charged before Postigan could react. He caught the man in a tackle and drove him backward and towards the open doorway.

Postigan groaned in pain as his back slammed into the door frame and then he and Rory struggled for control of the gun. Tumbling into the burning room, Postigan landed hard on the floor, pulling Rory with him. The gun went clattering away along the floor. Postigan caught Rory with an elbow to the temple and Rory saw stars. Rolling over, Postigan scrambled for the gun.

Scrambling to his knees, Rory looked up just as Postigan reached the gun and whirled around, aiming it–

"Look out!" Nan yelled. She was standing in the doorway behind Rory.

Shifting his aim, Postigan pointed the gun directly at Nan, his lips curling into a sneer, "This is for my daughter."

The building suddenly shook.

Postigan looked down as the floor vibrated beneath his feet. Angry flames shot up through the old floorboards, enveloping Postigan's lower body. The floor gave way and the mad scientist screamed, disappearing into the flames below.

Chapter 47

RORY WAS CLOSE TO THE EDGE of the burning, gaping hole in the floor. He could see the remains of the madman's body burning on the next floor below. Rory looked around and yelled to Nan, "Help your father up. We need to get out of here, now!"

Nan darted into the hallway and bent down to help her father.

Rory scrambled to his feet and was out of the room in a heartbeat, right behind her to help. Time was running out.

Cordell Bacon had pulled his own masks off and had one hand on his shot leg - the other on the side his head.

Rory reached up to the shoulder of his own shirt and ripped and yanked the sleeve off. He wrapped it around Cordell's leg over the wound and pulled it tight, making a knot to hold it in place.

Bacon grimaced from the pain. It was a struggle to get him to his feet, even with help from both Rory and Nan. Once on his feet, he moved woodenly under their support.

Nan looked across to Rory, "I think he also has a concussion."

Rory nodded but didn't say anything. And Nan understood - there was no time for temporary rest, additional treatment or anything else - they began moving down the burning hallway, doing their best to weave their way back and forth around the flames, looking for a way out. They reached another cross hallway on the left.

"That's the hallway we need," Nan said.

But Rory kept them moving straight ahead.

"We need to go back," Nan yelled above the roar of the flames. She tried to turn her father.

Rory shook his head, "I don't think that's a good idea. There should be a stairwell at the end of this hall."

"No," Nan yelled, "we *need* to go back to that hallway."

"But I'm sure there's another stairwell in this direction," Rory yelled, pointing ahead.

"And I *know* there's a stairwell not far down that hallway."

Rory looked across at her. "Are you sure?"

Nan nodded vigorously, "That was how they brought me in both times I was here"

Rory put his trust, and their lives, in her hands. He helped to turn her father around and they headed back.

Flames were raging all around them.

The noise was becoming intense.

Black, dense smoke was rolling along the ceiling above them.

They turned down the hallway.

To Rory, it looked worse than the other direction. But they couldn't go back now. Flames were filling the hallway behind them

Within a few minutes they came to a door on the right.

"I'm pretty sure that's the door," Nan yelled.

Rory looked across at her, "You're pretty sure?"

Nan shrugged and nodded - but she didn't look totally convinced herself.

Rory shuffled around to get close to the door. He held his hand near it. He couldn't feel any excessive heat. He tapped the door knob quickly a few times. When his fingers didn't feel intense heat, he gingerly grabbed the doorknob and then turned it. He slowly pushed the door open. There was no fire right behind it. Rory pushed it open, left Bacon and stepped into a stairwell. Flames were licking at the walls and curling around the staircase but they could go down the stairs at least.

Rory gestured for them to come into the landing. Then he helped Nan with her father as they began moving down the stairs.

Cordell Bacon struggled with each step. It was obvioulys agony for the man, trying to hold his weight on his bad leg as he stepped down, but he persevered. Flaming debris fell around them as they reached the first floor.

"We need to keep going down," Nan yelled.

Rory looked across to her, "Are you sure?"

"Yes!"

Rory put his trust in her again and they began the trip down the stairs and through the flames towards the basement. It was slow going but they finally reached the bottom and made it out into the basement area.

The ceiling to the basement was on fire.

Dead ahead was the black van Rory had seen 'kidnap' Lillian Safford and then take Nan Bacon and her father. "Let's use that," he yelled as he pointed at the van. They moved as quickly as they could over to it. Rory slid the side door open.

Nan jumped in, pulling the folding seat up. Together they got her father inside and sitting down. She worked at buckling his seat belt.

Rory closed the sliding door and ran for the driver's side. He climbed in. The keys were still in the ignition and Rory tried to start it. The engine made a grinding sound but it wouldn't start.

Nan slipped up into the passenger seat, looking at him frantically.

Rory tried again. It still wouldn't start.

"C'mon, c'mon!" Nan yelled as she hit the dashboard in front of her with her fists.

He tried once more - it caught - Rory put it into drive.

"Turn around. There's a garage door behind us," Nan yelled.

Rory floored the accelerator. The black van squealed as Rory made a tight turn in the basement.

Burning embers and pieces of blazing wood fell around them, bouncing off the vehicle.

Rory could see a wide door on the far side of the basement and he gunned for it. The tires continued to squeal as Rory pushed the accelerator to the floor, driving the engine as hard as he could.

The ceiling began to fall in around them.

A blazing 2 x 4 glanced off the front windshield and Nan screamed.

The door was closed but Rory knew they couldn't stop to open it. "Buckle up!" he yelled as he steered with one hand and reached for his seat belt.

Nan reached for her seat belt and clicked it into place.

Rory gripped the steering wheel. Hang on!" he shouted.

The vehicle smashed through the wide door and pushed the pieces aside as it shot up a small, concrete ramp way. The black van soared into the air and hung there for a few agonizing seconds. Then it crashed back down to earth and shot forward across the parking area. The driver's side door flew open from the force and Rory fought to keep from being thrown out. He jammed down on the brakes. The vehicle slid for ten feet and fishtailed around to a stop, coming to rest, facing the old building. The driver's door banged shut.

Nan and Rory sat there, mesmerized by the building that was now totally in flames. The burning smell was heavy and acrid as black and gray smoke rolled into the sky, lit up by the raging fire. In the distance they could hear sirens heading in their direction.

"Do you think the fire will destroy everything?" Rory asked. He coughed, his throat scratchy and sore.

Nan Bacon's voice was soft, "I think so. I hope so. That's what the ancient puzzle said." She coughed into her hand.

A few moments later, Rory said quietly, "Skye has a flamethrower with her. That should work."

Nan just gave a feeble nod in reply.

An explosion of fire burst through the glass windows on the upper floor.

Rory and Nan both brought their hands up to shield their eyes from the flash of light and intense heat.

A moment later, Nan slowly lowered her arm, "Now I'm glad that we lost the urn in the fire back at the university."

Lowering his own arm, Rory watched the licking flames, "Yeah, I think it was for the best."

After a few quiet moments of watching the inferno consume the two hundred year old building, Nan reached over and turned the radio on.

"... difficult to believe what I am witnessing. One hour ago, after the President addressed the nation, the United States Army moved into the quarantine zones and began using flamethrowers to set the

buildings on fire. Flames are leaping into the New York skyline as entire blocks of Central Harlem and Spanish Harlem are burning. I am told Harlem Hospital Center and Mount Sinai, as well as the buildings around them, are also on fire. Reports say nearly one-quarter of a million people have died from the plague outbreak...."

Nan turned the radio off.

Fire trucks and ambulances were pulling up behind them.

Nan left the van to get a paramedic for her father.

Rory sat and watched as the roof of the old naval hospital caved in and flames shot higher into the air. He could feel the heat of the inferno as it destroyed the Fire Plague.

Chapter 48

XI'AN, CHINA

TWO YOUNG MEN were working just behind the Black Warrior in Vault 3 at the Terracotta Army Museum. They had worked for hours removing the hard packed clay from an unknown figure. As they carefully pulled away one large layer, the figure of a powerful horse was revealed. Both young men became excited as they looked at the remarkable features created by an unknown artist centuries before. They gently followed the lines of the bit and the reins that curved up over the powerful neck to the back of the black, Terracotta horse.

One of the young men stepped to the flank of the figure, where he saw the representation of saddlebags, carved onto both sides of the horse. "Look at his!" he whispered in awe as he gently slipped an urn from the saddlebag.

"What is it, Cheng?" the other young man asked as he approached his fellow worker and friend.

"I don't know," Cheng said in a quiet voice. He slowly traced the carvings on the upper side of the ancient urn. "Look Qiang. You can see people carved into the sides. Some of them are yelling."

"That's amazing," Qiang replied. He leaned in for a closer look at the intricate carvings.

Cheng looked at his friend, "Do you know what this means? We found it, you and me."

Qiang nodded and he puffed his chest out, "We're going to be famous."